Praise for Andromeda Romano-Lax's *The Detour*:

"As Nazi Germany passes from living memory, novels that allow the reader to travel its ethical landscape are increasingly important. Andromeda Romano-Lax has a fine feel for moments of clarity that are recognized only in hindsight, when chance and personal defects—moral and physical—combine to produce heroism, or mediocrity, or cowardice. A convincing novel, beautifully written."

—Mary Doria Russell, bestselling author of *The Sparrow* and *A Thread of Grace*

"A suspenseful tale of artistic ideals, culture and power, complex family bonds, and redemptive love with one of the most finely crafted narratives I've ever read. It's certain to earn Andromeda Romano-Lax a new level of readership. Vivid and heartbreaking, set against a shameful time in world history, Lax celebrates the resilience of the human condition, and its ability to heal against all odds."   —Jo-Ann Mapson, author of *Solomon's Oak*

"A wonderfully evocative and lyrical novel—a coming-of-age story woven into an adventure of art-smuggling under the Nazis. Romano-Lax brilliantly depicts a triumph over the seductive dangers of passivity when faced by love, art and the moral choices of life. A gemstone of a book!"   —Simon Goldhill, author of *Jerusalem*

"Both a thriller and a poetic journey of a young art specialist and an ancient statue through the deceits and dangers of the Third Reich. Plunging into crazy adventures in a truck on the back roads of Italy and fleeing long-buried memories, Ernst seeks the safe delivery of the statue and in the process discovers loyalty, love, and his own soul. Andromeda Romano-Lax is a unique and wonderfully gifted writer." —Stephanie Cowell, author of *Claude & Camille*

"Swept up in the intrigue and humor, adventure and tragedy of *The Detour*, a reader might overlook the deep understanding of history and art imparted by author Andromeda Romano-Lax. Set in 1938 Europe during the rise of Nazi Germany, the novel does what only literature can do, allowing us to experience moral complexity and struggle through a single beating heart. As Ernst Vogler travels across Italy to bring a famous marble sculpture home to Hitler, you will ride along with him through small villages and fields of sunflowers, through violence and love, through history in the making. And when you arrive at the end, you—like Ernst—will have been changed by the journey."   —Eowyn Ivey, author of *The Snow Child*

"With elegance and an eye for the unexpected, Ms. Romano-Lax distills the often overwhelming anguish of World War II into this elegiac tale of an earnest young art curator's journey into Italy, where he finds himself caught between his reverence for the past and the horrors of the future. An evocative portrait of one man's passage into maturity and the resiliency of the human spirit, even in midst of the unimaginable."

—C.W. Gortner, author of *The Confessions of Catherine de Medici*

"A marvelous adventure across landscapes both inner and outer, *The Detour* is a moving study in art and memory, history and geography, courage and compassion and every kind of love. Beautifully executed, deeply felt, and crammed with what feels for all the world like reality itself, it's a rare and valuable book indeed." —Jon Clinch, author of *Finn* and *Kings of the Earth*

"A poignant and important historical drama, as well as part road trip and compelling adventure, *The Detour* defies our expectations on every page. Andromeda Romano-Lax is a powerful and moving storyteller." —Jennifer Gilmore, author of *Something Red*

"It's 1938, and already the Sonderprojekt is at work, bringing the great art of Europe to Germany for the Fuhrer. Young Ernst Vogler, reeling from the news that his mentor has been marched off in the night, is sent to Rome to collect a valuable statue, the *Discus Thrower*. He expects to head straight for the border, but Italian escorts Cosimo and Enzo have other ideas, taking him on a wild ride that sets quirky and lively humanity against the grinding, impersonal forces of war, history, and power.... The book is no (inappropriately) jolly picaresque; Romano-Lax, author of the well-received *The Spanish Bow*, keeps the palette just dark enough to remind us of the terror that is there and the terror that's to come. Nicely paced, brisk with dialogue, and lyric at the right moment, this would be great for book clubs." —*Library Journal*

Praise for *The Spanish Bow*

"An impressive and richly atmospheric debut."
—*The New York Times Book Review* (a *New York Times* Editors' Choice)

"Time and setting, character and plot come together in this exceptionally appealing first novel about a master cellist and his complicated relationship with the country of his birth and the poisoned times in which he performs. Readers will be captivated by this delightful book, loosely inspired by the life of the great cellist Pablo Casals."
—*Library Journal* (starred review)

"This riveting historical page-turner moves inexorably toward a heartrending crescendo."
—*Booklist*

"For sheer scope and ambition, this is a tough debut to beat." —*Publishers Weekly*

"Extraordinary, gripping.... Encounters with actual world players, like Picasso, Adolf Hitler, Franco, Kurt Weill and others, constitute a feature of this many-favored book. Another is the author's obvious love for Spain and its colorful cities, which are unforgettably detailed.... In the end, *The Spanish Bow* suggests that fighting the manifest evil in the world can be even more damaging than tilting at windmills. And yet, and yet—there always remains the message and nobility of opposition in itself." —*BookPage*

"Andromeda Romano-Lax's powerful first novel, *The Spanish Bow*, is an account of Spain during the years of 1890-1940, as experienced by a Catalan child prodigy who goes on to become court musician and then the country's most celebrated cellist. Epic in scale it is full of richly detailed tableaux of Catalonian peasant life, bohemian Barcelona, the chaos of the Second Republic, and the rise of Francoist fascism.... [*The Spanish Bow*] excels as a portrait of a country at a painful moment in its evolution." —*Times Literary Supplement* (London)

"Can art save us from ourselves? In her elegant debut, Romano-Lax ponders this timeless question through the ambitious tale of Feliu Delargo, a gifted cellist born in turn-of-the-century Spain. . . . From the hypocrisies of the courts of Madrid to the terror of Nazi-occupied Paris, Romano-Lax weaves the upheavals of the first half of the 20th century into an elegy to the simultaneous power and impotency of art, and the contradictions of the human spirit."

—*Historical Novels Review*

"Vivid and absorbing. . . . Romano-Lax's passion for music is tangible but not daunting. The characters are convincing (Delargo and Al-Cerraz are based on historical figures) and by using Feliu's voice along with her own narration, the author can point up the shortcomings in his self-understanding. She exposes the tension among the characters with masterly subtlety."

—*Times* (London)

"Andromeda Romano-Lax's ambitious and atmospheric debut examines 50 years of Spanish history through the eyes of a fictional Catalan cellist, Feliu Delargo; en route she has much to say on the relationship between music and politics. "   —*Guardian*

"(A) vast, inventive novel."   —*Telegraph*

"An inspired portrait of the cello virtuoso's unique career."   —*Elle* (France)

"Can music transcend politics or must the musician's only true response to authoritarianism be principled silence? This question is asked throughout Andromeda Romano-Lax's ambitious debut, *The Spanish Bow*, a sweeping memoir of a fictional Spanish cellist, Feliu Delargo. His life, from his improverished upbringing in rural Catalonia, via apprenticeships in Barcelona and Madrid, to a glittering career as a European superstar, is the thread that leads us through Spanish political and musical history in the early 20th century."   —*Observer*

"Expertly woven throughout the book are cameo appearances by Pablo Picasso, Adolf Hitler, Francisco Franco, Bertolt Brecht, and others, but it is the fictional Feliu, Justo, and Aviva who will keep you mesmerized to the last page."   —*Christian Science Monitor*

ALSO BY THE AUTHOR

The Spanish Bow

THE
DETOUR

Andromeda Romano-Lax

SOHO

Published by
Soho Press, Inc.
853 Broadway
New York, NY 10003

Library of Congress Cataloging-in-Publication Data
Romano-Lax, Andromeda, 1970–
The detour / Andromeda Romano-Lax.
p. cm.
ISBN 978-1-61695-049-1
eISBN 978-1-61695-050-7
1. Germans—Italy—Fiction. 2. Art—Collectors and collecting—
Fiction. 3. Italy—History—1922–1945—Fiction. I. Title.
PS3618.O59D48 2012
813'.6—dc23
2011034072

Printed in the United States of America

10 9 8 7 6 5 4 3 2 1

To Tziporah, Aryeh, and Brian:

fellow travelers along old Roman roads,
with love and gratitude for our time together
in Italy and Munich

"We are becoming more Greek, from day to day."

Friedrich Nietzsche

"The day of individual happiness has passed."

Adolf Hitler

THE
DETOUR

PROLOGUE

The russet bloom on the vineyards ahead, the yellow-leafed oaks, a hint of truffles fattening in moldy obscurity underfoot—none of it is truly familiar, because I first came here not only in a different season, but as a different man. Yet the smell of autumn anywhere is for me the smell of memory, and I am preoccupied as my feet guide me through the woods and fields up toward the old Piedmontese villa.

When a salt-and-pepper blur charges out of the grass and stops just in front of me, growling, I stand my ground. I resist retreating; I reach out a hand. Foam drips from the dog's black gums onto the damp earth. I am in no hurry, and neither is she.

The sprint seems to have cost the dog most of her remaining energy, though. Her thin ribs heave as she alternately whines and threatens.

"Tartufa?"

The teeth retract and the quivering nose comes forward. Her speckled, shorthaired sides move in and out like a bellows.

"Old hound, is it really you?"

She sniffs my hand, backs away for one more growl, then surrenders her affection. These have been ten long and lonely years. Take a scratch where you can get it.

She guides me, as if I have forgotten, up to the old barn. Through a dirty window, I glimpse the iron bed frame, one dresser. But other items I'd once known by look and touch—the red lantern, the phonograph, any trace of woman's clothing— are gone. A dark stain mars the stone floor, but perhaps it's only moisture or fungus. In the corner, wedged into the frame of an oval mirror, is an old postcard of the Colosseum. I know what is written on the other side. I wrote it.

I consider walking up the hill to the villa's family burial ground to check for any recent additions—but no, even after coming this far, I'm still not ready for that. Tartufa trots ahead toward the side of the main house, toward the figure seated alone at the wooden table, a spiral of blue smoke rising from his thick-knuckled fingers. The door from the terrace into the kitchen hangs crookedly. Everything about the house seems more worn, sloping like the old man's shoulders.

He calls out first. "*Buongiorno.*"

"Adamo?" I try.

Now he sits up straighter, squinting as I approach.

"Zio Adamo?"

It takes a minute for him to recognize me.

"The Bavarian? *Grüss Gott*," he cackles, using the only German phrase he knows. But still, he doesn't seem to believe. "You're coming from the North?"

"No, from Rome. I took the train most of the way. Then a ride, a bit of a walk . . ."

"You are living there?"

"Just visiting museums."

"Holiday?"

"Repatriation of antiquities." And I explain what that means as he nods slowly, taking in the names of new agencies, international agreements, the effort of my own homeland to undo what was done—a history already begging to be forgotten. Wonder of wonders, the old man replies, how the world changes and stays the same. Except for some things.

After he pours me a glass of cloudy plum liqueur, I take a seat at the old oak table and ask him about his sister-in-law, Mamma Digiloramo. He gestures with his chin up to the hill.

"And Gianni and his wife?"

They occupy the main house with their four children, Zio Adamo explains. He lives with them, and though this villa has been in the Digiloramo family for three generations and Gianni is not even a blood relative, it doesn't matter—Adamo himself feels like a houseguest now. Fine, it's less of a headache for him. Fewer worries about the crops, which haven't done so well in the last few years. Surely I noticed the shriveled black grapes on the west side of the road, approaching the main house.

When I empty my glass of liqueur and decline a second, he says, "You haven't asked about *everyone*," with an emphasis on the last word.

When I don't reply he volunteers, "She moved to town. During the war, everything here went to pieces. Now she works in a café. She lives with her son."

Stunned, I repeat his last word back to him: "*Figlio?*"

I must appear tongue-tied because he laughs, clapping me on the shoulder. "That's about how her mother looked way back when, discovering the happy news. Not a virgin birth, but close. We celebrated without any questions."

"*È quasi un miracolo.*"

"Your Italian is much better than last time."

"I've been practicing."

"Why?"

"No particular reason. It's a beautiful language."

He runs his tongue over his teeth, unconvinced. "If you wait, I can find someone to take you into town—if that is where you are going."

"*Grazie.* I'll walk."

"It will take you two, three hours."

"*Va bene.* I could use the time with my thoughts."

"I don't recommend it."

"Walking?"

"No, remembering." He doesn't smile.

Gesturing for me to wait, he pushes to his feet slowly, reaching for the cane leaning against the table's corner, then escorts me back down the path, past the barn, to the track that leads to the dusty road lined with hazelnut bushes. Something is bothering him. At the end, he straightens his back, lifts his whiskered chin, and brushes his dry lips against my cheek. "That's as far as I go, or I won't make it back."

The dog has followed us, grateful for her master's unhurried pace. I reach down to pat her side and mumble a few final endearments, whispering her name a final time.

"That isn't the original Tartufa, you know," Zio Adamo says, looking a little embarrassed to be correcting me. "It's her pup—the last one."

"This, a pup?"

"A very old one."

"They look the same," I say, squatting down to scratch her ears again, patting her ribs, puzzling over the pattern of her coat.

He leans on the cane, face lowered to mine. "Certainly, you remember what happened to Tartufa . . ."

"Yes," I say, standing up to brush my hands on my trousers. "That's right."

"It makes me feel better that I'm not the only one who makes mistakes." Zio Adamo smiles. "I'm sorry for not recognizing you right away. Even after you sat down, it was hard to believe."

"No need for apologies—"

"It's not just your Italian."

"I couldn't put two words together back then."

"No," he insists, with sudden vehemence, enough to make me wish I'd accepted that second, courage-bolstering drink. "You were different in other ways."

"Weren't we all?"

But of course, I know what he means.

There is a temptation to say that the long-ago past is a fog, that it is nearly impossible to recall the mindset of an earlier time. But that is a lie. The truth is that more recent events, such as the days leading up to the surrender, are a fog. In and out of the army, where they sent me again once it was clear I had made a mess of things on what might have been a relatively simple professional assignment—all that is a fog. I passed through it in a half-numb state, registering few sensations beyond the taste of watery potato soup and the unsticking of dirty, wet wool from frozen, bleeding feet.

A year or two, or eight, can elapse that way, mercifully, while a fundamental childhood incident or an essential, youthful journey can remain polished by obsessive and dutiful reminiscence. It can remain like marble in one's mind: five days in Italy—harder, brighter, more fixed and more true than anything that has happened before or since.

Except I'd forgotten about the dog, and only now that I am reminded can I hear in my mind the stranger's fatal Luger shot and recall how we all stopped, stunned, watching—and clearly forgetting, *wanting* to forget—even as the sound rang out across the farm, the first shot of several that morning, my last morning in Italy, ten years ago. Of course.

And if I have confused that one detail, have I confused anything else? Am I remembering my final moments at the villa inaccurately—not only the bitter, but also the sweet? Am I imagining a tenderness and a sense of possibility that never were?

But that's too much to ask without time to absorb and reflect on what Adamo has said, what the quiet of this villa and the padlock on the barn suggest. I cannot truly remember *her*, cannot truly remember *then*, until I can remember the person I was that long decade ago—a difficult portrait of an even more difficult time.

On this afternoon, with acorns crunching beneath my feet, I have several hours and nothing else to do as I walk, inhaling the soft musk of the season, realizing with each footfall that I have little to lose given how much has been forfeited already. Is there also something, perhaps, to gain? No telling. Only the brittle sound of cracking shells, the memory of a different breeze on my face, the recollection of a less pleasant stroll, and all that followed.

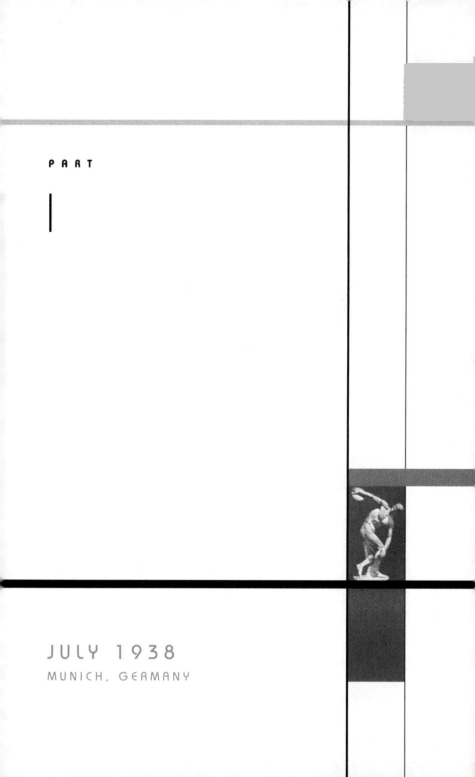

PART

I

JULY 1938
MUNICH, GERMANY

CHAPTER 1

A light evening rain had started to fall, but it brought no freshness, only the wafting odor of brewhouse mash settling like a brown shroud over the wet cobblestones. There was no question of the month—July—or the date—the eighth. I know this because I'd been counting the days since I'd last seen Gerhard, counting them with a mounting unease. On that damp and suffocating night, I took the longest possible route to my mentor's house, through Shirker's Alley, where I passed a man who had clearly gone out of his way to avoid the required salute at the SS-guarded *Feldherrnhalle* monument. And yet as we drew near, we each looked away at unnatural angles, and I told myself I had been stupid and would never take this route again.

For two weeks, Gerhard hadn't appeared at work or answered any of the letters I'd sent to his home. In the absence of formal explanations, no colleague dared make a comment, not even Leonie, one of our department's three secretaries, who—though fond of me—had avoided my every glance for several days, even going so far as to type without a sheet of paper in the roller the last time I'd passed her desk.

Standing now outside Gerhard's darkened door, rapping without expectation, I tried to pretend that he was out at a beer hall, even knowing that wasn't his sort of place. I was turning to go when a tuft of dirty-blonde, sleep-mussed hair appeared in the opening gap. The hired girl looked so anxious and eager that I immediately regretted having come.

"He hasn't paid me in a fortnight. I can't stay if he isn't returning."

"Returning from where?"

"*Bitte,* come in."

I stepped back. "Did he pack a suitcase?"

"I started to pack one for him, but he told me not to bother." She said this defensively, as if I might question her competence and fidelity, when that was the furthest thing from my mind. "And *they* agreed when he said it."

"They?"

"Two of them." She looked down at her bare, cold-reddened toes curling over the threshold. The building's heat had been turned down or off. There was no smell of cooking or any food at all coming from the hallway, only the dank, mineral smell of the tomb.

"Perhaps they weren't taking him far?"

This jogged a memory. "Not far—a town twenty or so kilometers from here, they were telling him. He recognized the name." She pronounced the two syllables, which seemed to mean little to her but plenty to me and to any other Munich resident who read the newspapers. *Dachau.* Just a quaint village, but one that had found a profitable new industry: imprisoning behind growing walls the unmentionable domestic elements—everyday criminals and political enemies, initially—that our government had determined must be contained. Gerhard was not a criminal, nor even politically active, I would have argued at the time, not understanding then what I finally know now: that everything is political—even a simple lack of discretion, or an opinion about art or aesthetics. Especially that.

The rain had started to fall harder, plastering my hair to my forehead, while I held my hat in my hands like someone delivering bad news rather than receiving it.

"But what does it matter, near or far?" the hired girl added, put off by my alarmed expression, standing straighter with her arms wrapped around her thin chest. "Either way he'd be wanting a change of clothes in all that time. And his medicine—his bag of pills—he can't go more than a few days without them, but they didn't let him take anything at all. Here, please. You're getting soaked."

But she wasn't offering me true shelter. She had nothing to give, only much to take away, just as I had much to take away from her, by explaining the things she might not wish to understand. We were all alone in this, and all of us waiting.

When I wouldn't cross the threshold, she withdrew briefly and returned with a book in her hands—a reference guide that I recognized from Gerhard's desk, the second volume of di Luca's *Sculpture of Ancient Greece and Rome*, inscribed to me personally. It was an unusual parting gift from a man who'd had insufficient time to take care of more basic details. But he'd been a wonderful mentor for this reason precisely: he never forgot his priorities. Art and beauty, beauty and art. No matter what was happening; no matter what would happen.

The first time we'd met was at a small, evening art reception with several dozen mid-level bureaucrats and military officials in attendance. I'd been hired just that week, and I was so nervous entering the floodlit gallery that even the soles of my feet were sweating. A banner on the wall over my head proclaimed: "Art is a noble and fanatical mission." I squinted at that odd choice of words—*fanatical?*—but thank goodness I was alone and anxious and not the type to make an impromptu wisecrack. If I'd recognized who had authored that statement, which would appear again at future art exhibitions, I wouldn't have risked any expression at all.

I'd just started heading for the main exhibit when an old man took me by the elbow, pinching it with a shaking, ring-covered hand as he whispered: "*Like it, love it, like it,* and as for the final painting, an undecided tilt of the head will suffice."

Wrenching my arm free, I turned to study his drink-flushed face. His jowls sagged above a pale blue cravat, the same shade as his eyes; his pale forehead gleamed, only slightly less shiny than his gaudy cuff links. I resented his pompous manner, but a moment later, when my new boss and the head of *Sonderprojekt*, Herr Mueller, invited me to survey the first wall of the gallery and tell him precisely what I thought, I recited like an obedient schoolboy what the opinionated elbow-pincher had said. From the pleased look on Mueller's face, I could tell I'd just passed my first test with flying colors.

The next morning, meeting him again in the *Sonderprojekt* basement offices, I thanked the old man and learned his name.

"We wouldn't want a disagreement of taste casting a pall over your first days here," Gerhard said, his pale blue irises twitching as they did in the hours before he calmed them with his first midday tonic.

"But what about the truth?"

"The truth is something we savor—usually in private. If you are lucky, Herr Vogler, you'll have many private pleasures in your life which shall make up for some public inconveniences, such as saying things you don't necessarily believe, and purchasing the world's most valuable art for fools who neither deserve nor appreciate it."

He wasn't the most popular man in our office. But *how* unpopular, I did not fully appreciate until that starless, inclement night in July, standing outside the domestic threshold he had not crossed in a fortnight with his poor servant girl eyeing me so desperately.

"He told me some people from his office might come by," she said. "But no one has come. Except for you, finally."

"I'm sorry," I said belatedly. "Vogler. Ernst Vogler."

That introduction seemed to give her no joy. It proved only how small her employer's world had become. He'd mentioned me perhaps more than the others, and here at long last I stood: an unimpressive figure, young, a little thin, no hint of power or privilege in my manner or dress, one elbow pressed against my rib cage, trying to avoid scratching that mostly-forgotten spot that itched in times of stress. I'm sure she had hoped for more.

"He said that if you came, I should give you this."

When I hesitated, she asked in a tremulous voice, "Don't you want it? At least he's given you something. He didn't give me anything—not even what he owed."

"Yes, of course." I fumbled for some *Reichsmarks* in my pocket and handed them to her before taking the book and sliding it under my jacket, out of the rain.

Our *Sonderprojekt* department, where I had been part of the art curatorial staff for just under two years, was located in the basement at 45 Brienner Strasse. Yes—*that* address; that's how important art was in those days, to the people at the very top. The Third Reich's very first architectural project was not a diplomatic building or some other temple of power but the House of German Art, a new museum completed in 1937. *Sonderprojekt* looked beyond that museum and beyond Germany to a larger vision, both artistically and geographically speaking. To what precisely, I did not yet know or need to know. My job was only to catalog the world's obtainable art objects and to add more items to the master acquisition list—a list based not on finite resources or some scholarly criteria but only on taste, and symbolic significance, and that least definable thing: desire. Whose desire? Usually our leader's, of course. But each of us also had objects we personally admired and longed to see or have a hand in collecting, for reasons as difficult to explain as the deepest merits of fine art itself.

The day after visiting Gerhard's house, I spent as much time as possible in the dark stacks and near the corner filing cabinets, pulling out and replacing one unread catalog card after another, trying to look busy while I puzzled over Gerhard's predicament—which, in his absence, had become my predicament as well. Section B of the master art acquisition list I was researching featured only sculptures; another researcher was assigned to paintings; a third to the special problem of avoiding counterfeits. Anyone watching me closely, as I fumbled in the wrong drawers, might have guessed that I was upset. But that was no crime, to be upset.

Neither was it a crime to laugh, and Gerhard had laughed—especially whenever an unimpressive item made its way into our hands: a statuette of a ballerina no more finely crafted or interesting than a child's music-box figurine, or a muscular male nude with a caveman's brow, or some other example of questionable art, hastily collected. He was supposed to have expertise in these matters. He was also supposed to find a way to share that expertise without humiliating others whose taste was not as refined as his own, especially others of high rank. But that kind of prudence had never been his strength.

Back at my gunmetal-gray desk, I was surprised to see Leonie waiting with a worn and bulging paper bag in her hands—a peace offering, perhaps, to make up for her recent avoidance of me. When I sat down, she pushed it across the desk blotter.

"Is it a sandwich?"

She laughed nervously. "No, silly. Candles—twelve of them. For you."

"I nearly forgot," I said, taking the bag gratefully. "I suppose they're sold out everywhere."

The natural blush on her cheeks showed, even from behind the stain of applied rouge. "I thought ahead and bought extras a month ago."

That night marked the start of the second annual German Day of Art, celebrating new displays of all-German art that turned away from modernism and harked back to the greater clarity and tradition of the past: images of peasants and working folk, landscapes, cows and horses (but only very strong ones), and the ideal and healthy human form. The art of the post-degenerate era. This focus was the cornerstone of our entire national cultural policy. It meant so much to our leader that he had funded many artistic activities from the profits of his *Mein Kampf* sales. His "struggle" had become the direct sponsor of art in Germany—the two things inextricably intertwined.

On this weekend-long "day of art" there was an exhibition of German works for sale, overseen by the Führer himself, who not only had rejected at the last minute eighty already-approved works but would go on to purchase over two hundred works that did please him. These purchases were separate from the more ambitious and distinctly more international *Sonderprojekt* collection that we basement experts were cataloging and beginning to acquire. The Führer's insatiable appetite for art objects was the reason we called him (always discreetly, for though it was not an insult, it still suggested an inappropriate familiarity) *Der Kunstsammler*—"The Collector." If we were not aware in 1938, we would soon become aware that *Der Kunstsammler* had the power to collect just about anything—or anyone—of interest to him. And the power to dispose of the same. How could it have been otherwise? But that isn't the voice of the twenty-four-year-old still learning his place in a new office, in a new profession. That is only middle-aged hindsight, which can be just as dishonest as the blinkered presentism of youth.

During the opening procession of the German Day of Art activities, all residents were required to display three candles in every one of our apartment windows. If anyone was expected to remember and comply, we members of *Sonderprojekt* were. There were dozens of ways to reveal your incompetence or disloyalty, and new ways were being invented all the time.

"Thank you, Leonie," I said, opening the bag of candles, realizing even as I said it that she had not only anticipated my faltering memory, but had remembered how many windows my lonely apartment had, despite having peered through them only a few times. She might have assumed, over the awkward winter months following our final date, that she had shown me too much, given too much away for free as the saying goes, and that's why I'd lost interest. But in truth, she hadn't shown enough. I didn't need a girlfriend who would change clothes only in the water closet and make love only in the dark, who would pretend not to notice the alarming changes in our departmental staffing just as she pretended not to notice the pink scar on my rib cage.

Still, one doesn't like to appear ungrateful.

"Leonie," I started to say, but she could see the question coming and looked down quickly so that I could see only the impenetrably thick spikes of her painted lashes. "At least look at me, Leonie. Please?"

But she would not. Someday, I would no longer be in that basement office, but she would be there still, typing without a sheet of paper in the roller, cradling the heavy phone to her soft cheek even after the lines had been cut—not because she lacked competence or intelligence, but because she knew walking away was no answer either. Perhaps she was smarter than all of us.

"It's a lucky day," she said quickly. "I think Herr Mueller is planning to call you into his office."

"Lucky? I doubt it." I tried one last time, my voice lower yet. "Leonie, I know you have a good heart. I know you liked Gerhard well enough . . ."

She whispered, "I know he was opinionated."

"But isn't that our job here? How can one curate art without having opinions?"

When she didn't answer, I pleaded, "You see the correspondence that comes through. You must have an idea . . ." But she was still looking down, studying her shoes. "Never mind. When I see Herr Mueller, I'll ask him."

Mueller was in an effusive mood on that Friday afternoon with a weekend of festivities ahead, including at least one event where he would spend time with topmost officials of the Reich, including *Der Kunstsammler* himself. (The rest of our small staff avoided such anxiety-producing "opportunities" whenever possible, coming and going by our own entrance, often forgotten in our subterranean lair.) Mueller asked me to sit but couldn't contain his own nervous energy and proceeded to pace in the windowless room. There was small talk about my family, cut short when I reminded him that my own parents had passed away—my father just the previous winter. The awkwardness didn't seem to bother him.

I was preparing to ask my question—to make a principled stand by asking *the* question—when Mueller sat down and slapped a file onto the desk and opened it, showing me the photograph clipped to the inside corner of the folder. "You know this statue, of course?"

I paused, tongue sticky against the ridged roof of my mouth, admiring the recognizable figure of Myron's ancient Athenian *Discus Thrower*: an image of the perfect male specimen, captured in a sporting posture of dynamic tension. "Yes, of course."

Mueller turned the file around, looked at the photo again. "*He* wants it. And he will have it, no matter the considerable expense."

I didn't say anything at first—not because I was too junior a staff member, or too inexperienced in this particular area to comment. On the contrary, I knew this statue well, better than anyone in the department. Gerhard's taste had favored the Italian Renaissance, especially Bernini. My taste, my self-education, my training, my fixations favored this: controlled, classical, iconic excellence.

I fell into a momentary trance, staring at the photo and imagining all that the photo itself could not capture. I loved this object as one always loves the most perfect example of an artistic period, the most realized projection of a cultural virtue. But "love" does not explain the feeling entirely. For what I felt most about the

Discus Thrower was a driving curiosity: a certainty, guided or misguided, that beholding this ancient statue in person, at close range, would answer an obsessive question and a personal need that had led me into the study of classical art in the first place.

I didn't like to see the folder shut, even though I knew exactly where to find a larger and better image: di Luca, vol. 2, p. 227—or any other classical art reference book in the extensive *Sonderprojekt* collection.

Mueller tapped the closed folder: "Herr Vogler . . ."

"Yes?"

"You don't have any questions about what we do here, do you?"

Questions? Those had been the specialty of my former mentor. Hard questions as well as soft, teasing ones. Rhetorical questions; questions posed over the smudged tops of wine glasses at parties; questions asked under the stark lighting of modern museums; questions asked with a flourish of Gerhard's blue-veined, aristocratic hands: "What are the foundations of civilized society?" And: "What purpose do these artistic images serve?" And: "Should all these European masterpieces really be gathered up by one people, in just one place?"

He had said the truth was a private matter, but in his own pointed questioning, he forced the truth where it did not fit or easily belong and so he had brought his own problems upon himself. Or so it would have been convenient to think, as one more way to avoid thinking.

Still, until I'd seen the picture of the statue, I'd been ready. Now, I discovered that the question I had prepared carefully and brought to Mueller's office had withered in my dry mouth.

"I don't know what you mean, sir."

"Do you speak Italian?"

"I am . . . moderately capable."

"What do you think about going to Italy?"

That would have been Gerhard's assignment. He had not explained the particulars, but I recalled the elliptical conversations, beginning when *Der Kunstsammler* had met with Mussolini for the first time, in May. Presuming he'd be tapped to return there at the behest of our culturally acquisitive leadership, my mentor had begun to revive his own memories of that fabled, sunny country: The hill towns and piazzas. The ruins and vistas. The frescoes and fountains. And a certain woman he had met somewhere—I think it was a town called Perugia, or maybe Pisa. The relationship had lasted no more than a few days but had meant the world to him, and I had been bold enough in my naïve youth to ask, "But how can something like that matter if it only lasted a few days?" He had grabbed my hands in his own lilac-scented ones and told me that, in his life, some of the times that stood out the most had been only a matter of hours, not days, and if I had never experienced that, then I needed Italy far more than he did.

At best I could say to Mueller: "I'm not sure I'm the most suited to the task, intellectually and artistically speaking. And—how do I say this?—I'm not much of a traveler."

Herr Mueller started laughing. I couldn't understand why.

"That's fine," he said, clapping me on the shoulder. "We don't need an expert traveler. We just need someone who won't screw up."

CHAPTER 2

The train stopped for an unexpectedly long time at Bolzano. It nearly lost heart altogether at Chiusi. It gathered for a final burst of effort before it delivered us, grimy and gritty from the trip, through the tight pelvis of girdling roads, and finally, with a squall of brakes and a sob of steam, into hectic Rome.

As it turned out, despite what the local Fascisti claimed, the trains didn't run on time, after all.

It was nearly bedtime when I checked into my pensione, where the resident signora invited me to dine, despite the questionable hour, with her other European guests. When I declined, she must have decided I wouldn't need breakfast either because the next morning, following a night of fitful sleep, none was provided.

I made my displeasure as plain as I was able, given some conjugating difficulties, and returned to my room, where I took a position in front of the rust-spotted mirror, distracted by the discovery of a small stain on my shirtfront. Another inconvenience. But given that I planned to be in Italy for such a limited time—a single day in Rome, another long day returning—I assumed my second dress shirt would suffice. Perhaps I would give the signora my first to wash, but perhaps not. I would evaluate her competence only after she delivered a suitable breakfast. Putting her in the position of the one to be tested made me feel momentarily better, as I was out of the pupil's examination chair for a moment myself, on a day when I expected the tests to be challenging and the examiners unforgiving.

It was while I was most vulnerable, half-dressed and fighting the temptation of further ruminations, that the incident occurred. There was a quick knock—no calling out, no request for permission to enter—and the bronze knob turned. In shuffled the bowlegged signora with a small wooden tray in one hand, catching me standing in front of the mirror, unclothed above the waist. My clean shirt was just beyond my reach, laid out on the sagging bed. Our eyes met, her chin dropped, and there—on my bare rib cage—her gaze rested and stubbornly remained.

She lowered the tray onto my nightstand, refusing to look away, chattering insistently, without any comprehension of my distress. I reached for the clean shirt and struggled to push each fist through the tight sleeves in an effort to shield myself. But even through the fabric, I continued to feel the heat of her curious gaze on that jagged, pink scar.

Artists are careful with raw materials because they know no amount of technical ability can make up for faulty marble or poorly mixed paint. The raw material of the moment was my own psychic equilibrium, not to be regained.

Of course, how much easier it was to blame a flash of insecurity than anything that had preceded it; how much easier to focus on a stranger's indiscretion, rather than any personal complicity or weakness in days prior. But it was all wrapped into that moment, somehow. And why shouldn't it have been? The question of a body's classic beauty—or its deep flaws—was integral to my artistic training, related to the item I had come to see and transport, and was in all other ways inseparable from why I had come to Rome. In any case, I did not appreciate her staring and reminding me—least of all on that day.

As soon as the signora backed out of the room, I finished dressing, left the breakfast roll untouched, and grabbed my essential materials, including my sketchbook and the di Luca volume two—but not the dictionary, which I left behind in regrettable haste.

My interests in Greco-Roman statuary, interests born humbly but cultivated with great sincerity, predated even the beginning of *Sonderprojekt* by seven years. Yet it would be made evident in just a few hours that I was to be treated here in Rome not as an art expert, not as an authority working on behalf of *Der Kunstsammler*, but as a courier. A mere courier.

But I didn't know that yet, so you can imagine my pride and carefully contained excitement as I climbed the time-worn steps to the side entrance of the museum where I had been scheduled to meet with the minister of Foreign Affairs and my own German Cultural Affairs contact, Herr Rudolf Keller, at 8:30 A.M. The seller himself—perhaps dispirited by local criticism over the controversial sale—had declined to take part.

I waited in front of a security desk, where a heavy, untidy man with slicked-back hair attempted to convey a message.

"*Dieci*," he told me. My watch read 8:15.

"*Dieci*," the guard repeated, grinning obsequiously as he held up all ten sausage-shaped fingers. Yes, even without the dictionary, I understood that. I had been warned about Italian manners. The meeting had been delayed an hour and a half, until 10:00 a.m.

"*Dieci*," I parroted back, and the man's smile cracked wider yet. He pointed to a bench and held open a cigarette case, but I shook my head and made for the open door.

Four blocks away I found a pavement café and waited in line for a table, or attempted to wait. The two bustling waiters were following no procedure that I could understand. An elderly man arrived several minutes after me and was ushered toward an empty chair in front of a dirty table. Pigeons darted between people's feet. The ground was strewn with crumbs and mottled with sticky patches. The warm air carried the strong smell of coffee—well, that was good, at least. It only made me wish I were somewhere more familiar, so that I could make my own needs clear.

Finally, an apron-clad waiter exhaled a string of musical syllables, barely waiting for my reply. Where had my week of language cramming gone? *Prego . . . grazie . . . per favore . . .* Damn that forgotten dictionary, even if I would have looked like a tourist carrying an entire library in my arms. I pointed at a square-shaped pastry on a man's plate nearby and then jabbed at my own palm and jiggled the change in my pocket, walking away a minute later with a sorry breakfast to eat on the hoof.

Except that I refused to eat on the hoof. I walked on, trying to stir up a breeze, looking for a pleasant bench or a clean step. At 9:20, according to the public clock that was ten minutes fast, I wiped the crumbs from my hands and opened the sketchbook I'd brought, intent on drawing the object in front of me, a dry fountain topped by a statue of two cherubs holding hands. It was not well made, and there are few things more forlorn in a once-great city of aqueducts than a fountain without water—proof enough, I told myself, that Italy had more art and architecture than its citizens could appreciate. But sketching was something to do, and I'd finished half the picture when three children ran loudly up to the cherubs and began climbing up their fat legs and swinging from their chubby, linked arms.

"Get off," I called to them in German, but they only laughed and scrabbled about, pleased to have an audience for their daring. "Go away. *Haut ab!*" Their laughter turned maniacal, even more so when I jumped to my feet, waving my arms above my head. They were no more afraid of me than the pigeons, which startled into the air and then settled again, bobbing their gray heads as they walked.

I slapped the sketchbook shut and reached in my jacket pocket where I had stored the three postcards I bought at the pensione, all destined for my sister Greta. She had made it a practice, ever since our father had passed away, to write me regularly from her home in Bamberg, two hundred kilometers from Munich, and she expected me to do the same. Her letters always followed a strict protocol: the greeting, the description of the current weather, an inquiry into the recipient's weather, followed by carefully filtered news, nothing upsetting. I found my pen, set a postcard on top of my journal, and looked up at the sky: blue and cloudless. I greeted her and her husband, skipped a line, and wrote:

It is . . .

I paused, thinking that "hot" would sound like a complaint *. . . pleasant.*

But I didn't feel like writing anymore, and I didn't feel like being a tourist. Until I accomplished at least some part of what I'd been sent here to do, I'd have nothing to report. I did not even want to recite the formulaic pleasantries that would be expected.

I put the card away and pulled out the di Luca guide. I rubbed a hand across the book's padded green cover, opening it without looking at the now-familiar gift inscription. I tried to immerse myself in the illustrations and old photos I'd studied so often, the lines and shadows I knew by heart. It was a calming exercise, so calming that I soon forgot my irritation, and jumped with surprise when a small leg rubbed against mine—the overheated appendage of a bold child, maybe five or six years old, one of the climbers, trying to see into this magical book that had commandeered my attention.

I ignored him, but he kept looking. Out of the corner of my eye I could see his round cheek and the long, black eyelashes batting every few seconds. I could hear the soft, ticking sound as he failed to suppress a swallow. He reached out one finger tentatively, toward the wine-colored ribbon trailing from the bottom of the book, marking a place several pages further on.

"You want to see that page? Well not yet. I'm not done here." I said it in German, but he did not appear surprised by the unfamiliar sounds. I welcomed my chance to have a first genuine encounter with a Roman (the pensione lady and the waters, paid to serve me, didn't count)—one who was willing to let art be the universal language drawing us into a brief fraternal bond. The brown finger touched the bottom of the bookmark, then pulled back, hovering near the open page.

"This is the *Venus de Milo*," I said, and paused, waiting to see how long his attention would last. A minute later, I continued, "You've probably seen an image of this before, or perhaps a replica. But did you know that it was discovered in an underground cave, by a farmer?"

No reply in any language—yet he kept staring.

"Good. You're not going to ask me why her arms are missing. I'm glad."

He blinked, his long, dark lashes fluttering rapidly like butterfly wings before he froze again. I turned the page and felt him lean in closer, and more of his small, curly head came into my sidelong view, so that I could make out the tendrils—moist from the sweat of clambering all over the piazza—framing his round face. I could just see a stripe above the boy's soft jaw-line, where a trickle of sweat had made a pale track across an astonishingly dirty cheek.

"That is *Nike of Samothrace*, from the Hellenistic period. I can tell you like that one better, and so do I. You're impressed by her large wings. One can imagine the wind blowing against the feathers and against the draping folds of her clothes. Just the thought of it can be cooling, on a day like this."

He was even more still now, listening, if anything, more intently. His lips closed and I could hear the little whistle of his congested nose as he breathed softly through it, trying not to make a sound.

"It isn't easy to convey movement using the medium of stone. An artist has to be talented to do that. But which artists first *thought* of doing that? We take it for granted, seeing a dynamic posture in a statue . . ."

I cleared my throat and prepared to turn the page, to reveal the most special of all pages, the one marked by the ribbon. In a flash, the chubby hand shot out.

"I was just about to show you—wait!"

The boy was scrambling away, his legs pumping so hard that his scuffed heels nearly spanked his own rear.

"Don't go!"

Only then did I realize what the wicked cherub's flurry of motion had accomplished. He had stolen the bookmark. He was running with it, joined now by his two friends, waving the thin red ribbon over his head without looking back, screeching and chattering like a pleased monkey, while I sat with my book in my lap, incredulous and finally resigned.

Back at the museum a half hour later, I was shown into a conference room where half a dozen men were gathered around a large table. Minister Ciano stood with his hands resting on the back of a chair. As soon as I entered, four young Italians in dark-blue uniforms walked away and waited on a balcony, where they lit up cigarettes.

Herr Keller looked up from the table's far side, his arms folded across his chest and rested atop the paunch that had formed over the course of his Italian residence of the last two years. The shopkeepers of Rome had sold him ridiculous soft-soled shoes; the barbers had neglected to trim the slick waves that now fell nearly to his fleshy earlobes. But they had not managed to convert him entirely to their culture of indolence. He exhaled with impatience: "We've been waiting for you."

"But I was told ten by a man at the desk, and it *is* ten o'clock, sir—or rather, a quarter to—"

"But we have been here since eight thirty. The reception clerk said he asked you to wait ten minutes—"

Oh, *Scheisse.*

"—and you vanished. We're short for time, now. There are important matters to arrange."

I strained to recall the receptionist's expression as he held up his ten fat fingers; I regretted my insistence on wandering away instead of waiting inside. How much Italian had I claimed to speak back in Munich when I had accepted this assignment? I had not used the word *fluent*. Only *capable*. Capable enough to translate museum labels, anyway.

The minister nodded toward the men smoking outside on the balcony. Another man, younger, in a fine suit, translated. "Do you agree?"

Distracted by my past errors, I had let my attention wander. "Do I agree?"

"That the packing materials are sufficient. In which case, we can have these men load the crate for transport. But it must be done quickly, now. The train leaves in one hour. "

I unbuttoned my suit jacket and reached for the pencil in my pocket, nodding smartly. "That's not much time. But let's begin the inspection. I will do my best to meet your schedule."

No one spoke. Out on the balcony, one of the men turned away and blew a forceful stream of smoke and kicked with the toe of his black loafer at a loose iron rail, until he realized how quiet everything had suddenly become, and stopped kicking.

"Herr Vogler, we finished the inspection one hour ago."

I looked around then at what I had seen without thinking and what I had missed. There, on the conference table: four hammers and a nearly empty box of nails, as well as a road map of Italy. In a far corner, near the door I had entered: two more Italian men, in rather plain black suits—looking less sharp than the translator, less sharp even than the uniformed policemen. On the floor, beyond the conference table and nearly out of view: a closed wooden crate, more than two meters long, a meter and a half wide and equally deep. Here and there, beneath my own feet, stuck to the bottom of my right heel: scattered wisps of straw.

"You sealed the crate?"

The Italian minister found amusement in my distress. He stifled a smile, gestured for his translator to follow, and walked away from Herr Keller and me, toward the smoking policemen on the balcony.

"We supervised the packing and sealed the crate," Keller confirmed quietly in German. "An editorial against the sale ran just this morning in the main city newspaper. I've put off returning several telephone calls as long as I can. People change their minds, you understand? Time is short."

I lowered my voice. "But my instructions—to make a status report before the packing and transport, for comparison with the arrival report, to ensure the most careful handling—"

"Reports . . ." He looked down at me almost tenderly, his soft chin tucked into his sunburnt neck as he dropped his voice. "Herr Vogler, reports are not held in the same esteem here as they are back home."

"But they will matter on my return, if I am to keep my job."

"Our payment," he continued, "*that* has been followed with close attention. But all the rest changes like the weather." Dropping to a barely audible whisper, he added, "In fact, the weather has grown gloomy in the last twelve hours. You will ask Enzo and Cosimo, when you are in the truck together, and they will explain."

"Enzo and Cosimo?"

Now the two men in worn black suits appeared at my elbow, reciting their names as they offered to shake hands in that peculiarly Italian way, with slouched backs and hands held at groin level, infusing the gesture with an excess of discretion and masculine drive. Enzo Digiloramo, as he introduced himself, was about my age and the stockier of the two, with a loose mane of curly blond hair. He was the first to shake my hand, and he held it twice as long as did his brother Cosimo, who was quieter and less flamboyant. His hair was also fair, but cut much shorter than Enzo's, the golden, nubby curls tight against his skull, almost like an albino African's. I caught this Cosimo sneering at me until our eyes met and he attempted a crooked half-grin. Then I realized his sneer was only a permanent, pugilistic asymmetry—his beakish nose pressed firmly to one side, his left cheekbone a little flatter than his right.

A clap of Keller's hands sent things into motion again, reminding everyone of how much time had already gone to waste. Enzo was dispatched to my hotel to get my things. I called after him, "Explain to the signora—explain that everything was suitable, more or less." Though it hadn't been, not really. "And there will be a shaving kit on top of a dresser, and a dictionary on the bed—"

I stopped, realizing I was speaking in German and there was no reason to assume he would understand. But he did. And only now was I beginning to intuit what would be verified later—that Enzo and Cosimo were not part of the pack of blue-suited Roman policemen, though they were also policemen, plainclothes from the northwestern Piedmont, and on friendly terms with the Italian minister, and perhaps on even friendlier terms with Herr Keller.

Cosimo was on his knees, propping open both double doors with small wooden wedges. The minister had accepted a cigarette from one of the four Roman policemen, all out on the balcony. Keller and I were as alone as we ever expected to be, and he used the moment to indulge second thoughts, quizzing me again.

"You were occupied this morning, perhaps meeting with someone?"

"No. I just went for breakfast—not much of a breakfast. I couldn't get a table."

"And this took you over an hour?"

"I walked. I sketched."

"Making a little something on the side, maybe? I know many are ready to sell, dealers who will make all kinds of introductions. Have you met—?"

"I arrived only last night, Herr Keller. I am here in Rome for one reason only."

The truth should have been the easiest thing to tell, but I'd never held up well under scrutiny. Or maybe it was just the day's heat. I could feel the moisture beading above my lip. Herr Keller's eyes were fixed there, too, on the perspiration, or perhaps on the tense set of my mouth.

He smiled. "You'll forgive the questions. But you're aware that the best items in Rome have been spoken for."

"Of course. That has been my job, for the last two years—cataloging items for potential acquisition."

"So you've had a head start, haven't you?" He lifted his chin in the direction of Minister Ciano, who was peering into the room, the sun bright behind him, the sounds of the street below louder now: the squeal of brakes, trucks rattling by with poorly secured loads, the shrill goose-like honk of some miniature vehicle pretending to be an automobile. "All right. Here we are, then. No time to waste, is there, fellows?"

The four Roman policemen stubbed out their cigarettes and reentered the room, rubbing their hands, preparing to hoist the crate and carry it down one wide flight of stairs out to a large truck that would be driven by Cosimo.

One of the blue-uniformed men kept saying something that sounded like "seguire," and somewhere in my addled, disappointed mind, that verb—"to follow"—fought its way out of a conjugational haze and I understood that the Romans were going to be following us to the nearby train station in their own truck, an even larger model, military style, with olive-drab canvas flaps. We trailed after them outside the museum and loitered near the truck, watching them muster their energies for the required heavy lifting.

Herr Keller, preparing to depart before the crate was fully loaded—eager to return to his meals, romances, and profitable deals, no doubt—clutched my hand, speaking softly. "The border—three days. That is what I have guaranteed Herr Mueller. That is what he has guaranteed the statue's new owner."

The Collector. Our leader. We all avoided the name, and Keller did, too—a sign of his own nerves, or the fact that while he salivated at opportunities appearing on the horizon, he bristled at the limits that were equally drawing near. In today's Germany, there was no such thing as an independent art agent. A man like Keller could call himself a "freelancer" or an "expat," but in truth, he had one person to answer to, and one valid passport.

"Three days?" I asked Keller.

"Not a single day more."

"But the train to Munich takes only one."

His eyelids grew heavy with condescension. "Enzo will explain about that. But the rest—the importance of maintaining the timetable and avoiding any problems en route—do you understand?"

"Yes, of course—"

"If problems arise, some improvisation may be called for. Do you know what I mean by improvisation?"

"Not exactly," I said warily.

"Because it is not only the on-time delivery that is important, but the appearance of competence and order. There are people in Munich who don't understand that Italy is not Germany. Things operate differently here."

I was worn out by his opaque references. But at least he had made no mention of Gerhard; he had not pushed the point about why I was sent in the place of an older, more seasoned curator. Did he know about my former mentor? Here in Italy, the shufflings of rank in distant Bavaria may have seemed inconsequential—or not. Perhaps he was content to deal with a younger man who would be more easily intimidated. But why intimidate me? Were we not on the same side?

"The last thing we need," Keller continued, smiling, "is someone arriving to impose more order where that kind of order simply isn't a possibility. It would interrupt the order that already exists."

The order that exists: he and his own art-dealing associates. His network of art buyers and sellers, government insiders and disgruntled outsiders. This entire country was a treasure house with doors left unlocked, windows cracked, a man at the back gate allowing passage to the select few.

And now I remembered this also about Keller: museums had never interested him as much as private collections, and he thought official purchases of the best-known items came with too high a price tag. There were other, cheaper, and more discreet ways to buy artwork. In coming years, there would be ways to procure masterpieces by force of political pressure without paying anything at all. In the meanwhile, simple theft was equally commonplace. *Der Kunstsammler*, at this point, had no need to debase himself by stealing, but Keller was not *Der Kunstsammler*. I was still missing the essential fact: that Keller needed only to appear loyal in order to thrive. Like me, he was under the false impression that Italy was a world apart, a place beyond memory and consequence.

"Then, at the border," he was saying, with a born liar's bravado, "we take a breath."

"I will take a breath with the unpacking in Munich," I said, trying my best to exchange a brotherly, dutiful smile. "The final report—that is road's end for a delicate and ancient object like this."

"Yes. Well. The border, anyway," he repeated, rocking back on his heels, and I knew, in less time than it took for my effortful smile to fall, that I was a fool—though I still did not understand to what extent.

"But I *will* be following the statue from the border to Munich . . ."

"Will it go to Munich?" he asked, as if quizzing his own memory. "Not our concern. We will let them handle it at the far end."

"Let whom—?"

In response to his silence, I pressed harder: "Is it going directly to Linz?" In the wake of our annexation of Austria, the city of Linz had become synonymous with some plan, not yet fully outlined, for another new museum of art, perhaps an entire city of art, designed by the man who once dreamed of being an artist. "Am *I* being transferred to Linz?"

"Transferred?" The word seemed unfamiliar to him.

I lowered my voice. "Will *I* be going somewhere new, Herr Keller?"

"Going somewhere? You barely made it here, this morning. How am I to know where you will be going?" His throat filled with laughter once again. "But you have youth on your side, and strength. Those qualities are welcome everywhere."

Yes, welcome especially where ditches must be dug and where fields await their adornment of barbed wire. My stomach turned, but it must have been from the train trip and the unsatisfactory breakfast. Travel wasn't good for the digestion. Disturbed sleep, foreign water; even the air smelled different and more complicated. What was Rome's elevation? How did men manage to live in foreign cities, or in fields of war, for that matter? In barracks where—I recalled my own interrupted basic training all too well—men whispered and groaned, living out all their small pleasures and larger miseries in soul-wearying proximity. In diseased trenches of the kind that had swallowed my father's generation, twenty years earlier. *Youth and strength*, Keller had said, laughing just enough to make his soft jowls quake, just enough to make my esophagus tighten, to keep the acidic, undigested truths my stomach already feared from finding their way up to my brain.

In response to my silence, Keller cocked his head, half frowning, half smiling. "You looked a little lost when we first met." That had been two years earlier, just after the Berlin Olympics, when he had been lean and stern—in contrast with now, ten kilos and many deals later. I had been different, too, of course—only four years out of secondary school, still recovering from the annulment of my athletic ambitions, and not yet employed in my current field. And yet look how far I'd come. But that was one aspect of working in today's Germany. Those who fell vanished without a trace. Those who rose, rose quickly.

"Others were impressed with you," he chuckled. "I didn't share their enthusiasms, necessarily . . ."

When I didn't take the bait, he cleared his throat. "But there can be no chance here. The border in three days, or they'll come looking, and no one, north of the border or south of it, will be pleased. And don't look so miserable to be here."

He winced, like a father embarrassed to be seen alongside his unimpressive son—a gesture that was familiar enough to fill me with unease and the beginnings of a quiet rage. Struggling later to think why I did not see through Keller and his plot from the start, I would remember that condescending wince and my own withheld anger, filling my senses with steam, blocking the view of what should have been painfully clear.

I said, "I'm not miserable."

"You have no reason to feel inadequate or uncouth, if that is the problem. That whole notion of the sophisticated world traveler is a myth. You know why young men of more prosperous times went on the Grand Tour? Not to experience eye-opening epiphanies, but only to have their prejudices confirmed. And you? I'm guessing you've confirmed your prejudices already, in less than twenty-four hours. But see? We Germans are efficiency experts."

He touched my shirtfront with the tips of his manicured fingers. "That's a joke, Herr Vogler." A disappointed sigh. "Anyway, three days. And trust Enzo. Here he is."

Already the blond Italian had reappeared, right hand steering a small, buzzing vehicle with little more heft than a motorized bicycle, left hand clutching the handle of my small suitcase. Though he was a short man by northern European standards, this tiny scooter was too small for even his frame, and he was forced to buckle inward, like an adult folded into a baby chair. Dropping the suitcase at my feet, he revved his engine, drove the wobbling vehicle up a ramp with exhibitionist speed, and disappeared into the back of the truck.

My eye followed him, and I saw there was already one crate in the truck, identical to the crate that had been carried out of the museum, now resting at the bottom of a short flight of stairs. I watched Cosimo and Enzo and the four Roman policemen load the second crate, inside of which I had not been granted a single, ennobling glimpse.

It is difficult to photograph marble well. Nearly always, too much flash is used, and one is left with only a clear outline of the statue's shape, a lifeless representation suitable for non-expert cataloging, and nothing more. But of course, even the best photograph can't rival seeing a masterpiece in its original form. With marble, there are the unique striations in the stone itself. Plus—while not intended by the artist—the subtle pittings of age. Breaks may reveal the drama of history, as in statues flung from rooftops onto the heads of invading barbarians. Lines carved into the buried surface of a marble back may recall the blade of an oblivious medieval farmer's plow. Other lines may signal further weakness, threatening new breaks to come.

All this, despite the fact that only the best white marble is used in quality sculpture. It is marble's purity, as well as its relative softness for carving, and the subtly translucent quality of the topmost layers—a waxy quality that can fool the eye into believing it is seeing a living body, real human skin—that have made it so timeless and valuable to artists.

Beyond the stone, there is the carving, and one will never see truly identical copies of an ancient original. The smallest difference in each sculptor's ability determines everything, *is* everything; it is the difference between life and death, masterpiece and mere object, soul-filled body and dull corpse.

The British Museum owns a copy of the *Discus Thrower*, or *Discobolus,* as it is sometimes called—one of several Roman copies made of Myron's original Greek bronze, now lost. The

British copy, bought in 1793, was restored incorrectly, with the head facing forward, rather than turned to the side. (Forward or turned, the face is still the same—it is a simple, blank-eyed, classical face, without the brilliant, brooding intelligence of Michelangelo's *David*, for example. But the face is not the essential element here.)

The inappropriately positioned head is a major gaffe, often discussed, but more interesting to me, from the first time I studied photographs of the *Discus Thrower*, were the small differences: the lesser tension in the torso; a lighter quality to the tensed thigh and left calf; a disappointing smoothness in the arms and a less realistic grip on the discus itself, held high and far back, in the right hand, in that frozen moment just before release. Even the fingernails appeared different, especially the right thumb; even the tension in the toes, gripping the statue pedestal.

What was most remarkable about the Rome museum copy was all that was missing from the British one: the arms so finely formed that arteries were visible and perfectly articulated; the shadows that fell across the muscles of the right leg all the way up the buttock, over the hip, and across each delicately curved rib of the torso. The skin's mottling spoke not of marble, but of real skin: the faint capillary flush of an athlete in motion. The balled left calf shined slightly, catching the sun.

But perhaps I was wrong about such subtle and essential details. I had not seen the British copy in person. And now, as of this July day, I had not managed to see the more famous Roman—rather, German—copy in person. How could I say anything with authority? I could tell you what the German copy cost our government—five million *lire*. But could I tell you what the German copy was *worth*? Could I tell you whether it summed up everything that was best in the human form? Could I tell you whether it justified *Der Kunstsammler's* fanatical interest? Could I tell you whether a nation should have been escalating its acquisitions of fine art, rather than feeding its people, or finding some future for its youth beyond the trench, the munitions factory, or the museum?

I could not tell you, just as I could not tell you with authority how the heart might respond to the *Discobolus's* representation of a moment—not a moment in action, but a moment just before action, the moment just before the discus flies, when nothing has happened yet, when no one has been judged, and no one has succeeded or failed, won or lost. When everything remains possible.

CHAPTER 3

"**W**hy you are not speaking?" Enzo asked, catching me brooding. We were just outside Rome, heading north.

When I didn't answer, he waved a hand in front of my face. "*Ciao? Guten tag?*"

I nodded briskly.

"You are hungry?"

"Not very much," I said, clasping a hand over my stomach to silence the grumbling. To my left, Cosimo drove with the silent, focused attention of a barely literate man struggling to complete an essential government form, unhooking his fingers from the steering wheel only to scratch once at a spot under his tight, close-trimmed curls. To my right, his more hand-some and apparently carefree brother drummed on the dash-board, shifted in his seat, stared out the window, flipped open a square brass lighter.

And snapped it shut.

Open. And shut.

"*I* am hungry," Enzo announced after the twentieth flip of the lighter. "We do not buy sandwiches when we have a chance at the train station."

This would be a problem with Enzo—the relentless present tense, which allowed for no reflection or prediction, only statement and complaint.

There was an exchange in Italian between the brothers about who was responsible for the food, I was fairly certain. Enzo had three times as much to say, the mark of a guilty con-science. Cosimo exhaled slowly, extinguishing his frustration in a series of softening taps against the steering wheel.

"If you please?" Enzo continued a moment later, bending forward to squirm out of his black suit jacket. He loosened his satiny blue tie, slipped it over his head, folded it several times, and tucked it into the jacket pocket. Then he attempted to hang the jacket behind his head, over the back of the truck bench. But there wasn't much of a gap. The jacket wouldn't hang straight. He scowled as he tried to smooth out the wrin-kles, twisting left and right.

Cosimo also removed his jacket, but, less concerned than Enzo about wrinkles, he simply wedged it between his leg and the door.

"If you please?" Enzo said again, and this time when I

nodded, he draped the folded jacket across his lap and mine. "It is all right?"

"Yes," I said, assuming this was a temporary arrangement while he continued to get comfortable.

"That is very heavy material," Enzo said, rubbing the thick brown sleeve of my jacket between his thumb and forefinger. "It is too warm, maybe, for summer?"

"It is durable."

He touched a hand to my trouser leg just below my knee, the part exposed beneath the jacket he had settled atop my lap. When I flinched, his hands flew up to his face. "So sorry! I am only feeling—it is the same?"

"It is."

He clucked his tongue. "The shirt is nice, though."

Then he switched into Italian again, discussing something with Cosimo about *Roma* and *scarpe*, an increasingly bitter commentary.

"They have better uniforms," Cosimo finally explained to me in German, noticing me trying to keep up, flipping back and forth through the unwieldy dictionary that Enzo had successfully retrieved from my hotel room. "On this drive, Mister Keller asks us to wear plain clothes, to be less noticeable, like the truck." It was a modified Opel Blitz with a separated cab, which could pass for a tomato or produce truck except for the heavy-duty tires. It had been borrowed from the German consulate in Turin, to be returned by the brothers once our mission was accomplished.

Cosimo continued, "Our usual uniform, it is nothing special. Enzo says the Romans, they all have the same shoes. We have no special shoes. We buy our own. What can I say? Small town *polizia municipale*. We are not the *Carabinieri*. We are not even the *polizia provinciale*. Enzo does not like our uniforms—but this is even more humiliating, to wear no uniform at all."

I turned to Enzo. "In Germany, the Gestapo wear plain clothes, I believe."

"They get respect, the Gestapo?"

"I would say so. I believe they are very effective." Somehow, it gave me pleasure to say this at the time—me, in my brown suit, hot and coarse and unfashionable, out of place here.

A half hour later, Enzo's jacket was still on my lap, warmed by the sun and collecting more heat through the windshield with every passing moment; immobile, like a black, self-satisfied cat that couldn't be ejected without offending its owner. After a while, my knee tickled where sweat was collecting and dripping into the top of my sock garter.

Squeezed stiffly into the middle, trying to avoid touching either companion, I was unaware of how much I'd been squeezing my legs, buttocks, and even my toes until a cramp flared in the arch of my left foot. I tried to flex my foot inside my shoe, but the shoe was tied too tightly. The burn faded slowly into a dull ache. Cosimo's side was warm against mine, halfway between soft and firm, appropriately unresponsive; I could at least pretend I was leaning into the arm of an overstuffed chair. Enzo, to my right, continued to fidget. Every time I yielded another millimeter of space, he expanded into it and pressed for more, emanating more heat and—as the day wore on—the salty, pungent smells produced by heat. On the trip south, I had found my train compartment to be uncomfortably small, but now I belatedly appreciated its spaciousness and ease.

At long last, I cleared my throat and gestured to my damp lap. "Excuse me . . ."

Enzo looked up, startled. "Oh? Yes?" He recognized the jacket suddenly, as if it were an object he'd forgotten somewhere and rediscovered only now. "Of course! It bothers you? Is that better? Are you comfortable? We promise to Mister Keller to make you comfortable, all the way to the border."

Cosimo took his eyes off the road to glance at Enzo, who pretended not to notice. "Don't you worry," Enzo said. "Yes? Am I saying it correctly? Don't worry."

"Is there a reason I should worry, Enzo?"

"No, that is why I say it: don't worry."

Several hours had passed since we'd unloaded one of the two crates from Cosimo's truck, and, with the help of the four Roman policemen, loaded it onto the train. It had not been heavy at all, an obvious decoy. When the policemen had failed to transfer the heavier *Discobolus* crate to the train, I'd been only mildly surprised. Keller had mentioned improvisation. Minister Ciano's approval of the statue's sale had been strongly protested by many prominent Italians, including the minister of education, Giuseppe Bottai. Many were unhappy with Mussolini's waiver of a key export permit. Plenty of people would have been thrilled to see our transportation of the statue disrupted.

(I reminded myself that King Ludwig's purchase from Rome of the *Barberini Faun*, a century earlier, was beset by similar difficulties, requiring ten years of political finagling and attempts at confiscation before the statue itself could be whisked north, to Munich.) For the sake of art—for the *security* of the art we were transporting—I couldn't ignore all of this tomfoolery entirely, as much as I would have liked to. "Trust Enzo," Herr Keller had said. Did I have any other choice?

Now we were past the traffic snarls and blaring horns. We were driving alongside green fields. In the distance: the glinting curves of a blue-gray river, also fleeing the clamor of the city. I asked Enzo, who seemed to prefer answering for them both, "Are we driving to another train station, outside Rome?"

"As I explain: we are driving."

"But—to a different station, or all the way to Germany?"

"Yes. All the way to the border. It is better, because of the way things are today."

"And how *are* things today?"

"Not so good. But the weather is better away from Rome, as Mister Keller say."

"The weather, really?" The sky had been clear and blue all morning, uncomplicated by clouds or breeze.

Enzo smiled, pleased with himself. "Not really the weather. How do you say it?"

"The atmosphere," Cosimo said. His eyes flickered rhythmically, checking the side-view mirror every few seconds.

"Keller said I should ask you both about that—about some increasing gloominess. Has something changed in the last day or so?"

"Everything changes," Enzo said, and smiled. "Everything always changes. That's why it is good to keep driving."

"I don't understand."

The second truck, following closely behind, accelerated to pull up alongside us, driving in the path of oncoming traffic. One of the Roman policemen leaned out of the passenger window—"*benzina, benzina*"—exchanging words with Cosimo, who bared his teeth in a distracted grin, nodding. The Roman truck pulled all the way in front of us. Cosimo's chest swelled with a deep, anticipatory breath. Up ahead, the other truck took a small side road, crossing railroad tracks on its way into a small village where fuel was sold, just off the highway.

We could still see the loose canvas flaps beating against the back of the second truck, when suddenly, ignoring the exit, Cosimo stepped hard on the accelerator. It took a moment for the truck to respond, and when it did we bucked forward and I bit my tongue. The taste of iron filled my wounded mouth as the truck battled to gain the next hill, rattling and groaning with the effort.

When I pressed him for information, Cosimo interrupted by raising a protective arm in front of my chest, pushing me back into the seat. The truck slowed, reaching the top of the hill, lurched, and kept going—down the other side, much faster now, fast enough to make my stomach drop. A man on horseback, riding toward us, reached up to touch his flat cap in greeting, then thought better of it and leaned forward, urging his horse to the narrow shoulder. As we passed, the horse sidestepped nervously, stirring up dust, while the angry rider flicked the underside of his chin, cursing us.

Enzo had pushed his left arm out the open window and was grasping at handfuls of wind, whooping with glee. Now he pushed his entire head out, and his loopy blond curls parted, regrouped and parted again, like a golden field bending in a storm. When he finally settled back into his seat, his hair looked twice as long, with hanks standing nearly straight up, a great, leonine ruff.

"The other truck? We're not waiting for it?"

Cosimo gripped the shuddering steering wheel, pushing the truck to its maximum speed.

Enzo dug a finger into his watering eye, still smiling. "We cannot. The other truck—*inaffidabile.*"

Seeing my confusion, he brought his fingers together and bumped the tips gently against his lips, trying to kiss the word that was eluding him. "*Sospetto.*"

"*Suspekt?*"

"Yes, it's no good. Keller say to leave the other truck behind, in case they have friends who like this cargo."

"*Like* it? Want to steal it, do you mean?"

"Yes, maybe."

"You mean, the same policemen who were helping us?"

"No, no. But they turn their backs, they give information. You notice they want very much to stop in this place, even though we are just leaving the city. Let me tell you, some things that happen . . ."

And Enzo proceeded to describe another incident a month earlier when a cargo of newly liquidated seventeenth-century paintings had gone missing from the back of a police truck like the one following us. The truck had stopped for a midday break. The driver and one partner had stepped into a small restaurant. A third man had stayed in the cab but conveniently fell asleep in the drowsy afternoon sun.

"In any case," Cosimo spoke up, eyes flickering to the side-view mirror, "we will not stop. We will go until we lose them."

"But how will you do that?"

"It's not as exciting or difficult as you think," Cosimo explained. "We only take a smaller alternate route."

Enzo saw the turnoff to this lesser road ahead, and pointed with gusto.

"*Certo?*"

"*Sì, certo.*"

Cosimo seemed less sure, but he took the turnoff without decelerating, pushing me hard into Enzo's shoulder.

I asked, "But don't you need more *benzina*, too?"

"In the back, we have containers. Out of the cities it is not always easy to find."

"But this alternate road, it must not go too far out of the way because we have very limited time. And it must not be too bumpy, do you understand? We can't have the statue rattling and jostling the entire way."

"*Ja, ja,*" Enzo agreed, unconcerned. "All roads have bumps. And the train, it rattles as well." He tried to be reassuring. "Don't worry. This is Mister Keller's plan. Anyway, you have two good men traveling with you. They say you need us because my brother and I speak your language. But there is more. They ask us because we are from the North. We have different friends and responsibilities. Things in Rome are"— he paused—"very complicated."

"Complicated. That's a pretty word for corruption."

Enzo misunderstood or misheard and thought I was praising the landscape out the window, which, to be honest, I had not bothered to evaluate. "Pretty? Yes very pretty. This is a good drive for you, much better than the train. We show you our Italy, where Cosimo and I grow up. It is much better than Rome."

■

I kept my eyes fixed on the road, watching for the simple stone kilometer markers shaped like little gravestones, which proved we were putting distance between ourselves, the second truck, and all of Rome.

But Enzo suggested I was noticing the wrong things. He gestured toward scenic highlights—fields spread across rolling hills, a small church topping a rise. He had no facts to share, no history or architectural insights. He simply pointed and said, "There, look. There she is."

He said the same thing an hour or so later, when he pulled a creased photo from his pocket and showed it to me: a dark-haired girl, young and pretty, her lips—painted scarlet in real life—nearly black in the photograph. To be honest, she looked a little plump.

"There."

"Yes. I see."

"Yes? There. *Bella.*"

"That is her name?"

"No—*Bella. Schön.*" Beautiful.

Yes, well, to each his own.

Cosimo interjected without taking his eyes from the road: "Farfalla. That is her name. Not *Bella*, not *Schön*. She is called Farfalla."

He loosened his grip on the wheel for a moment to flutter two fingers, for my benefit. Ah yes, *Butterfly*.

"When you care for someone," Cosimo scolded his brother, "you say her name. You see who she is—a real person. Not just '*my* girl'; not just '*pretty* girl.'"

Enzo mocked Cosimo's rebuke, linking his hands and fluttering crazily. "Of course, Farfalla. You want me to say it again, to our guest? You want me to say it again for you to hear because you don't hear it enough? *Farfalla. Farfalla.*"

Then he dropped his hands just as quickly, sighing, and smiled, his gaze occupied by the view out the window. "When I see the fields like this, in the country, I think of her."

Ahead of us, a thin carpet of greening crops struggled to break through a dry crust of mustard-colored soil, dotted with troublesome rocks. Higher on a slope, silver-leafed olive trees grew in five or six stubby rows, blocked at the boundary of a neighboring field, this one planted with grape vines, more woody than lush. The patchwork had a haphazard quality in this corrugated landscape and many steep gullies were completely wild, clotted with scrubby growth.

"It is beautiful, yes?" Enzo persisted.

We saw all too easily into the backyards of tiny farmhouses, with their lines of laundry, free-roaming goats, and kitchen gardens, scraggly with tomato plants. These were not the noble villas of antiquity. Parallel to the route we traveled, chalky white tracks switchbacked in a half-dozen directions. I had thought the farms would be larger. I had thought Romans built only straight roads. But maybe that was because we were off the main route, heading away from imperial roads toward obscure valleys known only by *contadini* and their donkeys.

I gestured toward the accordioned map at Enzo's feet. He reached forward, then sat up straight again. "More easy when we stop, I think."

"But," I persisted, nudging the poorly folded map with my right foot, "please, if I could just see it."

Enzo made a halfhearted effort to lean forward, then sat back, shrugging. I reached again, doubled over, stretching myself across his lap, fingers splayed.

"Please—"

He studied me one more time, and then finally, seeing I was not going to give up, reached forward with good-natured enthusiasm, as if looking at the map had been his idea, after all, rather than my own. He wore a bemused smile, enjoying himself as he tested my irritation. With his golden locks and smooth, tanned skin and biceps, which challenged the fit of his dress shirt, I imagined that he got what he wanted most of the time and managed to quietly obstruct plans that were not to his liking.

When I had the map in my hands, I inhaled deeply, trying to center myself. "Where are we, exactly?"

"Outside Rome."

I made a guess, pointing at one junction where a thinner line veered away from the darker route.

"Yes, probably there." He turned to the window, bored,

his energies sapped: first by hunger, and now by a bittersweet heartache of some kind.

"Would you say we have gone a hundred kilometers by now?" Cosimo granted me a half nod.

"Certainly more than sixty?"

"*Ja.*"

I looked past the driving wheel, searching in vain for an odometer or speedometer, and located only a moving needle under a scratched dome of glass, jumping wildly, as if recording earthquakes instead of motor speed.

"We will call it eighty," I said firmly.

I reached for the unfinished postcard in my pocket and marked several lines along its edge using the map's key, turning it into a rough ruler. With a pencil, I made a light tick on the map.

"You don't mind if I mark up your map, Enzo?"

"*Va bene.*"

And why should he have minded when there were marks all over this map already? No doubt, some of these notations had been made earlier that morning while I was strolling the streets of Rome, eating a pastry and losing my favorite bookmark to a scheming toddler. Herr Keller—for I still assumed that he was a trusted contact, even if the policemen in the truck were suspect—stood around that conference table with Minister Ciano for a good hour, discussing how best to move the statue safely across Italy, and if I didn't know where each road led, it was because I had not been present for the discussion.

With every tick mark, I attempted to erase the sting of that failed meeting. Every hour, I would make a mark on that map again, estimating perhaps on the conservative side of kilometers covered, but there was no way to be perfectly accurate. One had to do something, after all. If one was demoted from curator to mere courier, then one had to be the best courier possible.

With every tick mark, I felt more certain that my superiors had chosen well by assigning me to this task—someone scrupulous, with no personal agenda, apolitical, rule-abiding; more than a mere courier, really, because who else understood the value of the cargo we carried? At the '36 Olympics, our nation had instituted the tradition of carrying a torch from Greece to the Berlin Games, in memory of the Olympics' classical origins. The value of each torchbearer became clear to anyone who saw the final runner pass. A statue is more than a statue; a flame is more than a flame. *To think any less*, I told myself then, seeking a strength from the symbols around me that I could not locate in my own life or feel from within my own imperfect body, *is to reject civilization*.

It was late afternoon when Cosimo's eyes began to look glazed. I tapped on his shoulder. "Do you think you need a break? Perhaps the drivers should change every hour."

"I am the only one that drives the truck."

"But your brother knows how to drive a scooter."

"It's not the same. He is a very good mechanic, but . . ."

Enzo twisted to face me, tapping me on the knee to gain my full attention, grateful at last for some trivial conversation.

"This is how I meet Mister Keller. He has a touring car, Alfa Romeo, you know this?"

"Alfa Romeo," I said, to stop the tapping. "Yes."

"1930 Zagato Spider. Very red, very nice. When he visits Bologna last year, I come to see him, and I fix it. This visit, in Rome, I help him look at another car, more expensive."

"He likes expensive cars, does he? I wonder how it is he can afford them."

To the east, a low range of purple mountains faded into the distance as we curved west, climbing past more fields and dusty silver trees and the occasional rustic village with a bell tower. There was a disturbing lack of signs, but I supposed that many of these hamlets were too small to merit inclusion on a national road map.

"Well, it is same as art," Enzo insisted, unfazed by my lack of engagement. "You want something, you find a way to pay. Your government pays a lot for this statue. They pay more than he pays for his new car."

"Collecting art is not like collecting cars, Enzo."

"Very special, very expensive—no matter, statue or good car. Someone has good taste; he knows what he likes."

"Fine art is one of a kind."

"Yes? But your statue is a copy."

"It's an ancient Roman copy. That makes it very different from a modern copy. It's irreplaceable."

Enzo asked Cosimo to translate something, but Cosimo was ignoring us, his eyelids heavy, the steering wheel tugging gently left and right between his loose fingers.

"So you are saying it is so special," Enzo tried again. "So special that maybe Italy should not give it away."

"Your government sold it. It was not given away."

"But Italy should not sell it."

"Past tense. Sold. Finished deal."

"So Italy should not sold it, you are saying."

"Obviously I'm not saying that."

But we had not been talking about art or automobiles; we had been talking at first about the tired driver, and whether it made sense for someone else to help with the driving. It couldn't be me. Except for one weekend of driving lessons, which only convinced me of the great value of public transportation, I didn't know how to handle a motorized vehicle. "Your brother might need a break, I think, if you could take over for a short while."

"He is a good mechanic, my brother—good enough for extra pay," Cosimo commented placidly. "But my brother doesn't know how to drive. It's better. This way, we have different specialties, and we each have a job."

"Well, that's fine as long as we make unhampered progress. Florence by tonight, for example? That isn't too much to expect?"

Enzo considered, frowning. "Florence maybe tomorrow. Earliest, morning."

"But I should think that Florence is one-third of the way. Isn't that true?"

Enzo began to nod, slowly at first, then with greater enthusiasm. He had found it in his heart to forgive me for previous disagreements, at least for the moment. "Florence is a magnificent city. You are there a while, on the way to Rome?"

"No. I traveled directly."

"But you are a student of the history of art? Florence has more art than any place in the world!"

"I did not have time."

"And you will be passing close by it again—and to not visit? To not see the art?"

"It doesn't matter."

He tugged at a loopy curl over his ear, fatigued by my contradictions. "It does not matter?"

"I did not prepare for Florence."

"You cannot prepare."

"Yes. One can."

"No," he said, as if I simply hadn't heard him. "For beauty, you cannot prepare."

"You read, you study, you determine in advance—"

"No, no," he objected, smiling.

"—you determine what you will see," I said, finishing my thought, "and you prepare to understand and appreciate it."

He shrugged. "So you do this next time. Soon. When you are in Italy again."

"I don't enjoy traveling."

He tallied on his fingers the famous enchantments of Florence: "You have the Ponte Vecchio. You have the Botticelli, the da Vinci. You have, of course, the *David*. Your *Discus Thrower* is not even as tall as me. But the *David*, he is twice as tall."

"It is three times as tall," I corrected him. "It is just over five meters. It was started by Agostino di Duccio and the commission was taken over by Antonio Rossellino—"

"No, friend, it is by Michel—"

"—before the commission was given to the young Michelangelo, then twenty-six years old." Just two years older than me, and already immortal. Not to suggest I had any lofty aims for myself, only that I recognized youth was a relative concept, and no excuse for anything.

"That is very good," Enzo said, smiling at my recitation. "Very good."

"That is nothing. I am unschooled in the finer points of Renaissance sculpture. These facts I have told you are just facts, as a tourist would memorize them from a guidebook. And anyway, more to the point"—I was speaking too quickly, causing Enzo to wrinkle his brow and lean toward me in an extra effort to catch and translate every word—"the point you are making about the *David*'s greater height is no point at all. We don't judge art by its *size*. We are not selecting modern *furniture*."

Even confused, he still managed to look at peace. Grinning, he said, "But to go to Florence and actually *see*. This is different from facts." Eyebrows lifted, he affected the high-pitched tone of an adult trying to pique a child's interest. "It is *tempting*."

"It is not."

And this made me feel better as well. Perhaps this was why I was chosen—not because there was no other choice, but because I was the kind of person who preferred to be home, who could not be lured by the exoticism of distant borders, the distraction of foreign offerings. I was not even inflamed by passion for art outside my classical specialty—and good thing, or I never could have crossed such a treasure-filled country on a deadline.

In the beginning, our *Sonderprojekt* department had been staffed by twice as many men as women, even in the clerical positions. But almost as soon as I'd joined, following certain new arrivals and departures, the balance had reversed. It occurred to me only now that Gerhard's had not been the first unexplained change. There had been other quiet demotions and outright removals, less apparent to me then because I'd been so new, less worthy of reflection of any kind in Munich, with its day-to-day concerns and distractions—whereas here there was only the sound and rhythm of the wheels on the road, and more time—perhaps too much time—to think.

As it turned out, one could have too much knowledge and experience in the arts to be the best match for certain kinds of employment. Someone older than me, who had worked in the field longer and under a different zeitgeist, would have developed many ideas and tolerances that were no longer acceptable. When I first started working in our office there had been several modern art curators among us, but invariably, their tastes became problematic. Perhaps they defended an artist, living or dead, or had certain ideas about embracing new possibilities, or weren't sympathetic to the anti-modern "degenerate" exhibitions supported by the government.

None of that involved me, not because of my own political or personal views, but only because I knew so little about modern art, had never written any papers, made any statements, or even attended many gallery openings of note. I had not been strategically avoiding controversy. I was simply not part of that intellectual sphere, due to my own inadequate schooling and my late discovery—one of those doors that opens after another closes—of art itself. My ignorance, in a sense, had made me safe, even while my lack of broader knowledge pained me. But this wasn't the time to be a Renaissance man. This was the time for the deep, clean, and relatively painless cut of narrow knowledge.

At this moment, I reminded myself, lest my own thoughts circle too endlessly, the statue was my only priority, followed by the job awaiting me back in Munich. Surely, regardless of Herr Keller's intimations, the job *still* awaited. If I had erred during the first hours of my assignment, injuring my reputation in some way, then surely that error could be overcome. I had done nothing wrong, at any time in my young career or at any point in my young adult life. But if doing nothing was some kind of magic armor, why did I feel so exposed and out of sorts?

Enzo had picked up on my pensive melancholy, or perhaps he was simply trying to shed his own. He suddenly sat upright. Something had caught his attention out the window.

"Close your eyes," he said to me.

"Your brother might need a nap, but I'm fine."

"No, quickly. Close your eyes. It is something incredible coming, but you should see it only closer. Do this for me, please."

I relented. I closed my eyes and kept them closed for several minutes, enjoying the heat on my eyelids.

"This is most incredible thing you will ever see in your life," he said.

"Is it a fancy car?"

"No," he laughed. "I am not only liking cars. This is something everyone likes."

A minute passed.

"Is it a pretty girl?'

This made him laugh again. "Pretty girl? She is very big pretty girl if I see her from so far away and we are not passing her yet after this much time. Don't you think?"

"Just tell me when you're ready."

"No. Not yet. It is better soon. Yes, now, open! Look!"

"I'm looking."

They covered the horizon. Fields of tall sunflowers: dark faces fringed with bright yellow petals, nodding slightly, all facing one direction, bowing to some distant altar. I had never seen so many in one place. I had never seen such a broad expanse of yellow and green, on the left and on the right, ahead of and behind us. An ocean that turned toward the sun.

"Yes?"

"I see . . . flowers."

His eyebrows were furrowed, his features clownishly collapsed. "That is all? You see flowers?" He reached across me to grab me by the shoulders, squeezing the shirt fabric of which he only somewhat approved.

"Yes, Enzo. I see flowers."

He released my shoulders. His face said it all. It was done. *He* was done—with me and my refusal to be charmed, my refusal to be like him. For a moment, I experienced the thin, taut pleasure of having stood firm, followed by a slow and sighing deflation—the sinking realization that one has declined in another's already-modest estimation.

Oddly, Enzo's disappointment seemed to relax him. He glanced away. No more knee gripping. No more hair tugging. In being mildly difficult, in proving myself unworthy, I had made something easier for him.

The hills had softened; the terraced slopes that came into view as the day progressed were more neatly and densely planted. Fewer houses stood near the road, but more clustered on the ridges above us, both left and right—entire Tuscan hill towns, densely built and situated in high, defensible locations with views across valley after valley, land folding upon itself again and again, the discarded robes of a lovely, long-ago time.

If the roads just north of Rome had seemed wild, scrappy, and far from imperial, we'd now passed into some other zone with a different ambiance, more expansive vineyards, larger bell towers visible from a great distance, under a blue sky— pale but clear—whose precise shade I recognized from certain famous Florentine paintings. In some of these churches, price- less frescoes sat largely unadmired, hidden in shadow. Behind high walls painted red by the late-afternoon sun, the traces of remarkable history resided. And a different traveler might have had the time and inclination to turn off, to climb higher, to investigate the places where a Michelangelo or a Machiavelli had first set pencil to paper.

Even *Der Kunstsammler*, in those striking news photographs shot during his spring trip to Italy, had looked dreamy, wandering among the famous sites with his more sober companion, *Il Duce*. World leaders, busy as they were, could afford to look ahead and behind—but not the rest of us, who were merely living day to day, trying not to slip up, trying not to embrace the wrong historical lessons or even the wrong teachings from our own recent personal histories. All too often, a quick glance over the shoulder could turn into a risky detour.

Speaking of detours, there was a very brief one that Enzo, motivated by hunger, insisted on making.

"*Lì*," he pleaded as we passed another village sign, and again as we passed a squat, black-garbed woman standing next to a donkey cart at an unmarked fork in the road.

"No."

"*Lì, lì, lì!*"

"No, no, *no*," Cosimo replied.

Frustrated, Enzo started to fold the map but then pushed the crumpled mass into the space near his feet. After muttering in irritation, he switched again to words I could understand: "I want a big dinner tonight. You say it, I have it. Meat, fish, soup, pasta, wine. Everything. This is where I am tonight."

Cosimo corrected him in German, for my benefit. "This is where he would *like to be* tonight."

Enzo narrowed his eyes. "Oh yes? Is this what I mean?" He switched his attention back to me. "Do you know what happens to a lady at a wedding? If she is married, she thinks of her wedding. If she is not married, she also thinks of her wedding."

"She imagines her wedding, you mean," I said.

Enzo's grin widened so far that I could see past his six or so very white, straight teeth to the gap where his left molar was missing—the only imperfection in an otherwise perfect smile. "Every lady."

Cosimo insisted on explaining. "The girl in the picture. Farfalla. Her sister is having a big wedding party tonight." He pushed out his chin, preparing to swallow something that wouldn't go down easily. "Enzo was expected there. But how could he be expected? This is a three-day drive for you—for us, even longer, with the return trip from the border. My brother feels that if he had gone, this would have been his lucky time with the girl—"

"My *lucky* time!"

I glanced over, surprised to see that the skin around Enzo's eyes had grown red and patchy, his lips thinned by outrage.

"My brother," Cosimo continued, his stare fixed on the road ahead, "accepted this trip to Rome and back, I think, forgetting he would be on duty for every hour and every kilometer until we deliver your statue."

Enzo objected, "This is what you call it: my *lucky* time! Is this what love is, you think? Luck? Chance? One opportunity and then nothing?"

"But isn't that what you're trying to convince us?" Cosimo shot back. "Aren't you telling us this is your only opportunity? If so, *fratello mio*, it isn't love. It's something else."

Enzo started to speak again—then, uncharacteristically, decided to let his brother have the last word.

Cosimo shrugged. "Never mind. Do you have a cigarette?"

Enzo relented, unfolding his jacket to pull out the cigarette and his brass lighter. He leaned over my lap as he assisted his brother, smoke pouring into my eyes with the first puff, the smell of Enzo's sweaty underarms released in full bloom as he continued to lean over me, brushing some ash from his brother's shirtfront with a habitual tenderness.

Returning the lighter to his pocket, Enzo said, "I buy this for my brother yesterday. Does he accept? He says, 'You spend too much. Matches are good enough for me.' But see now who is lighting for whom?"

Cosimo objected. "Because I am driving."

"Not only when you are driving."

"So we'll share it, then."

"Not everything is for sharing." Enzo cast a meaningful glance in Cosimo's direction, then in mine, making it clear we were not really discussing a cigarette lighter after all.

Ignoring the cloud of cigarette smoke enveloping us, I squinted at Enzo and tried to change the subject. "Did you get a good look at the *Discobolus* statue, in Rome?"

"I see it while we make it go lower, into the box, yes. Sure."

"And what did you think of it?"

"I say before, it is not very big. A few cracks. It is old enough. That is why it is so expensive, yes?"

He was still playing with the lighter that took a dozen strikes to light—the crummy lighter that was manufactured last year and wouldn't last until the next. Enzo wouldn't understand workmanship. I was surprised he could judge the quality of an automobile, or, for that matter, the inner beauty of a woman, the one he loved—perhaps also the one his brother loved. There was no reason I should want him to appreciate the statue. Better that he didn't appreciate it, one might have argued, given how many Italians protested the export to Germany.

"But what did you think?" I asked, ignoring my own common sense.

"What do I think—?"

"Yes. That's my question."

There was a long pause, long enough for Cosimo to flick his butt out the window and raise the pane halfway. "He doesn't think. That is why Minister Ciano and Herr Keller like my brother."

Enzo cocked his head, not sure if he was being teased or praised. He laughed. "True enough. But Cosimo, if we can't get some food, at least can we take a break?"

"A very short break. But no town, no people, no trouble. I know a place."

CHAPTER 4

Enzo started unbuttoning his shirt even before the truck came to a full stop. When he flung open the door, the pebble gray of the road's shoulder was still a moving blur.

"*Essere attento*," Cosimo cautioned, braking gently—but Enzo didn't wait. The silvery glint of the roadside lake was too alluring. We were not yet fully stopped when he jumped, tumbling forward onto his knees, then sprang up again, running and hollering, pushing his pants down to his ankles.

"Lots of energy," Cosimo sighed, turning off the ignition.

"How many years younger is he?"

"Years? No years."

"But isn't he younger than you?"

Cosimo sniffed once. "Most probably. No one knows for sure."

I turned, studying him closely for the first time. "How could you not know?"

Outside the truck, Enzo hopped and laughed, freeing one foot from his pants. He raised a fist in celebration, then stumbled forward again to liberate the second foot. Abandoning the pants where he stepped out of them, he jogged forward a few paces, then reconsidered, doubling back to grab the pants. An hour later, he'd be rubbing at their grass stains with a lake-dampened handkerchief, grinding the stains further into the fabric.

"Of course," Cosimo continued, "one of us came out a minute before the other. But our mother did not expect. And in the surprise, and looking so much the same, it was never certain."

He did not know the correct phrase for identical twins, *eineiige Zwillinge*, but he assured me, "Yes, we were copies. We looked alike when we were little children. And even when we were big children. And then the first fight"—he touched his finger to his twisted nose—"and a few more." He touched his cheekbone.

"Not with Enzo . . ."

"No." He turned down his lips, lowering his eyelids to half-mast. "Never with Enzo. Only with the boys who tried to *beat up* Enzo. I got the tough reputation, he kept the looks. I was more tough; more wanted to fight me. I won; they only wanted to fight more. He was more pretty, he had more girls—why should he fight? He was one road going this way and

I was the other road going that way. You know this—how sometime something happens a little and then, too late, it can't be stopped?"

When I nodded sympathetically, he asked, "You have a brother?"

"A sister. Just one." I explained that we lived in different cities, far apart, that she'd moved immediately after marrying.

"So you must be angry at the husband."

"No. Grateful."

He seemed puzzled by my tone. "There was a particular time you and she stopped being close?"

"A particular time? No, I don't think so." But it was a good question, because surely we had been close once. The image that came unbidden was the two of us, sitting under a nest of tipped-over wooden chairs covered by a quilt, and the feel of Greta's fingernails digging into my skinny upper arm as we giggled, listening to our father entering the house, a little worse for wear, bumping into things.

She must have been no more than twelve; her golden hair had been long still, not yet cut by my father's dull scissors. That would happen a year later, when he noticed that her beauty was blooming and he decided that she was becoming flirtatious, though she was really still just a girl. *Vater* was always taking things into his own hands, impulsively. I was too young to stand between them, but surely, when she protested, "*Vater*, I never flirt!' and turned to me to say something, I could have done more than what I did: nothing at all. As if my own turn wouldn't come soon enough. How many times must we watch others suffer, in how many different ways, before we realize that our time, too, will come? Greta left Munich as soon as she had a chance, accepting the first marriage proposal that came her way.

"The distance is preferable for us," I told Cosimo, not wanting to think of my sister anymore, or at least not that vision of her—so small and slim and innocently pretty, so defenseless in her youth. "It helps."

"Yes? That is very interesting." He patted his legs. "But I do not understand."

He wiped a hand across his nose again. "You want to look at me now? You are staring, now, in order to compare?"

"What? No." But he'd caught me.

Cosimo pushed the door open, looking carefully for any sign of traffic, and stood on the road, refolding his jacket. "Wait, there is shade. It will be better for us."

He climbed back in with slow deliberation and drove the truck forward a hundred meters, parking it under the only large tree on this side of the road.

"Maybe I was staring," I conceded after he set the brake. "You and Enzo are just so different."

"We were always a little different." He opened the door again, leaving it open as the fresh breeze blew past us, airing out the steaming truck cab. "I remember when we were small. Enzo was three years old. He got lost at the marketplace. The woman who found him almost kept him—she said she liked the yellow curls. But good thing he was a crybaby. She gave him back."

His lips twisted into a crooked smile. "Come to think of it, many women spend a little time with my brother, and then they like to give him back."

He waited for my reaction, his expression friendly but guarded. "Now I am more interesting to you. Before, just the driver. Now, a little more interesting. Like the statue."

"I'm not sure what you mean."

"Something to study, for an answer to something. The statue is perfect. Everything just right—the arms, the legs, the way he is about to throw. I am the opposite, yes? A good start, the same as Enzo, and then everything turned a little wrong."

He winked, but that only drew attention to the fact that one eye drooped more than the other.

"The *Discus Thrower* we carry," he continued. "This one is only a copy, yes?"

"A copy of the lost Greek bronze."

"And if it's so perfect, maybe the original was even more perfect? Because things go from good to bad, from bad to worse." But he was grinning as he said this, as if sharing a private joke.

"Why are you smiling? Do you think I believe everything goes from bad to worse?"

"I don't know. But I am thinking that you believe there is perfect, and then everything else. And you know the world is going a bad way, but you think perfect art will make it better, or maybe at least give you something to stare at, so you don't see what is not so beautiful all around."

Determined, I stuck to my original inquiry. "Cosimo, I know your brother doesn't care one way or another, but really, tell me what you truly thought about the statue."

He shook his head because he had no more to say and I hadn't understood his point.

I pleaded: "Try to remember, before it was in the crate, when you were waiting in the room with Keller and all the others." Enzo and Cosimo had had all that time to regard a masterpiece while I had been out wandering like a foolish tourist, out of my element, feeling rattled, with time running out even then, in ways I couldn't admit or understand.

He relented. "It makes you . . ."

"Yes?"

"It is as if you must . . ."

"Yes?"

". . . hold your breath."

"Yes," I said, satisfied with that reverential answer, pausing for a moment as my lungs stopped drawing air, as my own blemished rib cage and imperfect body remained statue-still, imagining. Yes.

"But then," he said—and I couldn't tell if he was teasing me, trying to impart some great truth, or simply revealing his own lack of artistic appreciation—"that is good for only so long. Life is waiting. Then you must breathe again."

By the time I scooted out the passenger side, Enzo was standing naked at the edge of the lake. Before I could register my own discomfort at the spectacle he was making—so near the road, where anyone might have seen—he had plunged into the water, toes curling before they disappeared beneath the sparkling surface.

Cosimo chuckled to himself, undressing more slowly. "*Va bene*. Fifteen minutes."

He walked slowly to the lake edge, dropping his white boxers. When he was knee deep in the water, he splashed at his armpits and then turned back. "Are you coming?"

"*Certo.*" I rolled up the bottom of my pants and waded up to my ankles, toes squelching in the soft bottom of the lake.

Cosimo floated on his back, eyes closed, letting the water lap over his forehead. "It's not bad. Clean enough."

"Enjoy yourself."

A second time: "Are you coming?"

When I didn't answer, he called back with effort, "I don't think we'll see any cars. No one has passed for a long time." Still floating on his back, he started to whistle. The tune was familiar and pleasant, something I'd heard Cosimo whistle for brief snatches while driving, but I couldn't place it.

I rolled up my sleeves, dipping my wrists in the cold water. On the far side of the lake, a solitary tree spread its branches over the lake. The water had a deep and musty algae smell, like the olive-colored water at the bottom of a neglected flower vase. The lake's calm surface reflected the blue sky and cumulus clouds high above, creating a mirrored version that was, in fact, lovelier than the real sky, like a painting that allows one to see something unappreciated in everyday life—only one of art's valuable qualities.

But my reverie was interrupted. Enzo exploded out of the water a few meters away, shaking his golden mane. He laughed at my startled expression. "How can you wash your body while you are clothed?"

"I'm fine."

He waded toward me, into increasingly shallow waters,

chest bared first, then well-defined abdomen. "Come on now. The truck is hot. We are there soon again, back in the oven." He dragged one leg at a time through the water, taking the slow-motion strides of a muscle-bound giant. Though I tried to avert my gaze, it was impossible not to see as his hips emerged, followed by his hairy pelvis, his penis shrunken by the cold water, his testicles shifting with each advancing step. When I turned further away, Enzo insisted even more loudly, "You feel better all the rest of the day. You want that we toss you in?"

"No, thank you. Certainly not." My hand went to the front of my buttoned shirt, clasping the cloth there, pulling it tight around my ribs like a nervous woman holding her bathrobe closed. Embarrassed by the gesture, I dropped my hands, dipped my wrists again quickly, then waded back a few steps and sat on the dry shore, pulling on my socks with difficulty. My feet were still wet. I was hurrying for nothing. Relax, relax, I told myself, and remembered the postcard to my sister in my shirt pocket, warped by my chest's damp heat.

We have stopped at a small lake, I began to write a few minutes later, safely distanced from the lakeshore, and with those words I could see this moment as it should have been seen and experienced: as a congenial, natural, unselfconscious diversion. Who wouldn't have wanted to take a refreshing swim on a day like this?

And as soon as I'd allowed the thought, as soon as I'd let myself think again of my sister not as she was but as she had once been, I imagined my mother. She was down on her knees so that we were face to face, lecturing me gently on the day I was to leave for a week of nature camp just outside Landshut.

"If you refuse to take your shirt off, if you refuse to swim, the boys will notice and be *more* curious. Don't let them start, and you will be fine." But my heart was pounding as she gazed deeply into my eyes, attempting to make a gift of her own confidence. She glanced over her shoulder to be sure my father was out of earshot. He was talking to my uncle, who would drive my cousin and me to the boys' camp, two hours away. My father had already been through my suitcase once, approving not only each item, but how it was folded and placed. Now my mother pressed something into my hand. Six small, tan bandages and a small roll of tape. The bandages would cover what must stay hidden, if I were to avoid shame, but every time one got wet, it would have to be replaced. "Only six?" I said, my voice breaking with pinched dread. She rested her forehead gently against mine and explained, "The seventh day, there is no swimming. Only youth assembly. Now quickly: pack them away." My eyes welled up. I was dizzy with relief. She had thought of everything, as mothers do. And if we had lived alone, just the two of us—three, with Greta—we would have been happy.

Enzo's voice boomed across the water: "Are all Germans like you—embarrassed to take off their clothes?"

"Certainly not."

"Enzo," Cosimo called from farther out, still floating. "Leave him alone. Let him make up his own mind."

"*Va bene*. But there is no lake again today, so close to the road. And the truck has a bad smell."

"Not because of me," I muttered.

Enzo was in water up to his knees—hands relaxed at his

side, soaked pubic hair catching the light—staring at me, or past me, toward the road. I turned away, exaggerating the effort required to pull on each shoe, oppressed by his display—not the nudeness per se, I was no prude, but the arrogance of his ease.

"Vogler . . ."

I grumbled in reply, pretending to be focused on my laces, wishing almost that I had disrobed entirely—it really wasn't worth all the fuss, not as it had been for me once, long ago. That was all over—forgotten, insignificant—the problem reduced to one small, residual blemish. The boys' camp had been a problem, but I had survived six months of labor service just fine. I could tell you, labor service had been a lot more problematic than the boys' camp. But now that I was fully dressed, it would have seemed more awkward to swim than to avoid swimming.

"Vogler—" Enzo stopped short, only his feet submerged. "Do you see?"

There was a distant figure—no, two figures—side by side, walking on the road. Toward the truck.

I pulled the laces of my shoe so hard that one snapped. "Get your clothes!" I shouted, and took off running before I could tell if Cosimo had heard or if Enzo was following. The flat dress shoes tore into the grass. I slipped once, gained traction on the gravelly road, stirring dust as I sprinted toward the figures: one larger than the other, walking alongside the truck, tapping the side of it, pausing near the driver's door. I ran so hard I couldn't breathe, but there was no need to breathe for this short distance, only to run—fingers pressed together, palms gently cupped, elbows crooked, chin lowered, as our coaches had always instructed—as fast as I could, hobbled only slightly by one untied shoe and my untrained physique.

The figures heard me pounding toward them. The old man's lips parted beneath his gray mustache. The boy's eyes grew wide.

"*Hallo! Halten Sie an!*"

The boy took a step closer to his father, eyes wide, clutching the burlap bag he was carrying.

I interrogated them: "What are you doing? Why are you approaching the truck? What were you expecting to see here?"

Cosimo had pulled on his boxers and rushed to catch up. Now he stood just behind me, one hand pressed to his side, panting as he rambled in Italian while I slowly took hold of my senses and remembered: of course these two couldn't understand me. They'd never heard anything but Italian this far south. They were villagers. They'd mistaken me for a madman.

Cosimo tapped me on the shoulder several times. In response, I slowly loosened my grip on the boy's arm. I had been pinching that soft, thin arm so hard that there was sure to be a bruise to show when the boy told his mother, sometime that night, about the *übergeschnappt* foreigner who wanted to interrogate him.

"But why are they so close to the truck?" I demanded when Cosimo seemed to be letting off the strangers too lightly. Cosimo stopped massaging the stitch in his torso and pointed to the burlap bag. "They thought we might buy some lemons. They were walking from their farm to the next village. That's all."

He patted my back a few times now, a casual motion, but there was communication in every touch—a brisk pat at first, then softer, softer. Everything calmer now. He was in control. In that moment, I felt certain that Cosimo had avoided even more brawls than he had endured, that the coming age would be—would have been—a better place with more men like him. It was a different kind of masculine symmetry he presented—not the symmetry of a beautiful face, but the equilibrium of stance and situation. When Cosimo took a casual step forward, closer to the boy and the farmer, I took a step back. The boy nestled under his father's arm, relieved to be out of my reach.

Now Enzo—half dressed, curls dripping onto his bare chest—joined us, oblivious to the minor, evaporating drama. He chatted with the farmer, eyed what they were carrying, held up a finger, and returned a moment later with some money for the boy, taking the entire burlap bag.

The lemony scent filled the truck. The edges of Enzo's fingers were drying white from the strong juice. He had eaten five of them so far and was now squeezing a lemon into his damp curls, working the juice through with his fingers. "It is natural—good for adding light color to the yellow hair."

A fat seed was stuck to his temple, but I said nothing. What kind of man bleached his hair in this way?

"You eat one?"

"Maybe one," I said, digging into the thick yellow rind and passing a wedge to Cosimo, enjoying the way the citrus scent chased away the odor of smoke.

Enzo pressed his elbow into my side and winked, happy not

only about the shared fruit but also about a shared confidence. Just before we had pulled onto the road, while Cosimo had been placing our folded jackets in the back of the truck, Enzo had lowered his head and whispered urgently, "It is not true."

"What?"

"I *know* how to drive. My brother thinks I can't. This is what he tells you, before. It makes him feel better."

"Why?"

"He does not want me to be"—he paused, looking for the word—"independent. He wants me to live in our family town, always. He wants to be partners and share, always. He does not want to be alone. But I *can* drive. He cannot fix truck, but I can drive very well. Of course!"

Cosimo had pulled open the driver's door, cutting short our conversation. But it had served its purpose in restoring Enzo's manly confidence. Now Enzo seemed certain I'd share my own confession in return.

"So, how did you do that?" he asked, after he had finger-combed all his sticky, golden-glazed curls.

"Do what, frighten the boy?" Even I couldn't help but smile at the memory of the boy's wide eyes. The statue was safe and sound, we were not really being followed, and—hunger aside—this drive was turning out to be easy, after all.

"No. How do you run so fast?"

"It was important, for the security of our cargo."

Cosimo took his eyes off the road. "Don't lie to us now. You are some kind of athlete."

"Well," I said, looking at my dry, juice-whitened hands in my lap, "maybe years ago."

It came back to Enzo now. "Mister Keller says he meets you in the summer of the Olympics in Berlin, yes? He sees you there?"

"No, no." To my own surprise, my face was warming. "I wasn't a participant in the Olympics. I was a sprinter when I was young, but I was not that talented. What Mr. Keller meant was that he was introduced to me through a friend, another man, an art collector—who saw me only in the audience at Berlin, only briefly. It's complicated."

"But how does this other man recognize you? Because you are already a famous athlete?"

"No, Enzo. I was never a famous athlete."

"Then how does he recognize you?"

"He did not."

Enzo leaned on one haunch, twisting to face me, his forehead wrinkled with confusion. "But he knows you are an art expert?"

"No. I chose to walk out of the stadium at a moment when everyone was watching to see a high jumper receive his gold medal, far below us."

Enzo waited for me to explain.

"And my awkward exit attracted too much attention. From everyone, all around. It was an inconvenient time to leave."

Enzo's brow smoothed. He granted me a complicit smile. "You are an aggravation. That is why Mr. Keller remembers. Mr. Keller hates aggravations."

"Actually . . ." I paused—but why had I begun? Enzo was clueless and unlikely to persevere. But then again, I was sick of the memory, which had not faded for lack of exposure.

Additionally—and this was significant—there seemed to be no risk in telling this story. Germany seemed unreal enough here; Italy would seem even more unreal once I was back home, in less than three days. Nothing I could say or do here would change anything.

"Actually," I confessed, "people around me were expressing approval of my exit, some of them anyway. A few clapped."

"*Sono confuso*," Enzo lamented, still perplexed.

"Well, I should explain: the medalist was a dark-skinned man, a Negro from the United States."

"Jesse Owens?"

I sighed. "That is the name people associate with the Olympics, but actually, this was a man named Cornelius Johnson. There were a dozen and a half of these dark-skinned fellows in Berlin, and two women also, if I'm not mistaken. Many of them very good, very fast. Many Germans applauded for Owens and for Johnson—excellence is attractive, charismatic. To everyone. It is recognizable in athletics, just as it is in art, which is precisely why the entire world can appreciate a Roman statue, not only Italians. But some of my countrymen were not happy to lose to him, not even happy to see his kind in Berlin—that should not be surprising. When I left, they thought—"

Cosimo spoke up quietly: "That you were a racist, yes?"

"I had never given a thought to racism, nationalism or internationalism, any of that," I said, puzzling over the memory honestly, and feeling no sting in Cosimo's question. "I was leaving because of an argument with the person next to me."

"A woman?" Enzo guessed, nodding to encourage me.

"No." I took a breath. "My father."

Enzo looked briefly disappointed, then nodded even more deeply than before, willing to accept this second-best answer. *Of course.* "*Il padre. Il babbo.*"

"My father, who had bought our tickets—very rare and sought-after tickets. We were sitting not far below the most prized seats where some high-ranking government people and special guests were sitting."

"So, many government officials see you leave."

"Yes."

It was all as sharp as yesterday: the apologies as I squeezed past men, the woman standing to let me pass, the low murmur of disapproval, and that strange moment when the pitch changed, when the murmur rose to a higher register, and the crowd—as if a single organism—reappraised the situation, deciding that I was doing something notable, even noble. Two hands, somewhere, clapped—the quivering antennae of a large and unpredictable creature—and faces turned. Then more began to clap, and it became obvious that the applause—not scattered and swift and lighthearted, as the applause for the athletes had been, but slow, methodical, a telegraphic drumbeat of a message—was indeed for me. For my exit. And several—not all, but several—who were not clapping were looking around for their own jackets or purses or programs, preparing to copy what I'd done.

How easy it is to start something. Too easy.

Just before I squeezed out of my row, I looked up to see in the seats above us three faces studying me, one of them nodding in deep, if mistaken, accord. The most famous face, I found out later, had already left. He had had enough and refused to be present for the presentation of a gold medal to this American Negro. So I was merely adopting the style of the day, without intending to—without even knowing *Der Kunstsammler* had made his own exit before me. I'm sure at least one other man in the seats above me wished he had left before I did, so that he could have trumped my exit and perhaps garnered some reward. How many people left *after* me? I have no idea.

"It was because of the misunderstanding," I finished explaining, "that I was introduced to my current professional situation. The man who saw me, a friend of Keller's, also spotted me later, outside the stadium, and then we happened to meet a third time, went to lunch, and had a conversation. There were inquiries about my background, my interests. Not much later, I had a new job."

Enzo considered, sorting through the details for the only points that mattered. "And you are here, in Italy, because of your job."

"Yes."

"So you are here in Italy because of a misunderstanding."

"Yes."

"That is not so bad." Enzo smacked my leg, congratulatory. "That is only Lady Fortune smiling."

But there is balance in everything that happens, isn't there? There is symmetry. The thrower leans further forward to balance the weight of the outstretched arm and the heavy disc behind him. Something bad is attended, we hope, with something good. And with greater certainty, when something good happens, it is followed by something bad—especially when the good was undeserved.

The lake swim had refreshed Cosimo. The promised dinner stop was still an hour or more off. Enzo's lemons—at last count, seven—had filled and upset his stomach enough that he had lost interest in chatting. Now his expression was pinched, his pursed lips reddened by the acid, the large white seed still plastered to his temple. So there was time, perhaps more time than I would have liked, to remember.

My father was disconcertingly proud of the Olympic track-and-field tickets. This was after Mother had taken to bed, the hard growth in her neck swelling, the doctors long ago sent away. But *Vater* had found a distraction of sorts. First: the pleasure of the hunt, when obtaining tickets seemed impossible. This phase lasted three or four months and involved evening visits to gymnastic clubs, beer halls, and the private homes of old acquaintances.

I had tired long ago of boozy socializing with my father. From the age of twelve, he had tried to make a man of me by dragging me along to the Hofbräuhaus, where we'd endure the intense heat of the long tables crammed with three or four thousand men draining immense tankards. On those interminable evenings, I would sip my own cider and listen as the men discussed the only two subjects they relished—the war that had ended eight years earlier, leaving men like my father wounded and bitter, and the miserable economy that had followed it. Pushed into a sweltering corner, I occasionally sank into slumber, to be wakened suddenly by the blare of an oompah band starting up, or the stamp of feet and pounding of empty steins as someone stood on a table to give a political speech.

By 1936, though, I'd done my time and had failed to develop any affection for either pilsner or political rhetoric; my father by this point made the rounds alone. One night when he returned home tipsy and empty-handed, Greta confided to me that she no longer believed he was trying to get tickets, only talking about it as a way to stay out of the house, away from the smell of disinfectant and chicken broth. Mother would rarely eat more than a spoonful, but it reminded her of winter days and the thin pancakes her own mother had once made—pancakes cut in narrow strips and arranged into pinwheels at the bottom of a shallow bowl and soaked in broth, which had to be eaten quickly, before the pancakes disintegrated. These were the things we talked about at the end, not about life or love or God or regrets, but only about a winter day's *Flädlesuppe*.

Vater must have sensed our disbelief about his intentions to procure the tickets. In the morning he would rail: "The swindler doubled the price on me!"

Did he say "Jew"? Probably not. A few years later he might have. He was one of those people who liked being stylish, *à la mode*. The truth is, he disliked many sorts of people equally.

Finally though, he achieved his goal and could enjoy those three weeks when he already had the tickets and could spend every day leading up to the event boasting to anyone who would listen. I would like to think it made Mother happy, to hear him crowing in the next room. I suppose it was better than hearing him weep, as he also did, late at night when Mother was tranquilized on morphine and he lay, fully dressed, on the damp sheets next to her, thinking that neither Greta nor I could hear.

But remembering is bad enough. I certainly didn't want to sympathize with him. He was the kind of man who would soften your heart just in order to grab it more easily, to squeeze it inside his purple fist. As he did the day of the major track-and-field events, during that first week of August. I had begged not to go. Attending a spectacle just four days after a funeral struck me as tasteless. But he had bullied and pouted, until even Greta cornered me, pleading for me to relent. Much better for her to have him off in Berlin for a few days, drinking beer there instead of at home. My sister had much to do—putting the house back into order, writing cards in response to the first round of condolences and yet more letters to far-off acquaintances who were still uninformed, sorting through the bills that neither parent had paid in the last eight or twelve weeks (bills to remain unpaid, given the cost of two train tickets to Berlin, even at the foreign-guest Olympic summer discount price, which *Vater* had obtained by faking the worst French accent I have ever heard in my life). Yes, Greta was right. She deserved a break from him.

The trip to Berlin; the stay overnight at a distant cousin's flat where *Vater* boasted the entire evening, trying to steer the conversation away from more serious family subjects; the day itself—I'd found all of it exhausting. I'd never enjoyed traveling, and this trip was no exception. And finally, the interminable hours once we'd found our stadium seats.

"That could have been you out there," he started as soon as we'd made ourselves comfortable.

"Not really, Father."

"Yes. Of course. If you had done a little more."

And now we had our *leitmotif*, the melody to which he would return again and again, every time a sprinter broke the tape or cleared a hurdle or climbed to the podium to bask in public acknowledgment of his mastery.

"I was never that fast."

"When you were fourteen, almost. When you were fifteen, yes. And getting faster every day."

"Not like these talented fellows."

"And think, with the best coaching, how much you could have done . . ."

I ignored him when I could. I stared out at the field, as everyone stared—a hundred thousand pairs of eyes and even more watching—miracle of miracles—by the innovation of television. While all around us people clapped and shouted and shook their little flags, I kept my jaws clenched tight, unable to partake in my countrymen's revelry and joyful abandon.

"The *opportunities* your generation has. Unimaginable in my time."

Opportunities, he meant, like the training camp for which I had been wait-listed and then accepted at the last minute, after four athletes had been excluded—three for their non-Aryan roots, one for rumors of homosexual perversion.

"But I did what *I* could," he said minutes later, as if there'd been no delay. His thoughts were clearly looping and cycling, around and around, like the runners below us, trying not to see what was in the center of the field, the dark hole of the truth of the funeral service we'd sat through four days earlier. "*You*, on the other hand . . ."

He extracted the flask from his jacket pocket, made a silent mock toast to the crowd in front of us, and sipped. The golden liquid clung to the untrimmed whiskers of his mustache. He had thought about cutting it shorter, into the short broom-end style of a certain eminent personage, but Greta had begged him not to, for there were some styles not meant to be imitated. *Vater*, who thought he was always just one step away from some bestowed favor, some bit of luck, some elevation in status, was—Greta and I feared—really just one step away from embarrassing himself, or worse.

He was attracting too much attention even now, as his voice gained volume and stridency. "You should have *gone* to that training camp. If not for your—your—*shyness*."

"Have you forgotten why I couldn't go, Father? It wasn't shyness."

"Bah."

"It was raging infection."

"Bah!"

There was a long pause in the events below, as we all waited for the medalists to take the podium. Cornelius Johnson, the Negro, had won gold; another American Negro, I forget his name, had won silver. At that moment, I think a few Germans might have been wondering if our Aryan rules had been a little too strict. We had excluded a number of our own excellent athletes from competing, such as the women's high jumper,

Gretel Bergmann, and here was the result right in front of us. Excellence rises above all—above prejudice, above politics. Excellence speaks for itself. And then, of course, there were many in the audience who weren't thinking anything at all but just enjoying the excitement of the day—the anthems, the crowds, and the amazing feats taking place. Innocent human pleasures.

The problem was, with no one competing at the moment, with no one cheering in the crowd, everyone could hear my father's voice. It didn't bother him that people were turning to stare.

"A good bandaging, and you could have gone!"

"Father—" My voice caught. "I had a high fever. I was unconscious. And then I didn't walk for days. The infection weakened me for several months. How could I have run?"

"You probably think I shouldn't blame your mother."

That was too much, hearing mention of her, and the way he said it—as if she were still at home, waiting for us to return, ready to take any amount of abuse. "Blame her?"

"It was her indulgence of your timid nature. It was her indulgence of your . . . oddity."

"Father." And this is when I stood up to go, to the consternation of the men behind me, straining to watch as the gold medal was placed around the American athlete's neck. "It was *your knife.*"

CHAPTER 5

Appetite is a funny thing. Sometimes, when you don't desire food, it's impossible to tell whether it's because you're not hungry at all or you're so overly hungry that you've tormented your stomach into rebellion.

One way or the other, I had lost my appetite during the last quiet hours of driving on the dry Italian roads, thinking of the *Flädlesuppe*, of the smell of spilled beer and sauerkraut in the dining hall where I retreated after storming out of the Olympic stadium only to realize I had brought little cash with me. I'd sat there two hours when a man who had just been served called out to me, and I turned and recognized his face as one of the stadium men who had nodded at my awkward exit. Though I could tell from his gesture to the barmaid that he was offering to buy me a beer, I wanted no company of any kind, and I promptly dropped some money on the table and fled. There was no choice but to return to my cousin's flat, to wait for my father's return later that night. *Vater* and I hardly spoke for the next three days, even on the train trip home to Munich. The full détente came only once I was offered my *Sonderprojekt* curatorial job several months later, my reprieve from the army, in September 1936.

But it was not as easy as perhaps I am suggesting—the years before that last argument with my father, when I dared to say what I had not managed to say for six years. It was only slightly easier now, in Italy. Despite Herr Keller's cynical pronouncements and my own initial doubts, it struck me on this trip that travel did indeed offer more than mere amusement or escape. The dry, clean air and blue skies of another country did lend some clarity. I could not know at the time the nature of events still to come, but what I was starting to realize—what I look back and confirm even now, testing the memories for the feel of truth and finding them convincing— was that distance alone could be a reprieve. Distance of geography and of time.

A reckoning with the past seemed possible at that moment. As unpleasant as the memories were, the steady drone of our engine, the rise and fall of planted hills as we passed, and the occasional appearance of ancient villages of closely fitted stone houses and maze-like streets all made me feel, at that moment, safely removed from anything that could harm me. It took effort to remember that, in fact, I was supposed to be on my guard.

We had made a short diversion into a small town in order to buy some basic groceries. Enzo seemed completely unconcerned about the truck we'd left behind us long ago. Cosimo, while willing to risk a stop, remained vigilant. He insisted on standing outside the back of the truck while Enzo shopped, and I stood alongside him, stretching my legs. From what he had told me in bits and pieces throughout the afternoon, I gathered it was Enzo who had arranged this unusual freelance job, Enzo who had requested permission for time off from their municipal police captain. Those facts seem to have increased, not lessened, Cosimo's sense of responsibility.

"It is an unusual assignment," he admitted, digging into a pack of cigarettes. "But too many times before, I told Enzo what to do. So this time, I try to be a good brother. But being good is not being blind." He pressed a fingertip to the skin just under his eye for emphasis. "I keep my eyes open, and then my job is done."

Cosimo was on his third cigarette when Enzo emerged, grinning with an armload of food and a bottle of wine. He set everything down on the front seat, then turned toward the store again and went to the doorway, where we could just barely make out a young woman wiping her hands on a small white towel and following him out as they extended their good-byes. Remembering something, she darted inside and came out again, handing him some biscotti wrapped in paper.

"What?" Enzo said back at the truck, returning Cosimo's indignant expression. "What?"

"One stop. Thirty minutes." Cosimo tapped the gas.

"Now we have food enough for more than a day."

"One girl. Thirty minutes." Cosimo engaged the gear roughly, making the truck lurch. "And was she as pretty as Farfalla?"

Enzo smiled innocently. "Just as pretty, but so many girls are pretty. Why pretend it's not true? Mr. Vogler, don't you think?"

Cosimo grunted, "Never mind."

Tension lingered in the truck. But it couldn't compete with the smells of meat, cheese, and fresh-baked bread—all wafting up from the bags in Enzo's lap.

We passed around the long, hard stick of fatty salami, the grease coating our fingers and the black steering wheel. We passed around crusty bread, crumbling cheese, olives, and a glass jar of what seemed to be dark brown mushrooms soaked in olive oil. We were too impatient to make sandwiches; we just bit and ripped and spread the food around—and yes, it was all better than I had expected. My appetite had returned, and each swallow was satisfying. Eight hours had passed since I'd last eaten, and everything tasted delicious, even while Enzo kept apologizing, "This is not a meal. This is nothing," while he watched me from the corner of his eye, basking in my pleasure.

"More bread?" Cosimo asked Enzo.

"Here, I give you the heel."

"Any piece."

"No. My brother likes the heel. You want me to put on it the *crema di olive* or you want just the *olio*?"

Cosimo asked, "Mr. Vogler, you ate a good dinner in Rome last night?"

"I arrived late. But I had a sandwich I'd brought with me on the train, from home."

Still chewing, he let his mouth fall open. "You brought German food all the way to Rome? All the way to Italy, and now you are going home, and you have not had one good prepared meal?"

"This is good enough. I'm not just being polite. It is excellent. Thank you."

A dark, oily mushroom had fallen onto Cosimo's lap. "I can steer for you," I said, reaching across to grab the slippery wheel while he extracted a handkerchief from his pocket.

"Yes," he laughed. "I'm not letting this little fish get away."

Fish? A mistranslation, perhaps. But it looked like a fish, with its little damp fungal gills.

And it was while my hands were on the wheel and Cosimo's attention was focused on the oily item on his lap that Enzo broke out in a shrill frenzy of cursing—"*Maledizione! Al diavolo!*"—as if he'd just been stung by a wasp. I startled at his unexpected outburst, tugging the wheel so that we veered nearly off the road, and then everything was shaking. Two of our four wheels were on the grassy, overgrown shoulder.

Cosimo reacted quickly, grabbing the wheel from me in a confusing, slippery motion of four colliding, greasy hands. We were bumping along and swerving, the view through the windshield blurry and confused. Cosimo overcorrected, and we were back on the road but almost to the other side now—"Too far, too far!"—Enzo still cursing at who knows what, and Cosimo cursing back even more loudly. The truck swerved briefly through a thicket of corn growing close to the road. Green stalks filled our field of vision.

In the anticipation of what would come next—a rollover? a

collision with a low stone wall?—everything slowed, became taut and somehow fine, stripped of irrelevance. *I never got to see it*, I realized at that moment. *I screwed up, and I missed my chance to see it.* Yes, to save my own hide, I needed to deliver the *Discobolus*, but what I had wanted most, what I thought would deliver me, was just to see and to know what perfection looks like. Whether it made imperfection more or less sufferable. That's what made it worth so much—not to him, *Der Kunstsammler*. Not to anyone else. But to me.

My heart thumped wildly: twice, three times. Followed by a loud thump that wasn't my heart. It was the answering cry, the centrifugal response, from behind us, as the crate slammed once against the inside wall of the truck. This boom was answered by a softer slide and thump as the heavy wooden object shifted again, hitting the other side of the truck's interior before settling.

"*Scheisse.*"

Cosimo cursed as he braked gently. "Maybe it was just the scooter falling against the crate. But the crate is well built. It should be all right."

"*Scheisse!*" I repeated again, trying not to imagine the fracturing of marble fingers and toes, the split of ancient stone.

"No, no," Cosimo tried to reassure me. "It's all right. Give me one minute and I will find a good place to pull over, slowly."

"Cosimo," I said, taking deep breaths now, "I apologize for losing the wheel."

"Everything will be fine."

But Enzo's face was in his greasy hands, distraught. He'd said nothing until now, but suddenly a whimper broke through, like a popping bubble rising from the pursed lips of a baby on the verge of sobbing: "You have to go back. I lost it."

"Something at the food shop?"

He moaned, shaking his head.

When Cosimo interrogated him in Italian, I could make out only "*lago*," which I understood, and "*anello*," which I didn't. At the mention of this last word, Cosimo stepped on the brake. He yanked the door open, stepped down, and stood at the front of the truck, glowering through the windshield. Enzo followed reluctantly.

Outside the truck, they resumed their argument. Enzo stood with hands in his pockets. Cosimo paced back and forth on the road, waving his arms, gesturing up to the sky, no longer able to keep it all inside.

I got out slowly, stepped around to the back of the truck and crawled inside. The crate was there, with no visible sign of damage from the outside, not a dented board, not even a splinter. The marble was surely harder than the wood, and it was packed well, one hoped—*I* hoped. Yes. Of course it was. The slamming sound hadn't even been that loud, more of a soft bump, really. And the statue itself had survived worse insults than this. The scooter, tipped to one side, was now wedging the crate more firmly within the truck—a good arrangement, which I dared not disrupt.

My stomach settled; my breath deepened. If anything, I felt a giddy sense of relief: the worst had happened now, the fulfillment of a nagging premonition. A near accident, averted. As if we had made a small offering to the gods—a little sweat, a little terror. All could proceed without incident now. *Ohne Zwischenfall.* At the border, at the end of day three, the crate would be opened and I would see it then, I would have my unhurried moment in good light, before the *Discus Thrower* took its role as an object for other people, for other purposes. All day I'd been letting my mind wander through time, indulging memories, when perhaps I should have been concentrating on just that glorious moment. The near accident snapped me back into focus. I was here to do one thing only, and to do it dutifully.

Our jackets, near the truck's back door, had shifted and come unfolded. As I pushed Enzo's jacket back into place, something slid out of the front pocket: his folded blue tie, and with it, the picture of Farfalla.

A moment later, I approached him to ask, "Is this what you think you lost?"

The argument paused. Cosimo was still trembling with anger, his face tinged grayish purple with a cloud of capillaries ready to explode, in contrast with Enzo's face, merely flushed pink and more healthy looking than ever.

Enzo sighed, taking the photo from my hand. "No. But *grazie mille.*"

He studied the photo, rubbing the corner gently, as if he could feel the girl's cheek beneath his thumb. "*Che bella.*" And then, emboldened despite his brother's anger: "We go back to get the ring. It is simple."

"A ring?"

"An engagement ring," Cosimo explained to me. He turned to his brother again. "How could you lose Mamma's ring?"

"It falls out of my pocket when I run to the lake. It is my fault. But we must go back."

"We can't go back," I interjected. "Cosimo, it is impossible. We don't have extra time, and we don't want any unexpected encounters or additional difficulties. We cannot go back."

He nodded once, eyes on his feet. Then he gestured back to the truck. "*Andiamo.*" End of discussion.

More food was distributed, but it was eaten with less praise and less abandon. Enzo brought out the wine bottle and passed it around—a sip for Cosimo, a few sips for me, and most of it for himself as he wallowed in the corner of the cab. Wanting to avoid eye contact at any cost, I stared out the windshield as if I were studying the landscape, memorizing it for some future sketch, though I hadn't sketched a landscape in some time.

"A little more wine?" Enzo asked after he had polished off more than half of it.

"*Grazie.*" I reached for it casually, still avoiding eye contact. The wine warmed my stomach. It didn't take much for me to feel a little tipsy, and the tipsiness felt good, especially after the bit of excitement we had endured.

Ohne Zwischenfall. Without incident. Well, perhaps that wasn't accurate. The day had been at least a little eventful. But everything would be fine. It sounded better in Italian, more melodious and certain: *Tutto va bene.*

The sun's slow descent had painted the rusty hills. Bowls of purple separated fields of red soil. Night was collecting; everything was becoming softer. Just when you thought the canvas was done, that the light had finished playing its games and now darkness would fall, there would be another ridge highlighted with sun, another valley cast into even deeper shadow. This countryside appealed to me much more than the countryside around Rome, but maybe it was my state of mind. Maybe it was the wine. Maybe it was the fading, changing light and the natural colors that begged for artistic representation.

I had tried watercolor painting for a year or so, on my own without a teacher, but I'd had no talent for it. I fought the flow of water against the page, the drip of changing hue obscuring my pencil guidelines. Any watercolors I attempted seemed to have their own ideas. I couldn't relax and find inspiration from them. Worst of all was being pleased with some minor painting at the midpoint of its execution and then seeing it fully dry—there, changed again. Unsettling.

I drank a little more wine, then I finished the bottle. Why not? Enzo had already had his share; Cosimo needed to be alert. There was nothing else to do but sip and watch the sun go down, appreciating our recent brush with disaster.

Outside the window, there was an entire landscape with its own ideas, changing with every moment, so different from the statue we were transporting, a model of ideals that never changed, in a medium of reassuring solidity. A sculpture was what it was, not only mid-process, but before the chiseling had even begun. Michelangelo had believed that a statue's shape was hidden within the stone, to be revealed rather than created. Much as a person's true health, inner strength, character—call it what you will—is revealed.

And yet, this ephemeral moment was beautiful, too; one could argue it was even more so, for its lack of permanence. There was more to see at this sunset hour, and more to imagine: that soft hill there could be the rounded hip of a woman lying on her side, with that shadow obscuring her sleeping face. *Bella. Schön.*

There had been moments with Leonie, but no—we were looking only for reassurance from each other, for dull physical comfort, and the lack of chemistry was clear from the start. It had been best to discover that sooner rather than later. But why hadn't I tried to find my better half, the person whose honesty and beauty would help me feel more open to moments like these? Why hadn't I found someone to help me face what was not pleasant or beautiful in our lives? And how could I begrudge another man his eyes and heart for being more open than mine?

When I set down the empty bottle safely near my feet, a guttural sound escaped from Enzo's chest, and I peeked at his left hand on his left knee, flexing and tightening like a beating heart. Of course the hills reminded him of his girlfriend. They were all women, a nation of women—sleeping, dreaming, beckoning—out here beyond the noise and confusion, the scheming and ambition of cities, the stupid plans of men. And men did have such grand, ambitious plans: the acquiring, collecting impulse that could, unchecked, become something entirely different—a rapacious appetite for controlling things and ideas and posterity itself. And no matter how good it sounded—an "expanded homeland" or even an entire "city of art"—it somehow became the opposite of those things. The opposite of home and security, the opposite of culture and art. The opposite, too, of truth and beauty and love . . .

"Perhaps—" I said, clearing my throat, "perhaps we have made good time. The stop for food was quick. We carry our own fuel. I don't see how we could be far from Florence. We might even be ahead of schedule."

The justification, I thought, was sound: as long as the decision was mine, as long as the backward detour was a short one, I would be repaid in loyalty and efficiency. We would drive further into nightfall, and tomorrow there would be fewer unnecessary stops. Otherwise, I never would have compromised.

The lake was at least sixty minutes behind us. Two hours round-trip, though Cosimo had made it clear he was going to cut the loss to one hour, give or take, by driving nearly twice our previous speed. The truck, which had been whining already on every uphill climb, responded unhappily to Cosimo's increasing demands. Grinding the gears, he cursed under his breath. The whole truck was vibrating at this unwholesome speed—and *that* was not good at all. A constant vibration could do more damage to the statue than a single unfortunate bump.

"An hour lost is really not so much," I ventured, to an unresponsive audience. Clearing my throat, I made my point more plain: "We cannot drive so fast. You must slow down."

But Cosimo was barely in control of his own breathing. He inhaled, held it, and exhaled through his mouth in little bursts. His foot tapped the accelerator and we shimmied up the next hill, even faster than before.

"Then again," I said, feeling angrier now, the warm haze of the wine fading with every passing minute and every backward kilometer, "perhaps we should not have turned around for a ring, after all. Perhaps you should have gone searching for it on a subsequent journey."

"No, no," Enzo reassured me. "Tonight. It must be tonight." He glanced at his brother, speaking in German again for my benefit. "But yes, Cosimo, you must not go so fast."

When they resumed arguing in Italian, the dictionary was no help.

"Cosimo, the truck," Enzo said in German. "You are cooking the engine." He turned to me, smiling weakly. "Yes, I lose the ring. But do not be angry with me if we have no truck tomorrow."

We passed the next hour silently, breathing in the smell of a hot engine, spilled olive oil, our appetites ruined. But then we saw the glimmer of the lake, the same shoulder where I'd run so hard to catch the man and his son, the place that already seemed to belong to a long-ago past. The vegetation seemed higher, wilder, impenetrable. The lake had darkened from silvery green to nearly black.

Enzo hurried away from the truck and into the grass where he had first struggled free from his pants. He rummaged around in the dark, crawling on hands and knees. His lighter flicked on and off, on and off.

"Of course, he wanted to take this route," Cosimo muttered, watching his brother flit along the lakefront like an undaunted firefly. "Of course, we take the road to Siena. Of course, we park the night at the turn-off to Monterosso, conveniently. Of course!"

"I thought we planned to drive as far as we could. You didn't tell me that you and Enzo had already planned where we'd park for the night."

Cosimo didn't answer.

"You and Enzo—?"

"And Mister Keller," he conceded.

But why hadn't I been informed? "Don't tell me that Monterosso is near Farfalla's village. I thought it was only a fanciful longing. I thought he realized we wouldn't stand for it. Don't tell me that Enzo is really thinking he'll be proposing to Farfalla *tonight*."

"Let him have the nerve to try."

"I don't care about nerve, Cosimo. I care about the statue. And about my own well-being—"

"It doesn't matter. He won't find it," Cosimo insisted.

"Keller wouldn't have agreed to that, given the importance—"

But our conversation was interrupted. Enzo's face appeared suddenly in the open passenger window, his entire face lit up with an ear-to-ear grin: "Lady Fortune!"

He clambered back into the truck, shaking his head at his good luck. "Now I put it here. There she is. Good and safe." And he made a grand display of pushing it deep into his front trouser pocket, patting the circlet affectionately.

Cosimo grumbled, "*Congratulazioni. È quasi un miracolo.*"

Then we were driving again, with an orange scar of sunset to our left, a deep purple sky overhead, and the hills to the north and east uniformly black. The air had gone from cool to cold. We rolled up our windows and Cosimo broke the silence with his brother. "You are coming with us all the way to the border, no excuses."

No answer.

Cosimo dug deeper. "You are not leaving my sight."

A little shrug, lips turned down in distaste. Enzo lit a cigarette, failing to offer one to anyone else.

We drove in silence. We passed the place where we had turned around two hours earlier. Our road took us through a valley, dark and quiet and oddly unpeopled, while up on the high ridges to the left and right, the dim lights of farmhouses were twinkling doubles of the stars overhead. But none of those lights were strong enough to puncture the gloom on the road we were traveling. It was a moonless night. A weathered sign loomed up, barely lit by our feeble headlamps: Siena, 30 KM.

The road was so black, we couldn't see far ahead, and when something did appear, it appeared suddenly: here, a sheep; there, a white-plastered shrine, forcing Cosimo to swerve or step on the brakes. But then he would accelerate again, aggressively.

"Is there some particular place we are looking for?" I finally asked.

In unison, Enzo and Cosimo answered: "Yes."

Enzo cleared his throat, affecting a casual tone. "There is

a place, soon enough, a turn-off that is signed Monterosso. There is a shrine and a good place behind it to park, with a water tap. It is a well-known good place."

Cosimo added nothing.

"And this," I pressed for confirmation, "is where we're stopping for the night? There are no other options, even if we are making good progress?"

They were waiting for the right moment, anticipating a brothers' showdown, long and slow in coming. But perhaps, it occurred to me, the battle could be thwarted.

"Enzo, let me have the ring."

"Maybe later. When we park."

"If I hold onto it until we get to the border, there might be less temptation to make any additional side-trips. We might avoid a difficult situation."

"No, *grazie*. It is not helpful."

Cosimo took his eyes off the road briefly, glancing at me, and then, more skeptically, at his brother. A realization dawned; a decision was made. "At least you can show it to him, *fratello*," he said, ridicule sharpening his voice. "Let him appreciate your romantic intentions."

Enzo returned Cosimo's skeptical glance, then dug slowly into his pocket, inhaling, as if even he had doubts about the forces he was unleashing. The ring, cradled in the crease of his palm, was gold, set with a very small diamond and flanked by two even smaller glittering chips.

"There," Enzo said, speaking past me to his brother's unreadable face, all cards on the table. "Is this what you wanted? Are you satisfied now?"

We passed the sign to Monterosso. We passed the shrine. Still, no one spoke. Twenty minutes later, Cosimo found a small, dusty turn-off more to his liking—some compromise between conforming to an earlier plan with Keller and Enzo, while still exerting his own driver's prerogative, unaware of the original parking place's full significance. He pulled off the road. Then, spotting a larger tree, he continued a little farther, snugging up into the soft shoulder, under the low-hanging branches, refusing to set the brake until he had parked just where he wanted to park. "*Va bene.*"

The rasp of Enzo's hand against his unshaven jaw was audible. No one hurried to step outside.

"You bring a razor in your suitcase, Mister Vogler?"

"It was left behind at the pensione, when I wasn't given the opportunity to pack my own things. But that was understandable. The statue was awaiting transport and we were in a great hurry," I said, hoping now to communicate that sense of urgency we'd all shared not so very long ago. "Do you remember?"

Enzo exited the truck, stretching and brushing the crumbs off his white shirt. Cosimo and I followed him around back. Enzo opened the back door, set up a wooden plank, and wheeled his scooter out of the truck. "More room for sleeping." He gestured. "There."

But Cosimo was watching, too—wordlessly, arms over his chest.

I was waiting for the confrontation, waiting for Enzo to admit what he was planning, waiting for Cosimo to demand more explanation and impose our shared opposition. But maybe I'd been misunderstanding Cosimo all along. Maybe, deep down, he did share some of Enzo's way of thinking. If Enzo believed this was the best possible night for testing Farfalla's love, Cosimo seemed to think it was the best possible night for testing Enzo's fraternal loyalty.

I tapped Cosimo on the arm and gestured for him to follow me around the side of the truck where we could talk privately.

When we got there, he spoke first. "It isn't Mamma's ring. All that time in the truck, but he didn't explain." His voice was low and stern. "Hers was a simple band. No diamonds."

This should have been good news. There would be no argument over which brother should have the right to their mother's ring. As for who had a right to Farfalla, that was another matter, but far beyond my influence.

"You do plan to tell him again that he can't leave us tonight."

"I can't speak to him. Let him speak to me."

Behind us, the scooter started up.

"He's leaving right now," I said, turning toward the scooter, which had—I realized only now—no functioning headlamp. Wherever Farfalla's family farm was located, on steep side roads climbing into the black hills, it would be a long, dark trip on a moonless night. "We have to get going in the morning, early. What if he doesn't come back tomorrow? What if we need his mechanical skills and the truck breaks down?"

I took a few steps toward the scooter, a few steps back to Cosimo, pacing. "He went into that food shop and stayed for a half hour, and that was just flirting with a pretty stranger, never mind proposing to a woman and then trying to leave her family, her bed . . ."

The scooter motor died; Enzo pushed it onto the kickstand with a metallic groan before approaching. I exhaled, so relieved I wanted to embrace him. But he walked past, ignoring me. He stood next to Cosimo, muttering into his shoulder, requesting something. Without making eye contact, Cosimo shrugged himself out of his own jacket and handed it to Enzo, took Enzo's jacket and pulled it on, looking miserable.

It took me a moment to find my voice. Enzo was already behind us again, back on his scooter, revving it.

"Cosimo—you gave him your jacket? He's still leaving, and you traded jackets?"

"Mine was cleaner, maybe." Dragging his hand across his nose, Cosimo angled his face toward the black sky as if willing the new moon into a fuller phase. "Maybe he'll change his mind. He drives a little while, in the dark; he thinks a little while. *I* would change my mind."

"You told me how different you are. Two roads going two different ways, remember?"

"Only the outside. Inside, we are almost the same."

"He isn't changing his mind, Cosimo. He's on the scooter." I stubbed my foot against the gravel of the road's shoulder. "Keller shouldn't have tempted him. There were other routes, other places to park. Keller knows about Enzo's girlfriend?"

Cosimo nodded. His eyes met mine, alight with a recognition he wouldn't share, except to say: "I can't stop him. I've never been able to stop him."

But it was too late for that, anyway. Our ears filled with the sound of spitting gravel, the whine of the scooter's motor, and then the fading mosquito buzz of Enzo's departure, leaving us both in silence on the road, only gradually aware of the insects chirruping, only gradually aware of the penetrating cold of a night in hilly country.

Cosimo offered me the front cab, but I didn't want any favors and I was edgy about being too far from the statue. I insisted on taking the back of the truck.

First, though, I excused myself to empty my bladder, a little ways down the road. When I returned, Cosimo was in the back, pulling at wisps of straw sticking out of the crate. The slats were extremely narrow; he managed to harvest only a few wisps. In his hand was the burlap bag that had come with the lemons, with barely a handful of straw at the bottom.

So this was why Enzo had to hurry off to propose, I thought to myself, less than charitably. And this was why, perhaps, the Italians were better off selling some of their national art. Because they too often thought: *What's the difference?* A few kilometers off the main road, a few hours off schedule, a few pieces of straw from the crate. Everything was flexible, everything emotional. Decay and disaster, one small step at a time. There was no hard reasoning: the packing material had been there for a reason, just as the schedule had been there for a reason. One more bump and the statue might shift, an outstretched marble finger might make contact with wood—and break. *That finger, Cosimo, outlasted the rise and fall of civilizations, outlasted attacks by barbarian hordes. But it might*

*not outlast your brother's desire to get under a woman's skirt
on a moonless night.*

"A peace offering," Cosimo said, handing me the straw-filled burlap bag, a rough, pathetic imitation of a pillow. "*Buona notte.*"

Cold toes and stiff legs. A hip wedged painfully against the hard floor. A piece of straw, as sharp as a porcupine quill, poking directly into my cheek. The memory of my father's voice: "You haven't felt cold until you've slept in a wet trench in November. You have no idea what discomfort is."

There's no way to sleep, I thought, trying to rearrange my jacket over my shoulders. The temperature in these hills was surprisingly cold once the sun was down, even in summer. *No way even to nap*, I thought, *no way . . .*

And then it was morning. Warmth heating up the metal floor of the truck. A crack of bright light alongside the bottom of the retractable door.

I sat up suddenly, squinting into the light. What had happened to our early start? What had happened to dawn? I rarely managed to sleep through a night at home, and this was when insomnia finally took its vacation, on a night when I should have stayed alert?

I scrambled to climb out of the truck, still trying to orient my senses while telling my bladder it could wait just a moment, seeing as it had made no effort to get me up any earlier.

"Why didn't you wake me?" I demanded of Cosimo, who was pacing the road's shoulder, an unlit cigarette hanging from his lip. "Where is Enzo?"

"It is light two hours already."

"Precisely!"

"Something is wrong."

"Yes, something was wrong as soon as Enzo decided to run off last night."

"No. Something is more wrong." He rubbed a hand against the bristles sprouting from his jaw. "Maybe last night I should have told you. When we traded jackets, Enzo said to me, 'Don't worry. Just go along.'"

"*Just go along?* Well, that's precisely what you did. You didn't even argue."

"I am afraid there is more. I have been thinking about it all morning. I'm afraid it is worse."

I prepared for our debate: drive north and leave Enzo behind versus drive toward Monterosso and wake the young Romeo from his blissful and irresponsible slumber. But Cosimo was in no mood to argue. He walked to the truck cab, and I followed several paces behind. He started the ignition before I slammed my passenger door.

"The back is secure?"

"Yes, but you may not make any decisions without me."

"It is not a decision. There is no choice."

"I don't understand."

"I had a dream, early this morning." He was struggling with the words that had been haunting him since before dawn.

"It was a dream about my brother. He is lying down, looking peaceful—"

"I think we know that he is lying down."

"But there is tall green grass all around him, and he is alone. He is not in any bed. And he is saying, 'I am sorry, brother.'"

"That's all?"

"'I am sorry. Look in my pocket.'"

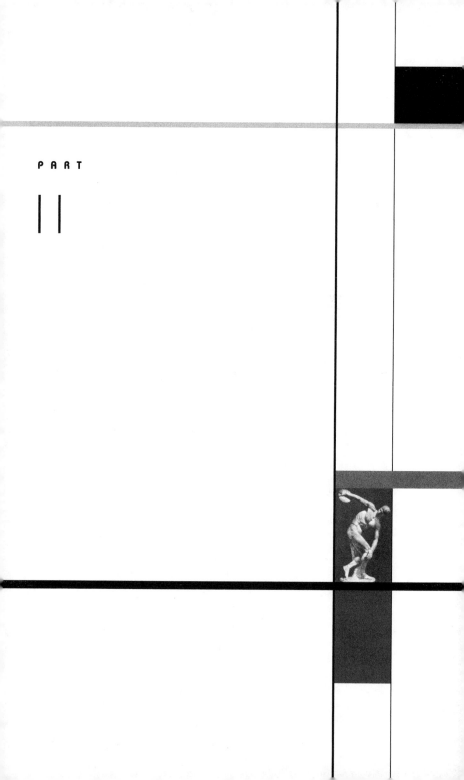

CHAPTER 6

A rusty, pale blue Fiat slows down alongside me and a local man in a black wool vest and a matching billed cap rolls down the window, startling me out of my reminiscences. He asks whether I need a ride into town, still several kilometers away. I tell him *grazie, no,* the weather is fine, I really don't mind walking, I'm in no rush. It's only when he catches my accent that he leans back into his seat, upsetting his cap, which he pats back into place with a quick, embarrassed tap.

"The shops close in less than an hour."

I try to smile. "That's not a worry."

"They stay closed for most of the afternoon," he says, as if to discourage me from walking into town at all. "If you plan to go to a shop or a café, you may be disappointed."

"Not a problem, thank you. I will walk until they open again."

Who knows what an accent like mine means to him, where or under what conditions he might have last heard it, how close or distant, how forgotten or eternal the war that ended three years ago seems to him now.

He takes a while to engage his clutch and drive past, watching to see whether I really mean it—whether I am to be trusted ambling past these rural fields and modest vineyards, whether I am really enjoying my walk. I feel like a fraud, trying to inject some lightness in my step, when just moments ago I was strolling furiously, head down, overwhelmed completely by my memories—by memories *of* memories, really, a paired set of mirrors in which one could get lost and never return.

Back in Munich, I'd thought of my 1938 trip so often that it had seemed more vivid than the present. But even so, more than I realized, some of the details were lost after all, only recoverable here, where the light and the smells and a thousand other things I cannot name bring so much more back: perhaps the scuff of my shoes against the warm, chalky path underfoot, or the slim shadow thrown by a cypress rising up toward a heartlessly blue sky. Now I pass a hand along a low stone wall covered with a trailing, woody plant that looks like rosemary. And yes, rosemary it is—there, pungent and undeniable, but quickly fading from my fingertips—and I am struck by both the power of the scent memory (I remember in a flash what I have allowed to remain forgotten for so long: the desire to be rid of a revolting smell and to replace it with something cleaner and more sweet) and the fact that I am now a different person, unable to entirely reinhabit the past, unable to step into the same river twice.

Aside from the later smells that the rosemary effortlessly conjures, what I remember most clearly from that morning of our second driving day is a sense of self-recrimination, perhaps for all the wrong reasons (a narrowly defined duty, a refusal to face certain facts), but self-recrimination nonetheless. It was my fault we'd gotten into such a mess. I had lost my focus. I had become sentimental, allowing Enzo to retrieve the ring. I had failed to keep Enzo and Cosimo dedicated to our task. And then, somehow and suddenly, Enzo had left, forcing us to go in search of him—a detour resisted but not denied.

As Cosimo steered the truck around each switchback, white dust rising and spreading behind us and painting each passing olive tree a duller silver, the present moment's worries insisted upon yoking me to other worries I had hoped to leave behind. I did not want to think about Gerhard. I did not even want to think about Enzo. The quickening of my heartbeat and the sour weight in my stomach reminded me of my intolerance for suspense—a poison that my system was no longer capable of handling.

I hadn't always been so high-strung, I recall thinking that summer morning, as we rolled along, slower and slower as the road became even rockier and steeper, as the sun beat down on our arms and faces and our eyes burned with the

dust, the heat, and the tense effort of looking for something—
someone—I didn't fully expect to find.

There had been a time, eight or nine years earlier, when to
be poised in the starter position, with the full track ahead,
was to be ready and eager for an explosion of joy. That anticipatory moment was so exceptional that even after my own
serious athletic prospects were irreparably damaged in the
summer of 1930, I still wanted to run. I recovered my health.
I bided my time over the winter. And that following spring of
my seventeenth year, I joined a track team again.

I remember the first race day, when I took a small spade in
my hand and started digging the holes in the cinder track—the
little starter holes we used, instead of starter blocks. I pushed
the toes of my thin-soled running shoes into the holes, got into
position, and prepared myself for the starter pistol, which for
some reason was slow in coming, as it sometimes was. Then—
suddenly—even before the shot came, a plug was pulled. The
happiness drained away.

I looked to my left at the boys who were stronger than me,
who had spent the winter staying in good shape. I looked to
my right at the boys who would beat me. I told myself it didn't
matter, I would run just to run, just to enjoy my own relative
speed and returning health—but I had lost something, some
kind of mental steadiness. I told myself it was the starting position, that my body had simply changed, that I'd lost a little
muscle and gained a little fat. But that wasn't it at all. It was
my mind that had changed. Now, the anticipation was nearly
sickening. And when the pistol went up, I reacted jumpily, like

a person afraid of being ambushed—which is indeed how I had felt ever since the previous summer.

Which is all a long and unwieldy way of saying that I did not like surprises anymore. *Ohne Zwischenfall*, without incident—that was the preferred state. I did not like waiting and wondering, the strain of not knowing, most forms of conflict or novelty which are essential aspects of many things—competition, for one. Love, for another. The only kind of passion I had managed to sustain was my passion for art, itself a substitution for other losses. And yet it remained to be seen if that passion would itself be my undoing, and if there would be nothing left to hold onto, if even the most carefully carved marble would prove itself to be inconstant, insignificant, ultimately worthless.

It was a month after I'd quit track altogether, a year after the incident, when I showed up at the library one late afternoon in my seventeenth year. The old man behind the desk was seated with his face just in the shadows. What I could see best were his hands, folded on the desk, underneath the bright glow of his desk lamp. My request was a little odd and I felt out of place, so I concentrated on those hands: soft and powdery white, ribboned with blue veins like tunneling worms.

"Books—about bodies," I muttered to the librarian. He scooted a little closer so that his face came into the light. He looked up over his glasses, noting my age, my blotched adolescent skin, my clear discomfort at stating my interests clearly.

"What about 'bodies'?"

I had no idea how to put it into acceptable words. "Variations?"

Here he laughed—only slightly, and with forgiveness, but his mirth was plain. "Between the genders?"

The librarian closed the book he'd been reading and removed his reading glasses. "You don't mean reproductive systems, do you?"

"No," I assured him. "Not that."

He waited.

"Perhaps diseases," I ventured. "Rare ones. But not the kind you catch."

He would have waited all day, but I had no more clues to impart, so he loaded my desk with some impressive medical tomes. I'd never encountered such thin onionskin paper or such small, dense type. Much of it in Latin. No photographs and only a few illustrations of concepts too general to be useful: circulatory systems and skeletal charts.

One might find my curiosity strange, now that my father's erratic actions had solved one problem for me (replacing it with another, that summer of infection, the subsequent year of healing), but yes, I was still curious. Even more so. Though he had attempted to remove the small proof of my difference, leaving me scarred in the process, I was even more driven now to discover how deep and permanently within the human body flaws are marked. I wanted to know what remained after he had removed the surface flaw from my flesh.

I was nearly ready to leave that day, my fingertips dirty from the endless turning of pages, each tired breath moving my ribs, evoking the little twinge from my bandaged side. The librarian showed up: the soft, white hands again, under the light of my own study carrel. No wonder Gerhard would seem familiar to me when I would meet him some five years later: he had the same soft, white hands.

The librarian saw my finished stack of books. "Did you find your variations?"

"No, sir."

"Perhaps we have begun from the wrong end of things. Perhaps we are being too technical. You know, when I was your age and interested in the human form, in its most ideal and masterful depictions, I began not with modern science but with the Greeks and Romans . . ."

He had lost me entirely. But he was speaking from his own memories, with evident pleasure. "And best of all—yes, why didn't I think of it sooner?—they provide us with something more than text; they provide us with images. After all the reading you've done, you might find some pictures to be a tonic. Wait here, young man."

He returned with yet larger books, opening them to show me illustrations of the great Greek and Roman statues. "There you are. I'll stop back in half an hour, and then I must collect these and set you on your way."

He disappeared tactfully back into the shadows, leaving me to puzzle over these naked forms. I'd seen the occasional classical illustration, of course, but I'd never had the privacy to make a thorough, close-up inspection. Rather than glancing quickly—at a small penis centered over a scrotal sack, or at the lines and curves where the secrets of womanhood remained hidden—I could stare now until my eyes had had their fill, then follow the graceful lines of chest and pelvis, thigh and calf, bicep and forearm, belly and breast.

In these pictures I found no clue to my own strange variation, but I found something else: a fascination that would grow during the many library visits to follow. The classical artists had captured perfection—athletic, aesthetic, even moral perfection—and perhaps if I understood perfection I would understand its opposite. I would know which flaws were only minor details, which were deep and ineradicable. I was completely unfamiliar with genetics at this time—my school was about fifty years behind in its teaching of science—but I am not sure genetics would have provided the answers anyway, not in a form that spoke to my own athletic background, my own respect and regret for the minor aspirations I had set aside. Yes, I recognized that wonderful dark line running along the back of a tensed hamstring. Yes, I recognized the commanding realism of *The Spear-Bearer* by Polyclitus, an ancient Greek statue of a muscular man walking with a spear over his shoulder, one leg just beginning to lift from the ground. Yes, I recognized the calm, focused faces of the athletes—who, much more than gods or unlikely heroes, offered real insight into the human condition.

"You haven't visited the Glyptothek?" the librarian said to me one day, after my weekly library visits had become routine. "Your parents have never taken you there?"

My father? "Never."

"Oh, my boy," he said, deeply apologetic for having failed to mention that we had our own excellent museum of classical art in Munich. "You must go. You know, of course, where the Königsplatz is?"

Nearby, at 45 Brienner Strasse, the Nazis had already built their party headquarters, the Brown House. In years to come, the party would choose this location for some of their enormous rallies. But once I came to associate the Königsplatz with art, with the Greek and Roman masterpieces and the magnificent Glyptothek itself, nothing would ever convince me that the heart of Munich could be anywhere else. Even if this part of the city became the heart of something else, too. Even if one couldn't walk thirty meters without being expected to offer a *verdammte* salute.

Meanwhile, Germany was facing the currency crisis, bank failures. Here I was, entranced by old bronze and stone, oblivious and increasingly unemployable. Perhaps if I had attended a more rigorous secondary school, I might have gone on to a university such as the one in Erlangen, where that same year a student committee made a request to the Ministry of Culture for the creation of a chair of race science. Some subjects were deemed worthy of national support, even with a failing economy. But I didn't dare dream that, in a few more years, art history would be deemed worthy of public support as well. It doesn't always hurt to have a failed artist as Führer, many art lovers might have reasoned in those early years—before life became more complicated, before reason itself was left behind.

When I graduated from secondary school in 1932, the jobs I managed to find were low-paid and sporadic, though I was happy to get them. On weekends, I worked as a sports club trainer because nationalistic sports clubs were booming in Munich. Even in my unexceptional condition, and even though I had a reputation for being reserved and for keeping my distance from the boys in general and from the changing room in particular, I could still earn a few marks conducting warm-up exercises and running drills.

During the week, I worked as an assistant to a small-time art dealer and auctioneer named Franz Betelmann. This second job was much more important to me. I kept records for Franz and helped him evaluate and catalog the ancient statues, many of them with a Trojan theme, inspired by German archaeology being conducted then in Asia Minor. They were just copies, of course, and were being sold as such—nothing particularly valuable, only *objets d'art* to grace some city dweller's chilly entrance hall. But Franz wanted to elevate himself. He wanted to appear better educated than he was (as did I; as would anyone who had attended a *Realschule* instead of a *Gymnasium*) and he was eager to absorb what I had already assimilated.

He expressed no embarrassment that someone my age would be lecturing to him on the significance of the *contrapposto* pose in classical sculpture. He'd smack his leg, delighted, the pince-nez he wore for effect falling from his face: "So there's a name for that! I always thought those Romans looked tired, leaning on one leg."

I worked for Betelmann on and off for three years, for diminishing pay, as his own accounts became more irreconcilable. I enjoyed learning and sharing my increasing knowledge of art with my employer, and even with the customers. I sketched on the side, not with any artistic ambition, but only to develop my own eye and memory and appreciation of famous objects. My father wanted me to work for the German Labor Service—yet another unpaid job, and this one promising only toil, but one he thought might lead to some paid job when the economy improved. I put it off as long as I could, but in the summer of 1935, the six-month labor stints were made compulsory. So at the age of twenty-one, I joined thousands of other secondary school graduates. We were each given a bicycle and a spade, and a brown uniform symbolizing the earthiness of our pursuits, and on the uniform—this struck me as funny, somehow—was a cap patch featuring a spade and a special belt buckle featuring, ah yes, the spade again.

They were serious about this spade business. So serious that they made us carry the spades, drill with the spades, keep them shiny and clean, and present them for inspection when requested. I think we all knew what this was preparing us for—not just future employment as construction workers or assistant engineers. No matter what the Treaty of Versailles said, no matter what limits had been placed on our standing army, thousands of us were being whipped into shape, taught to follow orders and get along, to carry heavy wood-handled implements over our shoulders as we bicycled or marched. And all while singing the typical group-unity drivel:

> Our shovels are the weapons of peace,
> Our camps are castles in the countryside.
> Yesterday divided by class and standing,
> Yesterday the one avoided the other,
> Today we dig together in the sand.

There was a military briskness to the entire program, from our rousing at 4 A.M. to our dormitory life and bland meals, and our long, callus-producing hours spent in sun, wind, and rain. My regiment was building an autobahn: one of the early highways that would someday connect with other autobahns, connect all of Germany, perhaps even minimize our regional differences—in other words, a peaceful pursuit. But also a multi-pronged strategy. Good highways could serve a wide range of purposes. We did nearly everything by hand; there was rarely a construction machine or heavy vehicle in sight because the more human labor we required, the more people were temporarily fed, housed, and exercised. Elsewhere in the nation, regiments were draining swamps or reclaiming soil.

It wasn't easy, but in a sense, I was glad to have served in the *Reichsarbeitsdienst*. For one thing, it made me theoretically eligible for university. Due to changing national priorities and ideologies, university enrollment was no longer strongly encouraged and admissions had been restricted, though of course not eliminated. I had no idea, to be honest, if I qualified in other ways—I was now older than a typical applicant and my earlier education might not suffice—but it was still a dream of mine, one encouraged by the art dealer, Betelmann, who was kind enough to praise my potential.

But there was another reason I was glad to have served. Having heard my father's war stories, knowing how much he had changed as a result of that terrible conflict, and having spent so many of those childhood beer-hall hours listening to other men who were similarly haunted, I had truly feared military service. But the Labor Service was like the military, and—remembering that I had already healed from my injury and now looked even more like everyone else—I made it through.

So when, just after the Berlin Olympics, I was drafted into the Wehrmacht Heer, I wasn't as upset as I might have been. It wouldn't be so bad, I figured, and someday I'd have my own stories to tell—in university, when all this was done, or back at the art dealership where I might find a way to earn commissions selling not copies but authentic classical objects.

That accepting attitude got me through the first five weeks of training: firearms instead of spades, and finding my place among my fellow *Landsers*. Then, one night, I heard three men in my *Gruppe* talking about another man they disliked, a farm boy named Ackerman, a kid who had attracted teasing from day one for his dedication to the platoon's rabbits. Ackerman had informed on them for taking the wire cutters he used to maintain the rabbit hutches. They'd stolen the tool to cut a gap in a barbed-wire fence, hoping to exploit the break on an upcoming evening when they planned to sneak out of camp and visit a brothel in the neighboring town.

This simply wasn't done. When it was time for that sort of entertainment, a field brothel would come to our camp, we had been told. An order would be followed: a health check for the rifleman, issuance of a condom, and a can of disinfectant spray that had to be returned empty. These three in my *Gruppe* were rebellious and impatient in a way that would be unimaginable a few years later, but this was only 1936, and these were new recruits—fellow Labor Service boys who thought they already knew it all.

Even after getting caught for messing with the barbed wire, even after serving their punishment—reduced rations, extra latrine duty, prohibition from sending or receiving mail to girlfriends back home—they still planned to try to sneak out the following Friday. Invited to come along, I told them I'd think about it. I'd learned that the middle path was the safest: breaking some rules, but not many; eating some tripe, no matter how green or suspect; taking part in some schemes, but not others, and never tattling. I had at least one excuse for not going out that coming weekend: an officer in camp had seen some nature sketches I'd done and wondered if I might draw his portrait on Saturday. I'd told him I was no good at drawing real people, but you can bet that I started practicing with an electric torch under the covers every night that week.

Now the three others challenged Ackerman to cover for them, should anyone come poking around their bunks after midnight—a major task, given that our superior officer was now more alert to mischief. And if Ackerman didn't cover? *They would make him a Jew.* I'd heard of ways to make a Jew a gentile—feed him pork, make him claim allegiance to Jesus— but not vice versa. How does one turn a gentile into a Jew?

"Just make sure the blade is good and sharp," someone at the table said. "He's bound to squirm and you'll hurt yourself as well as him."

"Oh—" I said out loud, hand dropping to the table with an audible *thunk*, unable to conceal my horror. With the other hand I clutched my own side, that tender, scarred spot, in sympathetic pain. Without that wound, I might have believed the men were only joking, showing off. But unfortunately, I knew what a person, armed with a knife and some asinine ideas, could do.

The man next to me smirked at my expression of dismay. "Oh?"

"I forgot something."

"What?" He was still testing me, probing for any indication that I would stand in their way or report what I had just heard. "You didn't forget who your friends are, did you?"

"No, no," I stammered. "I only forgot that I don't have enough charcoal or high-grade paper. I'll have to get to an art store somehow, if I'm going to sketch Hauptmann Becker on Saturday."

Pushing away my plate, I hurried directly to the officers' tent and explained my enthusiasm for our upcoming portrait session. Becker was occupied Saturday, as it turned out. Sunday would be better. I needed more supplies, I told him. All the better, he said, I could use Saturday to go shopping. He not only gave me a pass to leave camp, but arranged for a ride—not just to the closest village, but all the way to Munich, my hometown, nearly ninety minutes away. I should get oil paints as well, he said. This time I had the sense not to mention that I did not paint with oils. Now I had my entire weekend booked with excuses.

Whatever my *Kameraden* did, it need not involve me. Whatever happened, I could not be asked to handle any knife. I left a cryptic message for Ackerman telling him to be on his guard, but honestly, once I left that note on his bunk, I pushed the matter out of my mind—not thinking I'd be punished someday for that cowardly amnesia, not thinking that this was only one such decision life would send my way and there would be many others, not realizing that moments like this were like a sculptor's tools, revealing the shape of the true self locked within. What I did not—perhaps *could* not—yet understand was that character, rather than genetics or racial differences or minor biological oddities, is the real mystery of life.

At the time, I felt only lucky, and bound to get luckier with every kilometer traveled away from our camp. In Munich that Saturday, wandering the aisles of a small art supply store, fingering the brushes and caressing the tips of soft gray pencils, inhaling the clean smells of paper and paint, I heard a man call out to me. He was well dressed, in a crisp suit, wool coat, and white muffler, holding a large, brown parcel—a freshly framed artwork of some kind, retrieved from the corner of the store where an old man cut mats, hammered wood, and touched up the gilt on antique frames.

"Berlin," he called out, shifting the package from his right hand to his left in order to shake my hand. "The Olympic stadium. I saw you there. I applauded your moral act. I would have made my own departure, but I was another man's guest—such difficult tickets to acquire! And besides, I was hoping to sell him a painting later."

"Oh—yes?" I wanted my hand back, but he was still massaging my knuckles.

"And then, in the beer hall near the stadium, I happened to spot you. I called out, but you didn't hear. Isn't that strange? Three times now—a lucky number. One shouldn't ignore signs. Are you an artist?"

"No, sir."

"But you're buying art supplies."

The sketchpad and pencils were tucked beneath my left arm.

"Come to lunch next door," he insisted. "I'm meeting a friend who is an art dealer, very well traveled—Italy, Greece, Egypt. His name is Keller."

"I should be getting back to my *Zug*."

He was a big man—mustachioed, red cheeked, well fed. He insisted on standing close to me, touching my arm with his free hand. "What's the hurry? Let me be honest—Herr Keller keeps a Mediterranean schedule. I don't know when he'll turn up late or on time, so I show up on the dot and end up waiting more often than not. It gives me indigestion. But here, you can tell me some stories. We can discuss the finer things."

Before I had even caught his name, our arms were linked and he was guiding me out of the art supply store. That is how I ended up dining with the mining magnate-turned-art aficionado Heinrich Röthel, who would go on to help organize one of the first Third Reich art "shopping lists," which would become the starting point for the art curatorial office, *Sonderprojekt*, in which I would ultimately work. Much later, this list would be expanded upon by top museum professionals. Röthel was no professional himself. If anything, the scholars and major museum directors intimidated him, but he had strong opinions, he had lots of money, and he knew a lot about people and politics and slightly less about European masterpieces.

The maître d' seated us at the table Röthel had reserved, a small round table for two under a nineteenth-century painting of two water nymphs—romantic, probably Austrian, but the nymphs' diaphanous robes were painted without fidelity to gravity or lighting, and their hands, so difficult for any artist to paint, were conveniently hidden within the robes' folds. I hurried through my first course, expecting to make a quick exit as soon as Herr Keller appeared.

Röthel asked, "Do you know why the Louvre has so many great artworks?"

I had never visited Paris and couldn't have ventured an opinion about any of the great museum's collections.

He supplied the answer: "Napoleon! Most of that artwork is looted German art. Have you ever thought of working in a museum? Perhaps when you finish up in the army?"

"I've only begun my basic training."

Without apology to Keller, my generous host ordered the next course. He expounded upon four centuries of German art, culminating in the work of Arno Breker, sculptor of impossibly wide shoulders, bursting forearms, and improbably square jaws—all works that were not in my area of expertise, nor aligned with my own artistic taste. Röthel kept quizzing me and feeding me; I had nothing to supply in return, so when the conversation turned briefly to Ancient Greece, I was grateful.

"The Olympic Games and fine sculpture—the Greeks started it all, didn't they?" Röthel said.

"The two, hand in hand," I agreed, setting down my fork at last, feeling I should say something rather than just keep shoveling food like the hungry, unrefined soldier-in-training that I was.

"I see we've hit upon an interest," he said, smirking as I wiped my mouth. "Tell me. Don't be shy."

"Well, all right—though I don't know very much." Saying those words, I heard and saw myself from a distance: the self-educated son of a working-class man, the hesitant laborer and dread-filled recruit, a person who had only a few more chances—maybe only one—to rise above his present station. Sport and art were all I knew. Of those, only the latter could guide my life now, but of course, the art I loved best incorporated both sport and the human form.

I began to explain to Röthel that the first classical statues were *kouroi*, stiff and unrealistic nude males, copied by visiting Greeks from the Egyptian style in the seventh century B.C. But the classical marble nudes we know, the sculptures we have come to love, were created back in the city-states and inspired by the Greek culture of competitive sports. Later, the Romans would treat sports as entertainment.

"For the Romans, everything was entertainment," Röthel agreed, flagging down the waiter for more wine.

"But for the Greeks, it was more primal," I explained, losing any self-consciousness to excitement. "A contest, a struggle, where losing was out of the question. Sports were really a preparation for war. Every citizen had to be prepared to defend his city-state. Athletic victors were allowed to have sculptures cast in their images. Hundreds, probably thousands, of such sculptures were made. Finally—sculptures of real people, not of fertility figures or abstract gods. Methods were improved; standards were established. Realistic sculpting of the human body reached its zenith. So we have a connection between war and sport and art—"

The lozenge of veal that Röthel had ordered for me had gone cold on my plate, under a lid of rubbery sauce. I had gone on too long.

Just then, Herr Keller appeared at the table. The maître d' rushed to fit in a third chair.

"No, go on, don't stop," Herr Röthel urged me, as soon as quick introductions had been made. "This young man was impressing me." He turned to Keller. "Do you remember in Berlin, the lady documentarian—Leni—who was filming the Games? She kept going on about the athletic Greek statues as works worthy of emulation and acquisition. This generated interest at the highest of levels."

"Of course," Keller said, taking a menu. "There has always been interest. That goes without saying."

When I stood up to relinquish my seat, unwilling to disrupt the lunch party any further, Röthel held onto my wrist. "If I'd had you at my side, a young voice passionate about history, we might have talked some important people into loosening their purse strings."

Herr Keller, eyes hidden and chin tucked into his neck, grumbled to himself. "Demand is never the question. Supply is the question."

"Of course it is! We're not negating the art dealer's role. But what the Reich needs—outside of the existing museums—is an entirely new apparatus, a small staff to research these issues."

"There is work being done in Berlin."

"Must everything always be done in Berlin?" Röthel pointed

to the bag beneath my feet, my parcel of paper and pencils, which I had been unwilling to have checked because I wanted to be able to make my exit freely, without fuss. "Tell me again, who is your commanding officer? How much longer do you have to serve in the Wehrmacht Heer? How would you like to meet some interesting people?"

I said I would, and Röthel would go on to prove himself and his connections, many times over, as I knew he would. As I recalled our fortuitous encounter later that night, lying on my bunk back at our guarded compound, I already felt more free.

And what happened to Ackerman while I was away from camp? A little skirmish, but he had fought back and achieved some sort of tense stalemate with our comrades. What bothered me most upon my return to camp was how he tried to thank me for the meager warning, as if I'd done him some favor. If anything, I'd learned the wrong lesson: that a middle ground—dare I call it a pose?—between paralysis and action was possible.

My antiques job with Betelmann had never impressed my father. My new job, to which I reported barely a week later thanks to Röthel's apparently effortless pulling of strings, most definitely did impress him. He would have much preferred me as a top athlete, but second to that, a government career wasn't bad—especially when I explained to him how the top Nazi officials were art collectors.

"Really? All of them?" he asked.

"Yes. Each wants to imitate the other, to see who can collect the most," I replied. Well, this sort of basic competition my father could understand.

"Your luck has turned, my son," he said, sounding the happiest I'd ever heard him. This was perhaps the only moment when his hand on my shoulder felt non-threatening, like a simple exchange of joy and warmth. "A little dignity and reward for the Vogler family, at long last."

CHAPTER 7

"Can't we go any faster?"

"No. We'll miss something."

"But the faster we go, the faster we can get to his girlfriend's farm and wake him up and be done with all this."

"He isn't at the farm."

"How do you know that?"

"He isn't sleeping."

Cosimo spotted the shrine we had passed the night before and made a swift turn. But once stopped, he seemed hesitant to open the door.

"This morning," he explained, "I walked up toward the main road, away from where we parked—I was just off the shoulder, taking care of morning business—and I saw a red car go by."

"Interesting," I said as flatly as possible.

"He did not see me. He did not see the truck."

"Which *he*?"

"Keller. That was his prize car that I saw. His red Zagato Spider."

"And the Roman truck, too?"

"No. He told us they were *suspekt*. But maybe that was only to get us away from them, traveling the road alone, so that he and any others he has hired could take the statue without being seen."

While I skeptically resisted absorbing this news, Cosimo opened his door and gestured for me to do the same. We walked past the shrine to a water spigot that had been dripping slowly, dampening the dusty ground. He leaned down to pick up a cigarette butt, squeezing the end between his fingers. Thirty or forty of them littered the ground.

"At least three or four men waited here last night for us to show up."

"Or one chain smoker."

But Cosimo was serious. "He would need that many to move the statue. Keller assembled a team to take the statue and to sell it to whatever buyer is waiting."

"A team of four."

"Or five." He returned my stare. "My brother could never have afforded that engagement ring."

"He said that Keller paid him for helping to choose a new car."

"Keller paid my brother enough to buy his *own* car. My brother bought an expensive ring. He can't even afford a good pair of shoes but suddenly—diamonds. Don't you see?" Cosimo sniffed his fingertips: "Turkish tobacco."

"We should fear the Turks, now?"

He gave me his heavy-lidded look. "Many German smokers prefer Turkish tobacco."

"And many Germans," I countered, "don't smoke at all. We're discouraged from it, as a matter of fact. It's not even allowed in our offices. You Italians light the second before you throw away the first." A ridiculous argument, but I still didn't want to believe. "Even if Keller were in charge, even if this were his own private heist, wouldn't he have mostly Italians helping him?"

Cosimo began to swear, cursing Keller's name again.

"You knew something was wrong last night," I reminded him. "You knew it as soon as you saw the ring. You knew when Enzo told you, 'Don't worry, go along.' Why didn't you do more?"

Cosimo inhaled deeply. "I hoped he would change his mind. I could not change it for him. But now it is bigger than that. I fear, Mister Vogler, that it is bigger than both of us."

Back on the road, we traveled in silence to the Monterosso turn-off, and I kept my eyes fixed on the di Luca guide in my lap, fingers tracing the embossed letters on the thick, green leather spine while Cosimo, driven with what I hoped was only paranoia, steered us ever farther from the main road.

Goats bleated from the shade of a chestnut tree. Above us in the hills, a rooster crowed its dawn alert several hours too late. Just one of many reasons not to live in the countryside.

"I need to visit the bushes," I said.

When I walked back to the truck, Cosimo was sitting with a photograph balanced against the steering wheel, studying it as his lips moved silently—seeking comfort or guidance, it seemed, which was only further proof that Cosimo was taking his own dire premonitions too seriously.

A raven-haired woman stared back from the center of the curling photo with one blurry hand lifted to her forehead, sweeping back a piece of hair. She had prominent cheekbones, a wide mouth, and an impatient but somehow not off-putting expression, like someone who didn't want to be photographed. That explained the blurry hand. This woman, attractive as she was, had no desire to be admired, or to wait for a man's approval.

"Rosina. She would know what to do," he said, acknowledging my presence, eyes still focused on the curled image in his hand.

Rattled by Cosimo's superstitious gloom, I feigned a lighthearted tone. "I wouldn't say it if Enzo were around, but she is much more beautiful than Farfalla."

When Cosimo responded with a dismal expression, I continued uncertainly. "Intelligent eyes, a wonderful smile."

"She isn't smiling."

"But she wants to smile; she is considering, but perhaps she isn't easily persuaded."

"Trust me," he said, "she isn't a woman who can be persuaded about anything."

The more I looked, the more I saw it. In the photo, the woman appeared undecided about whether to berate the photographer or burst out laughing.

"I'm not teasing you, if that's what you think. I'm trying to make you feel better. You haven't broken it off with her, have you?"

"No," he said, pushing the photo back into his pocket. "I see her all the time."

"Well, then—one ray of hope in dark times, yes?"

"Mister Vogler," he said, starting the truck again, tapping the gas until the guttering roar eased back into a steady rumble, "she is my sister."

We saw a young boy tugging a goat alongside the road, the animal's satiny blue collar glinting in the sun.

"There." Cosimo swung toward the shoulder, jumped out of the truck and stood next to the boy, questioning and pointing while the boy pulled his goat nearer.

"We're close," Cosimo explained, back in the truck.

"To the farm?"

"No."

"What did the boy say?"

"I gave him a coin and I asked him if he saw a yellow sports car early this morning. He said yes, maybe. I asked him if he saw a silver sports car. Yes, also. And a blue one—that, too."

"You paid him. He was trying to please you."

"But when I asked him if he saw a red car early today, he said, '*Assolutamente no.*' The problem is not that I paid him. The problem is that someone else already paid him more."

"But surely you're not going to take a little boy seriously—"

"You think I was only listening? I was looking. I saw the collar on the goat. The boy told me he has owned it since the goat was born."

"So?"

"It was Enzo's necktie."

I hurried to look over my shoulder at the boy, getting smaller on the road behind us. It was possible that the tie had fallen from Enzo's jacket pocket the night before, while he was riding. But Cosimo was impervious to doubt. Tense with dread, he was sitting up so straight that no part of his spine touched the back of the truck seat, and he was driving slower yet, at barely more than a brisk walking pace.

"This is very important," he said after a while. He instructed me to look on the right side of the road; he would search on the left. "If we find his scooter on my side, he was coming back from the farm. If we find it on your side, he never made it."

"If we find his scooter at all. If it isn't parked safely up some dead-end road kilometers from here," I added, but Cosimo showed no sign of hearing.

In some places the shoulder was clear and climbed directly up to farmlands or dry, unplanted hills. In other places there was brush and high grass. I scanned with concentration, arm hanging over the sun-beaten windowsill, sweat tickling my neck. But we found no sign of anything in the next two minutes or in twenty.

And of course, this search was taking us farther away from the bigger road along which we'd been traveling. We were losing time. Even the addled roosters had stopped crowing, silenced by the day's building heat. Our *benzina* supply: diminishing. Our own energy for the long drive still ahead: draining away. This was idiotic. We were going the wrong way, damn it all. We were digging ourselves deeper.

"Anyway, is there a difference?" I finally asked. "Does it matter, if he was coming or going?"

Cosimo would say no more.

Irritated as I was, I was not immune to the contagion of his superstitious imagination. As the hot, slow minutes ticked by, the paired possibilities took shape in my mind: Enzo making it to the village, halfway through his future in-laws' celebratory dinner, making a grand entrance, being enfolded by the arms of Farfalla's brothers and sisters and aunts and uncles. Fitting an extra chair at the table. Bringing another plate, another glass. Enzo apologizing for his appearance—the dirt of the road, the golden hair standing on end. And then toasting and dancing for the bridal couple. Enzo cornering Farfalla's father, and then returning to the table and tapping a glass. A proposal to the bride's younger sister. I imagined her saying yes, and everyone turning a blind eye when Enzo fell asleep not in the main parlor, where a half-dozen male relations shared a nest of blankets, but somewhere else—a cellar perhaps, or a farmer's shed. Somewhere with Farfalla.

But that was only the first possibility. The second possibility was a night ride, dusty eyes straining to see the outline of road, an obstacle—rock or stick or wild animal—and then the spinout of scooter against chalky road. The scooter sliding toward the shoulder and into high grass. No party, no Farfalla. No memorable night in the cellar. At the last minute, in that coldest part of the night just before dawn, a thought sent out into the starry ether, toward the only person who could receive it.

(Did I believe that twins could be connected in such a way? Given my own genetic anxieties, I had to believe it was possible. Do I still believe, a decade later? If the world holds no mystery at all, no romantic possibility, then my second trip to the Piedmont is futile—so yes, I choose to believe. War takes away nearly everything, but perhaps not that final illogical tendency that allows us to continue living.)

Scanning the road for any sign as the truck continued along at its creeping pace, I weighed the scenarios, wondering which was better or worse: to leave behind a ruined woman, following a night of pleasure; or to miss that night, but in missing it, to spare her considerable grief.

"Where are you hoping to find him, Cosimo?"

"To anyone who has felt love, it is clear."

It wasn't clear to *me*.

There was a long pause as Cosimo stewed before surrendering the answer. "Left side. Coming back. To have one night with her at least. To have one night with a wonderful, beautiful woman. Of course I must wish this for him."

The truck swerved and braked. Ignoring my questions, Cosimo jumped out and paced along the left side of the road, where he'd evidently glimpsed something. I copied him, pacing along the right. But he seemed so certain that I couldn't stop looking over my shoulder, watching as he pushed a long stick into what looked like a trampled stand of thick roadside grass. He crouched. Dropped the stick. Reached a hand into the grass, near the ground, and left it there.

Even from across the road, I recognized the look on his half-turned face: the same look that Greta had worn the day I'd come home from my part-time job with Betelmann and she'd come to the hall, holding a handkerchief that had belonged to our mother. "The doctor just left. *Vater* isn't back yet, he doesn't know. You should go see her now, have your own moment, before he gets back and turns the place upside down." But it was hard to take the next step. "Go now." It was hard to move from that in-between realm of knowing and not knowing, accepting and not accepting; that frozen place from which every step is a step toward unhappiness.

Nearing the spot, I saw that Cosimo's hand was resting on Enzo's ankle, just above his black shoe. The laces had come untied, and after a moment, Cosimo tied them, slowly and carefully, making the loops even and snug. That tender gesture held my complete attention as the rest of my mind raced to catch up with what I was seeing, what I was not believing: the shoe and the foot, the trampled grass, the motionless body.

Then Cosimo patted his brother's ankle again, leaving his hand there for a moment, until he nodded for assistance.

Waving away the flies that were already buzzing around, I reached forward to help Cosimo roll the body over and struggled to resist recoiling. Enzo's thigh was slightly stiff, but even through the cloth of his trousers I could feel a greasy emanation of heat. Yet there was no pulse. I'd expected a corpse to be cold. This was worse.

"Normal?" I heard myself ask Cosimo, losing somehow the "is" and the "it," along with the basic rhythm of breathing and swallowing, which now seemed to require considerable conscious effort. When the body in front of me lost solidity, I had to look away just to force open the shutter that was closing in my mind, blackening the view in front of me.

Cosimo winced at the road rash on one side of his brother's face. "There is warmth—for twelve hours, sometimes more." His voice came out in a warped staccato, tinny and uneven, as if it had traveled over a long distance through a metal tube.

He turned to cough into his sleeve before facing the body again, wiping at a bloody temple with his handkerchief, dabbing at Enzo's matted, sticky hair, each touch tender but tentative, as if he could barely bring himself to make contact and then barely bring himself to break it.

When Cosimo began to cough again, face hidden, I moved away and busied myself by pushing the scooter back onto the road. A string bag was still snagged on the left handlebar on the scooter, filled mostly with glass shards now, as well as some food items wrapped in newspaper. The ground was stained grayish white from what I realized was milk—milk that had been collected just hours earlier and handed to Enzo with a farewell clap on the shoulder. Milk in a glass jar, for Cosimo. That famous statue—of the twin boys with their cherubic, upturned faces, nursing side by side from a she-wolf. The founders of Rome. Romulus and Remus. Fifteenth century. Which brother slew the other and why? I couldn't recall. It was the simplest question, but my memory wouldn't cooperate.

The countryside was quiet. No vehicle traffic or animal noises. No shepherd's distant bells. A faint breeze failed to lift our clinging shirts from our damp backs.

Cosimo stood next to me, a few meters from the accident scene, fumbling to strike a match and keep it lit within his cupped palm. Finally, he managed to light the cigarette and took his time smoking it. When the final ash fell, something more would have to be done. That part of the future seemed—for an odd moment—endlessly far away. Until the moment was now. Then it seemed too soon.

He gestured for me to approach, and while he reached down for his brother's top half again, I tried to take the bottom. But the trousers kept bunching and slipping. I worked my way higher up his legs, trying to get my shoulder under his thighs to push him up. As I was pushing, something edged out of his right trouser pocket: a corner of a banknote—a thick, folded pile of currency.

Cosimo had seen. He ordered me to set the body down, crouched low to the road and emptied the pocket slowly—first, the folded Italian *lire*—one clipped-together bundle, then a second. He looked at me, and then pushed his hand into the pocket again. The third bundle was a thicker fold of *Reichsmarks*.

"I thought Keller ran him off the road, but now I am not sure," Cosimo said. "Keller knew he carried money. If they saw the crash, they would have checked his pockets."

"You're saying it was just an accident?"

"Maybe he saw them coming in the distance, maybe he recognized the sound of the Spider coming around a curve. He panicked and skidded out."

"So you're not blaming Keller."

He stared at me, eyes blazing. "Of course I blame Keller for talking Enzo into this. I will kill Keller if I see him."

"No, no," I stammered. "We don't need any of that."

Cosimo resumed digging through Enzo's other pockets. I looked away, trying to give him a moment to do what he needed to do, trying to give myself a moment to breathe, to think. When I turned around again, Cosimo's lips were pressed together, a fresh unlit cigarette between them. He held something toward me: Enzo's lighter, shaking violently.

I looked at it for a moment before understanding. I took and lit Cosimo's cigarette for him.

He inhaled once before holding out the other hand. The diamond ring rested in his flattened palm.

"He didn't propose?"

Taking the cigarette from his lips, Cosimo pushed his face into the crook of his elbow, wiping once. "She said no."

"Maybe he didn't even propose."

"I am certain. He would not fail to propose."

"You're certain he asked?"

"This was Enzo. Of course he asked. You can see that he made it there—the milk—and he was coming back. But she said no."

Cosimo crouched near Enzo's body again, a little unsteady on his feet. "I have seen bodies before," he said after his breathing had become more even. "But it isn't the same."

"Do you need to rest for a moment?"

The suggestion alone seemed to irritate him, bolstering his resolve. He was stoical beyond belief—an effect of his police training, I could only imagine. Again, he lifted Enzo under the arms. I struggled to hoist his lower half, my arms wrapped around his stiffening calves, feeling repulsed by the slightly pliable feeling of skin over hardening muscle, the curly hair pasted down with grit, dried sweat, trickles of brown blood. The bad smell wouldn't leave my nose. It wasn't the smell of death—not yet—only spoiling milk. Gripping Enzo's legs, I tried to ignore the dizziness building in my head.

We brought him to the truck, set him down on the ground. Both of us tried to look away, to see any part of Enzo but his stained face.

"A minute, please," Cosimo said, and I willingly walked toward the front of the truck and rocked on my heels as I listened for Cosimo to call me back again. I heard him jump into the back of the truck, rummaging and clanking around. Then a long pause, followed by quick steps, a thud as he jumped to the road, followed by an anguished moan.

Racing to the back of the truck, I saw Cosimo doubled over, vomiting into the dust. I led him, still doubled over, farther away from the truck, farther away from Enzo's body, to a low stone wall that ran along part of the road. He did not want to sit, but I made him, as I wiped his face with my handkerchief. I took each of his hands, guided them to a mat of herbs growing just behind the wall, and urged him to rub the old smell away, replacing it with the scent of rosemary.

"A little better?" I asked.

He had caught his breath. "It should have been me."

"Cosimo—"

"No, please. Say nothing. It is better that way."

When my mother had died, I had said nothing helpful to my father, nothing even to my sister. When my father had died just before Christmas, I had such mixed emotions I was afraid to open my mouth, fearful of what would escape, the compressed emotions of my youth unrelieved by his passing.

"It's a common reaction," I told him now, searching for the right phrase. "But there is no way to trade your life for his. You cannot bring him back, Cosimo."

"Truly," he said. "It should have been me."

"It doesn't help—"

"You don't understand." He was firmer now. "It should have been me. Not me to die—me to propose. Farfalla and I were supposed to be married."

"She was yours? Enzo stole your girl?"

"For a while. With Enzo, it was always for a short while."

"But this time . . ."

He stood up from the stone wall. "What could I do? He is me, the same—but better."

"No, Cosimo. You and he were not the same . . ." I found the anger building so suddenly, so irrationally, that it was hard to finish. "And he was *not* better. Don't make it worse by believing that."

Cosimo was attending to his own obsessions, his own wounds: "But last night, she must have said no to him. That is what the dream meant, when he apologized and told me to look in his pocket. Not for the money, for the ring."

He continued to nod, trying to absorb all that had happened. It was like watching a heavy man pull himself, hand over hand, up a thick rope, feet kicking and sliding, failing to get solid purchase.

"She said no. But that is the worst thing, because now, I can never ask her. I can never profit from this. I cannot be a replacement. So yes, it might as well have been me, lying there."

CHAPTER 8

"They'll be looking for us," Cosimo said when he was behind the wheel again, eyes dry and engine running. "They don't know about Enzo. They don't know if I was helping him or helping you. But Keller and his men know we have the statue."

"You're not well. Let me drive."

"You don't know how to drive."

"It can't be that difficult."

When Cosimo ignored me and began to turn the truck back toward the main road from which we'd come, I picked up the empty wine bottle from the floor near my feet and raised it shoulder high. "You *will* let me. That way, there will be two of us, driving day and night if necessary."

He leaned back, eyeing the raised bottle in my hand. Cosimo was a little bulkier than me. I was a little taller.

"Your mistake," he said after a moment, looking back at the road, "is not breaking the top of the bottle. I can tell that you've never hurt a man."

"And this means I never will?"

He hesitated. "You're right. I can't tell. Sometimes a quiet man is the most violent because he has been holding back so much for so long."

Cosimo brought the truck to a gradual stop and got out so that I could slide over and take the wheel. He watched as I made an inventory of the dashboard, the view out the front window, the view out the sides—there couldn't have been any lonelier section of road. The engine stalled and I restarted it. I tried again, got the truck rolling, struggling to remember how to shift and steer.

"We'll choose a route to the border, together," I said over the screech of the grinding gears. "We'll look at the map at our next stop."

I dared not take my eyes off the road in order to check his expression. I had driven forward only a hundred meters when the engine stalled again.

"Enzo's body—we'll figure that out," I said, trusting that Cosimo's red-rimmed eyes were on me still. "We need to bring him somewhere close and then keep going. We've stolen nothing; we've done nothing. All we have to do is deliver the statue. If it goes missing, we're suspect. But if we deliver it, they'll believe us."

"The Italian government?"

"The Germans. *Der Kunstsammler* himself—he wants only the statue."

Again, he said nothing. The gear stick wouldn't respond to anything less than brute force. I grunted, trying to jam it into the correct position.

"We still have two days to cover seven hundred kilometers. It isn't impossible. Twenty to twenty-five hours of driving altogether, even on the roughest roads. Are you hearing me, Cosimo?"

"The funeral," he said under his breath.

"Of course. After we get the statue to the border, or it will be our own funeral they'll have to plan next." There was a way to manage all this, to fit the pieces into place. "Should we have brought your brother's body to Farfalla's home? Weren't we almost there? We could have left the body and then kept driving."

"No. I am not ready to see Farfalla. And more important, you are not thinking of my mother and my sister."

"But where do they live, Cosimo?"

He reached out a hand toward the dashboard and rapped at a needle that appeared stuck under the scratched glass. As we struggled uphill, the truck lurched, gurgled, and bucked, aggravated no doubt by my incompetent shifting.

"How far does your family live from here? I thought you said it was very far—the Piedmont, didn't you say?"

"Not enough *benzina*," he muttered. "That is the bad sound."

"Yes?"

"We have more in the back, if you could please . . ."

"Yes, of course."

I was in the back, near the crate, handing over the fuel containers—one, then another, carefully, over the sprawled body of Enzo, crouched to one side of the truck, near the back door. Cosimo reached up for the second container and I stepped back slightly, strengthening my stance, and straining to hold the container high and level, not wanting to touch any part of the body as I leaned over it. Then suddenly, just when my hands were empty and I was standing up to stretch my back, the door rattled shut, plunging me into darkness.

"Cosimo!"

Metal rasped against metal—a latch securing the door.

"Cosimo, what are you doing?"

The truck started up, gurgling healthfully this time, not short on *benzina* at all.

"Have you lost your mind?"

I crouched, eyes wide, waiting for my vision to adjust, unable to see anything but a thin line of light where the retractable door didn't perfectly match the frame. The truck started moving forward and I reached out a steadying hand. I couldn't stay on my feet. I'd have to find some way to sit, without getting too close.

I remembered Enzo's lighter, which I'd slipped into my pocket after igniting Cosimo's trembling cigarette. I opened the lid and struck the flint wheel, and there was the crate, taking up most of the truck's cargo area; and there also, in the jumping shadows, was the body. I banged on the wall near the driver's side of the truck.

"Why are you doing this?" I slammed my fist against the wall. "You can't leave me in here!"

Three more slams, not nearly loud enough; three shooting pains that traveled from my knuckles up into my wrist and elbow.

Finally, he called back, the words just audible: "If I let you out, you won't let me put my brother properly to rest."

"To rest, where?"

The muffled reply: "There is no point in arguing."

We had left Rome on a Saturday morning. Today was Sunday already—late morning, or perhaps noon already. Certainly, noon.

"The statue, Cosimo. We can't lose our focus. The border, by tomorrow night!"

The back of the truck was uncomfortably warm. Hand aching, I sat down with my back up against the crate and alternately closed my eyes, to stop from straining to see, and opened them again, desperate to see, to make sure—what? That nothing had changed? That nothing had moved?

Each time my mind wandered to Enzo's body—and it did not need to wander far—my nose filled with the smell of spoiling milk. My heart accelerated, followed by my breathing.

Think of something else.

But it wasn't easy.

There is the crate, and the statue. Think of that.

We should have turned him over. We should have covered him up.

Create a mental sketch. Imagine each part.

I pictured the outstretched hand and disc. I moved down to the shoulder, down the chest with its gently grooved and lightly sculpted ribs. I tried to slow myself down, to remember all I could so that I wouldn't get to the bottom too fast. If I got to the bottom, I'd think of Enzo again.

So often, a statue is praised as lifelike. But a statue must be more than life, which ends so easily here, in death. It must be more and better, not a mere representation. But that was the wrong direction to go.

Not death, not life, just stone—think of that.

Back to the stomach muscles, and the two horizontal creases at the statue's waist, just where it bent forward, the navel and just above. The carved marble: an illusion of softness. The human body: transforming via rigor mortis but only until softness returned again. Only until there was decay and putrefaction. How long did we have—two days? Three?

My breathing quickened again. I couldn't bear the darkness, but I didn't want to waste the lighter. Cosimo's family lived in the North. Perhaps a day from here? A very long day?

I tried to remember the next part of the statue, but it had vanished from my mind. I tried to recall a turned foot, a knee, a hand. Nothing. I knew I'd feel better if I could just see the statue, in life or in my mind's eye—something to concentrate on, something clean and cool, unsullied, unstained.

Think—I told myself—*of the eternal.* By which I did not mean heaven, or wherever Enzo was going. I meant art.

Gerhard had asked more than once, "Does it bother you, that someone, a few people, should gather up all these masterpieces—"

I had deflected the question, but perhaps part of me was thinking: these few people, these powerful and politically connected art collectors, this entire regime—none of it would last long. So who cared if our Führer took some pieces here, and his head of secret police stored a few other pieces at his private estate? That was one generation. But we were speaking of paintings that were five hundred years old, and statues that were three or four times older than that. Whatever happened, the art would outlive the men. As long as it survived somewhere, it would survive.

Is that what I was thinking? Or was I thinking only of my personal survival? Or was I thinking nothing at all?

Di Luca was nearby—I recognized the padded cover under my blindly groping fingers—but even with better light, the book wasn't what I needed. What I needed to see—and what I was at the same time afraid to see—was directly in front of me.

I pushed my fingers into a narrow gap between the slats, halfway up the crate. I pulled out one piece of straw after another, pushing hard with my fingers to get deeper into the crate, scraping my knuckles as I pulled out more, thinking all the while that they hadn't used enough straw, hadn't packed it tightly enough, and I should have been there, on time, in Rome, to oversee things. The packing job had been insufficient. A truck hits too many bumps and ruts. A train at least travels a more smooth and predictable path. To trust a masterpiece to this kind of handling was insanity! But then again, of course—how many times did I need to remind myself?—Keller had not expected it to be on the road for long. Just the first day, just until Monterosso, and then it was meant to be intercepted and sent back. No wonder it wasn't packed adequately, and no wonder it was being carried in a truck that lurched and shimmied all over the road.

I pushed my hand in so hard between the crate's splintering slats that several times I nearly got my fingers stuck, but still I pushed and pulled, pushed and pulled, my fingers tender and damp with blood I could not see, working my hand in just to the knob of the wrist bone, where it could go no further.

Near the body, against one wall of the truck, I located Enzo's tool kit. Inside, there was a claw hammer. Moving back to the crate, I stood cautiously, barely maintaining my balance, and started working a board free. Some were too tight, and working in the dark, I was wary of pulling too hard and whacking myself with a flying board or a slipping tool. Shoulder height was no good because I didn't have purchase. I lowered myself to my knees and tried working another board free until it gave slowly.

I held the lighter up to the gap and peered in: glowing marble, a pattern of shadow and light.

Squinting into the dark crate, I could make out just a few illuminated inches, bare of straw: perhaps the triceps of the left arm at first, the lowered left arm. But no, the crate was turned the other way. It was the right hip. It was the right hip, and above that, the belt of muscle that bulges just up and over the statue's right hip and down across its groin. The beautiful iliac crest.

Few men are so perfectly proportioned, such the right mixture of muscular and slim, to have that kind of perfectly sculpted definition. The Greeks covered themselves with oil and exercised in the nude, scraping away the grime with a strigil when they were finished, their tanned bodies on full civic display—a testament not only to athleticism, but to a deeper kind of vitality and purpose. My own fellow countrymen, in search of answers and purpose and power, could find no better symbol than that kind of body, that kind of athleticism. "The Germans have joined anew the bond with the Greeks, the hitherto highest form of man." Someone had written that—Nietzsche—or I had heard it in speeches at the Königsplatz, or most likely both.

But philosophic mottos were nothing compared to what stood in front of me now, even if it stood in dark shadow. This was it. This was he. I was not disappointed; I was relieved and grateful, much as a religious person in desperation would be grateful for any sign or miracle that suggested something larger and more meaningful than his own wretched insignificance. I knew these centimeters of perfection better than I knew my own body. I loved this body more than my own body. But that was an easy comparison to make, when my own maturing body had brought me increasing grief, day by day.

The smell came back to me in the back of the truck as I slept. First, the nameplate on the door, DR. SCHROEDER, and then the wafting antiseptic smell.

I was fourteen years old. Greta, then seventeen, had been told nothing at all and made to stay at home. My father knew where we were going, but not what it cost, and Mother had not wanted him to know, because as much as he wanted the problem eliminated, he did not approve of spending any more than absolutely necessary.

In the aromatic waiting room, my mother sat at my side, gripping my hand, while I tried to read the ornate calligraphy on the certificates and then to count the tongue depressors and cotton balls I could see in jars on a far shelf. But Mother's hand kept squeezing and relaxing, a dying fish on my lap. When my fingers started to tingle, I looked up to see she had locked eyes with the woman opposite her, a woman who had arrived ahead of us with her son, an overweight, towering fellow who walked with a limp. Despite his height, he had the face of a boy, fat cheeks stained with tears. He was directed into the examination room, alone.

The woman waited behind, clenching a handkerchief that appeared yellow next to the gray-white skin of her thin, tensed hand. From the next room came the sound of feet on the floor, the deep-voiced boy arguing with the doctor. The door began to open, then closed. The woman stood, her face pale, torn between going to help her son and staying put as she had been told.

"Change places," my mother whispered to me, and moments

later she was holding a quiet and sympathetic conference with the woman next to her.

". . . yours?" I heard the woman say.

"Just a very simple procedure, I've been told."

"That's what I was told, before," the woman said, twisting her handkerchief. "A simple examination. I brought him in last month with a rash."

"It couldn't be treated?"

"Yes, easily. But the doctor got to asking me questions, discussing the future, and then . . ."

My eyes flickered to the poster above a desk on the far left side of the room. ANTHROPOMETRY, it said at the top, and there was photo after photo of a man in his underclothes being measured from every angle by a white-coated doctor.

Across the room, a second poster shouted in blocky, self-assured capital letters: HEALTH, A NATIONAL RESOURCE. If health were a resource that a nation needed desperately in order to survive, then the healthiest of its citizens were heroes. The unhealthy were bad people, the kind we heard about so often on the radio: *saboteurs*. I looked back at the anthropometry poster, suspiciously eyeing the doctor's large black calipers, long and curved like the back end of an earwig.

In response to my mother's well-meaning inquiries, the other woman responded, "It's better this way." She smoothed her skirt and patted her loose bun, which was sprouting black bobby pins that looked like tiny, electrocuted snakes. "It would only be harder in a few years, and that might be too late to hold off troubles."

"That makes sense."

"And anyway, he doesn't understand it."

"Do you understand it, dear?"

"Well enough."

We were made to wait a long time. When the woman was finally allowed in to see her boy, I moved back to the seat next to my mother. "What doesn't he understand?"

"He's being sterilized."

"Is he covered with germs?"

"No, that's not it."

The surgical room was open and we could see the doctor and the mother trying to help the wobbly boy to stand and proceed to a secondary recovery room in the back. But whatever anesthesia they had given him was still coursing through his veins, and the mildly degenerate young man—if that's what he was—kept collapsing back onto the table. With every thump, I felt my mother's grip tighten on my sleeve, and I finally understood her fear: that this eugenically minded doctor, full of new ideas and politically astute aspirations, was a danger to us, though I still didn't quite understand why.

"Hurry," my mother said, dragging me by the arm, gesturing toward the way out.

"But why?"

"I want to leave." The tension had finally overtaken her. Her face was damp and drops of tears were collecting at the tip of her red chin.

"But I'm not being"—I searched for the word—"sterilized."

"No, you're not. We came for our own procedure."

"But are they going to do it?"

"Not now. Let's go."

I wasn't entirely relieved. I was confused. Because a part of me did want this done and finished—"a simple procedure," my mother had been whispering in my ear all week, preparing me to be brave. A part of me was already looking ahead, thinking of the group hikes and swims I'd be able to attend later in the summer and feeling how much easier it all would be from this day forward. But there was also something about the smell in the air, the drunken stagger of the man-boy, and my mother's own sudden loss of confidence that all merged into an unspeakable dread.

Until this point, the problem had been a matter of surfaces and emotions—no small things, of course. My difference was a humiliation, but in some school circles, wearing the wrong outfit and hairstyle were nearly as problematic. But what if it went deeper? What if this thing, whether left in place or surgically removed, was a sign of something else, and that something required further treatment or quarantine? On the way out, I looked at the anthropometry poster again, and at the large calipers that the doctor in the picture was holding tight to the patient's head. He was only measuring, I told myself. Not clipping, crushing, or rubbing him out.

I woke in the hot dark with my hand pressed against my face and my fingers clutched around something hard and square, and the smell of antiseptic—no, lighter fluid—strong on my fingers and in my nostrils.

"Air!" I shouted. "I need air! It's too hot in here!"

No answer.

"You can't leave me in here all day, with a body! Cosimo!"

They say that kidnappers operate most comfortably in ano-nymity. I had made myself too anonymous to my captor, who had known me until now only by my last name, Vogler.

I took a deep breath and shouted: "Ernst!"

One syllable, lost to the whine of the engine.

"Ernst—that is my Christian name!"

Still no reply. I waited a few minutes, listening for any sound, and then gathered my energies to try again.

"Cosimo!"

But he was trying his best to ignore me. When I pounded on the wall, the engine sounds rose in pitch, as if he were acceler-ating slightly, and in that acceleration I perceived his stress as well. He could have left me on the road. He could have taken the statue and his brother's body and left me. But he did not, so I reasoned that he did, in fact, plan to help me still—only later. But what he couldn't realize, because he wasn't thinking, was that "later" would not suffice. If we weren't at the border by Monday at nightfall, we would be labeled as criminals. Keller would claim, conveniently, that we had evaded the Roman policemen in order the steal the statue—that we had planned all of it from day one—and that's how it would seem.

The heat and the dark and the constant bouncing made me feel drugged, obscuring how much time was passing, or how much I had slept. I set up a rhythm of pounding my fist and calling out, followed by periods of rest, during which I listened for any signs of Cosimo's attention. We slowed down, but it was only to make a sharp turn. We sped up later, coasting down a hill. Another steep turn, followed by another—we were zigzagging, the engine straining. A major left turn, perhaps heading west. Climbing further into the mountains.

I banged again and again with the edge of my aching fist, counting as I went—*sieben, acht, neun*—and was rewarded finally with a sound: not a voice, but a whistle.

It was tremulous and uncertain at first. Then it built, becoming the tune that Cosimo had whistled the day before at the lake. German opera. But what was that tune? Nothing epic or Wagnerian. It was simpler, lilting, and sweet. The association that came to mind was one of woods, children, a sandman and a dew fairy and angels, all watching and protecting. I could see the big old radio in our house and my mother next to it, with her hand resting on top of the wood because whenever she lifted her hand there was static. Somehow we thought it had to be her hand that was summoning music from the radio, that she was nearly magical, so Greta and I begged her not to shift. "Of course, you love this one," she'd tell my sister. "It is named for you."

Or nearly so. It was *Hänsel und Gretel*, by Humperdinck. The opera I couldn't quite place before.

It was a message. Cosimo was telling me that he meant no harm. We were not abandoning the precepts of civilization; he was not a rule breaker at heart. He was only insisting on his own values, as I had to insist on mine.

If there is something I feared as a child, while listening to *Hänsel und Gretel*, it was the thought of being pushed into an oven. It happened only to the witch in the end, but still.

It took a half hour or so to build up the courage and several attempts to get the lighter started. As the smell on my fingers attested, the fluid had leaked as I slept, and now there was not enough to guarantee many more strikes. I found my suitcase and felt blindly through it, searching for something flammable. My sketchbook and my dictionary remained in the front of the truck.

I patted my pocket, locating a large, poorly folded piece of paper: the map. I ripped it into long sections, fashioning each into a twisted horn, then applied the lighter and began to add handfuls of straw, which ignited easily.

"Fire!" I yelled, my throat tight with apprehension until I cleared it and accepted what I had done. "Cosimo! Fire!"

I crouched near the door, next to Enzo's body, ready to jump out. The pile of burning straw crackled. The burlap lemon bag had finally caught, filling the truck with smoke. I started to cough.

He shouted from the cab. "You're lying to me!"

"I'm not!"

The response came back muffled. "*Imbecille! Dummkopf!* Everything back there will burn!"

But it wouldn't. Not the statue made of marble. Ancient things have a way of outlasting us, as they should.

If the fire were left unchecked, the wooden crate would go up next. Then the body, or rather two bodies—but it wouldn't come to that, I didn't think. The crate was slow to catch, but catch it finally did—not blazing yet, only smoldering. Meanwhile, I could scarcely breathe.

"Fire! You must stop the truck!"

At the moment I reached out a hand and made contact with something I'd overlooked in my search for flammable paper—the padded cover. Di Luca. The most important reference in my collection. But more importantly, the only thing I owned that bore my mentor's name. Why did this matter so much if he was still safe somewhere, to emerge someday from these confused times, dignified and healthy and whole? My instincts knew what my mind refused to admit. If there was a moment of uncontrolled panic, it hit then, and I leaned over the book, its corners pressed into my chest.

I was coughing uncontrollably when the truck braked to a halt. A moment later, Cosimo unlocked and threw open the retractable door. He ignored me, attending to the fire instead, beating it with his jacket. Briefly, I had the advantage: I could lock him inside the truck and either he would fight the blaze or fail to fight it, but either way the statue would survive. But I couldn't do it. As duty-bound and determined as I considered myself to be, I could not do it, even then.

Smoke billowed but there was no visible flame. Cosimo's face was dark with grime and exhaustion. It would not have taken much to subdue him. He approached me, lumbering in a soot-covered half crouch, so disappointed and so disheartened, readying himself to jump down from the edge of the truck, both fists curled with contempt.

He pulled the truck's back door closed, leaving me standing as he returned to the driver's side door. I followed, uncertain, calling out, "Someone has to be committed to the larger things—to art, to the future!"

"Go around," he said, stabbing a finger at the passenger door. "Get in."

The hour hand on my watch crept past three o'clock, and then four. I noticed the roominess of the truck bench, the gap between us, where before we'd been so crowded. I cleared my parched, smoky throat and asked Cosimo where we were, but he reminded me that I'd burned the only map. A sign pointed toward two names I didn't recognize—Vignola and Maranello—but we continued along the smallest roads, always turning away from any town or larger *strada*. He would say only that we were heading northwest; that we had to avoid being seen; that he needed to concentrate to find his way on this indirect route he had traveled only a few times before.

The sun was low and hot in the burnished western sky when I patted my pocket and noticed the shape of the postcards meant for my sister. If I'd remembered them before, I would have used them for kindling. I took one out, and pushing hard against my thigh to keep the script smooth despite the road's bumps, I wrote:

We are past Florence . . .

Nothing else came to mind, until, with exasperation, I put pen to paper and scrawled quickly:

. . . which is a shame. It would have been wonderful to see, though I was not prepared to see it. But perhaps for beauty, one cannot prepare.

I read the card once and tore it up, ashamed of my own blatant ventriloquism. It would have been a gratifying notion, to think I had absorbed something from Enzo in the short amount of time I'd known him, that his impulsive nature, his *gioia di vivere*, had been somehow contagious. But it would not have been true.

Hearing the sound of tearing paper, Cosimo glanced at the ripped pieces accumulating in my lap. For the first time in hours, he tried to smile: "You're not starting another fire, are you?"

Cosimo accepted a piece of bread left over from yesterday's groceries, though I noticed he took one dry bite before pushing it back into the bag, his free hand pressed against his stomach.

He said, "I smell something."

I sniffed my own sleeve. "Neither of us smells very good."

"Worse than that," he said, wrinkling his brow.

Earlier in the day, the rear compartment had been hot enough; many more hours had passed since with the sun beating against the metal, raising the temperature as we drove.

"Something rotting," Cosimo said.

"The milk smell. It was on the ground. It probably splashed onto Enzo's clothes."

"Milk," he repeated. "No, that isn't it."

He pushed a finger against his temple, massaging in hard circles. After a while, the same hand went to his nose, which he couldn't stop rubbing. He tried unrolling the window and, weary of the clouds of hot midday road dust filling the truck, rolled it back again. Despite his attempt to be discreet, the compulsion built over time until I couldn't stop watching and he couldn't stop sniffing.

"Maybe a cigarette," I suggested.

"In a few months, it will be truffling time again," he said, ignoring me. "I have my best dog, Tartufa. Every autumn, we go . . ."

This was a good subject, neutral and safe, and I encouraged him for more details: the dog, the black and white truffles, the season, the sights and smells in the Piedmontese woods. And it seemed to work, for a few minutes at least, until Cosimo took what seemed at first to be a short detour but was really the path he was following all along, into a darker place.

"But Enzo never liked the woods," he rambled. "And I think now—it makes sense—this is why he didn't want to be a policeman. If it weren't for a body we found one day in the woods—a corpse, you call it, yes?—he might not have been looking for other different jobs, he might not have worked for Keller . . ."

Scheisse, again. "That's all right. You don't have to talk about it."

But he insisted. "It was already four days old, maybe five days. Flies lay their eggs, you know. Under the skin. Everywhere. When you find a body, you can tell when it died according to the insects. They teach us this in the training school."

"You're only smelling the milk, I'm sure of it," I told him, making a face. "Don't worry. If not a cigarette, maybe you could eat another piece of bread? Is your stomach bothering you?"

"They teach us about the little worms," he continued. "I don't know what you call them in German. They teach us about the stages, the problems you have, the third or fourth day." He pressed on, trying to find the foreign words that eluded him for the tightening clothes and the collecting gas as the body became a dark and rotting balloon.

"Take it easy."

"And when our mother, strong as she was, was ready to take the body—"

"*Your* mother?"

"I didn't say *my mother*."

"You did."

He frowned. "An old, local woman. When *she* was ready to take the body and clean it and dress it for the funeral—because that's what we do and what we've always done, we don't leave it to others, no matter the difficulty—"

"All right, Cosimo."

"So it was no wonder that Enzo did not want to be a policeman."

"It's only the milk smell that's bothering you. The closed space and the heat and the milk. That's all."

We came to a fork in the road with a field to our right and a low, crumbling bluff to our left, and in a hollow of the bluff, a green and mossy spot, in which there seemed to be a sort of basin and a small white cross. I assumed Cosimo was going to say a prayer or empty his bladder, or perhaps vomit again. But then he walked slowly around the front, came to my side of the truck, opened the door, and gestured me to slide over into the driver's seat.

"All right?" I asked him.

"Fine."

I spent the next twenty minutes reacquainting myself with the shifting, the struggle to coordinate feet and hands and eyes. When Cosimo groaned, I assumed he was expressing anguish at the damage I was doing to the truck's gears, until suddenly he called out and begged me to stop the truck. His door opened and I heard the retch and the splash, followed by a sighing moan.

He closed the door, wiping his mouth. "We should have wrapped the body."

"Is it still the smell? Is that what's getting to you?"

I started driving again, but he continued to press me about our need for a sheet or blanket, some kind of covering, especially with the sun nearing the horizon and the cold night coming soon. I stated the obvious: that Enzo wouldn't feel the cold; that, in fact, the cold would be better for transporting him. But during all that talk, I kept my eyes glued to the road. It was only when I finally started feeling comfortable with the steering that I made myself look over at Cosimo and noticed he was shivering, his skin pale and clammy, the whites of his eyes gone yellow.

"*Verdammt*—the body isn't too cold, you are."

He whispered into his damp sleeve, "I have a terrible headache."

"It's more than that. You're in shock." In my flustered state, I let the truck veer off to one side where it rubbed against a low thicket of blackberry bushes until I corrected my course. The sudden scratching noise made Cosimo's eyes flash open. "We need a doctor," I insisted.

"I won't talk to a doctor."

"But you need help."

"I only need a blanket." He shifted uncomfortably. "My stomach hurts—and my head. I just need to lie down, somewhere, just a few minutes . . ."

"I'll look for a town."

"No town." But after a minute, he relented. "A house. If you can find some farm, maybe . . ."

We passed alongside a field and, beyond it, a village of a dozen or so stone houses, huddled close, some of them with open animal stalls directly under human quarters. But as soon as we slowed down, dogs began to bark and a suspicious face glowered from an open doorway. There were too many people and too much life squeezed all together. Too much attention. Cosimo shook a dismissive, trembling hand and squeezed shut his eyes against the noise. We had to find someplace smaller. Someplace set apart.

"Don't fall asleep," I cautioned as I continued driving, my nose against the windshield now.

"Why not?"

"I'm not sure." But I had a feeling he shouldn't sleep yet, not without warmth and some food and a pair of eyes ready to watch over him better than I could manage while steering the truck down narrow roads.

"It's not a tractor you're driving there, friend," he said, teeth chattering. "You can go a little faster."

"I'm trying."

Ten minutes later, I loosened the grip of one inexpert hand from the steering wheel and gave Cosimo a shake. He had been moaning again. "Talk to me."

He opened one eye. "It's not my brother's fault that he was a romantic."

"Open your eyes, please. I must be firm. *Open your eyes*."

"You take everything so seriously, Mister Vogler. And I can tell you: I've seen worse than what I saw today. I've seen terrible things."

"Ernst. I think it is better now for you to call me Ernst." What was the point of convincing him he was in shock? What was the point in telling him that anyone would be shocked to see his own double in a state of imminent decay? He'd said himself that it was not the same as seeing another corpse, but Cosimo was intent in his professional self-regard, and blinded by his sense of duty. In that, we had something in common.

"Enzo would have wanted me to get you to a proper doctor," I said. "What do you think about that?"

Cosimo shook his head, not so easily fooled. A moment later, he asked in a groggy voice, "You think I was too easy with him?"

"Certainly. You gave him everything, even . . ." I was about to say, "even your girl," before realizing it was too strong a reminder. I finished: ". . . even your own jacket."

"That wasn't a favor to him. You might want a lifetime with a woman, but sometimes you settle for a night."

"Enzo didn't get even that," I said, if only to remind him of what he had not yet lost. But it didn't work.

He asked, "What do you think a night is worth?"

Nichts was my answer. Absolutely nothing. But I didn't want to upset him. I only wanted to keep him talking. "I don't know. Maybe one night can be pleasant."

His eyes were looking glassier; his speech was thick. "I wanted at least one night, but I settled for wanting my jacket back, smelling of her. He gets the girl; I get one smell. Her perfume—orange blossoms. Now you see?"

Cosimo tried to arrange his features in a grim smile, but the jostling over each deep rut pained him and he closed his eyes. We could take these bumps only slowly, and the little shack I'd spotted was high on the hill. Steering toward it with intense concentration, I told Cosimo that I thought he still had a chance with Farfalla. Now wasn't the time to think about it, but someday, he'd see things differently. And as tempting as it might be to imagine that another person's death required his own, the world didn't really work that way: a banal lecture never fully understood by the one who hears it, or even by the one who speaks it, but so it was then, and so it remains.

An old man in an untucked shirt, baggy trousers and hanging suspenders came to the open doorway of the small shack. Thick gray brows obscured his dark eyes—until the brows lifted in surprise in reaction to Cosimo's blue lips.

The shack was furnished with a cot, a table, and a kerosene lamp. One window framed a view of a larger villa, farther up the hill. Inside the modest dwelling, Cosimo managed only a few words, hard to understand through his clacking teeth. I pantomimed our need for a blanket and some kind of food, and I tried to explain about the pains in Cosimo's head and stomach. The caretaker shrugged, waiting. Perhaps it was my fault for speaking and raising the suspicion of these *contadini*—these country folk. Cosimo alone might have garnered more immediate sympathy. I patted my empty pocket for money, thinking of the large stash in Enzo's pockets—*forget that*—and tugged at my watch, unbuckling it. The man took it quickly in his rough palm.

Moments later, an old peasant woman appeared, pointing to the villa, but Cosimo shook his head. Too far; too many people. And now there was a flurry of activity, all of us crowded into this space not much larger than a gardening shed. The old man was wrapping Cosimo in a wool blanket, except for his feet, which stuck out at the bottom, uncovered. When I pointed to the oversight, the man waved me away. He brought out some strong-smelling salve and massaged Cosimo's bare feet and calves, filling the tiny room with the smell of olive and herb and pine. The peasant woman pushed spoonfuls of a white bean soup into Cosimo's mouth, and when he couldn't hold it down, wiped his chin and started again. Yet another woman appeared, having been called down from the main house with more blankets in her arms, and when I tried to step back to make room, I tripped on a bucket near the doorway.

The second woman, also gray-haired, pantomimed to me: *The man is cold. The man needs to sleep.*

"Of course. But not for long. He can sleep in the truck."

Overhearing, Cosimo shook his head at the next approaching spoonful of soup and pushed himself to a more upright position. "Leave me here. *Va bene.* Take the truck."

"With Enzo?"

"Leave him here, also. He'll be with me. This is a good place for us."

There was a sound of morbid finality that I didn't appreciate in that last remark. Just hours earlier, I had wanted to lock Cosimo in the back of the truck. I would have welcomed any chance to leave both him and Enzo along the road so that I might have had a fighting chance to change routes and make the border on time. But not now.

Cosimo pulled the diamond ring from his pocket and handed it over to the woman with the new load of blankets. Her eyes grew wide and she took it quickly. She and the old man wrapped Cosimo in more blankets, burying him behind the cocooning folds.

"He needs to breathe," I said, stepping closer to the cot again, but their ranks closed. The three peasants continued patting and tucking, and though I was taller and able to see over their heads, I couldn't seem to push past them. "Cosimo? Can you hear me?"

The response was a muffled but serene murmur.

"I'm not leaving you here!"

When I tried to push closer again, the older of the two women scowled at me over her shoulder and bumped me purposely with her hip, swathed in broad pleats of vulturous black. The man turned around and eased me backward, one shuffling step at a time, out the shack's narrow door. Visiting hours were over. I was being escorted away from the patient.

"*Dieci*," the old man said, holding up his narrow wrist, upon which my watch hung loosely.

"Ten minutes? Ten o'clock?" And the déjà vu of it made me laugh once—a half-crazed, unconvincing bark.

"*Dieci*," the old man said, revealing a mostly toothless smile.

"I'm not leaving!" I called out one last time as the door squeaked shut. "I'm just checking on the truck! *Va bene*, Cosimo?"

Outside, the sun was hidden below the horizon and the sky was losing its peach blush, turning pale blue to the west, deep indigo to the east, the hills and farms and distant woods reduced to silhouetted black shapes. I followed a footpath back toward the white track where we had parked, between the flowers I'd ignored on our way up to the shack: the flowers on their thick green stalks, all bowed in the same direction. Out of habit, I turned my wrist to check the time, and finding it bare, dropped slowly down to my knees and began to whimper—tentatively at first, and then louder, until I was groaning and rubbing at my eyes, and then simply sobbing, while the dark faces of the sunflowers remained turned away, embarrassed by the outburst.

PART

III

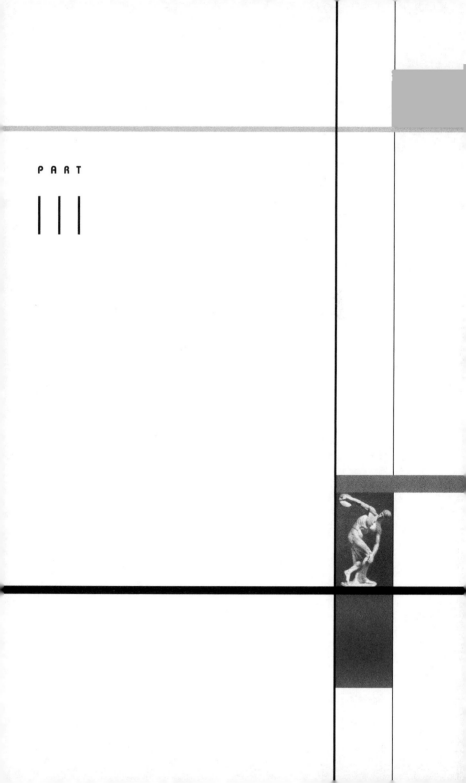

CHAPTER 9

Then and there, it must have been, my pretending came to an end. I knew there was no point in imagining that these Italian hours could stand apart from the rest of my life; no way to pretend any longer that the sun that rose and set there didn't also rise and set on the Germany of my past and of my future. Watch or no watch, I could look at the flowers and see that even brainless creatures are aware of the time. Enzo's death had, at last, penetrated; as had some other things—not all at once, and not completely, but like a rainstorm thrashing fields of bone-dry soil, soaking them well here and running off too quickly there. A wasted watering, where the ground was still too difficult and steep.

When the shack door opened early the next morning and Cosimo hobbled toward me on the path, red-eyed but pink-cheeked, I threw my arms around him. He returned my embrace but seemed perplexed by my effusive rambling about vultures and blankets, death and abandonment. The rest and warmth and food had done its work. He had simply needed some good *contadini* doctoring, he assured me, while pulling himself up and into the passenger side of the truck. He apologized for delaying us further and still did not seem to understand what his body had endured. But anyway, he asked me with undue tenderness: Was *I* feeling all right?

I was, I told him again and again. *I was.* He could sleep more and I would drive, as long as he provided the directions.

There was no argument about competing priorities, even when we came to a fork signed for Modena, a place-name I remembered from the old map. There was no discussion of the remaining day and a half it would take to get to the border from that juncture, or the day it would take to get to Cosimo's family farm. Traveling to the farm first, and only then to the border, would take three more days total, but in light of all that had happened, this math no longer seemed logically connected to any choices we might make. The choice had been made outside that shack.

We were hopelessly late for my deadline by now, and yet, for a time at least, not late for anything. We were simply driving. The sky was just beginning to leak its black ink, and the gray dawn was beginning to reveal wooded valleys and small, grassy, overgrown vineyard plots, cloaked in mist, more lush and tangled than we'd seen in the dry, hilly lands farther south.

When Cosimo said a word under his breath—"Nebbiolo"—
I asked him if it was the name of a town ahead.

"No, the local grapes. Named after the fog—*nebbia*. This is
starting to look like home."

We drove all day without any mention of the cargo we carried, or of much else that I would be able to recall ten years
later. Cosimo took over at day's end, when my own eyelids
were closing, but for most of the morning and afternoon, I
was the one behind the wheel. Probably the smartest thing
he ever did was let me drive most of that third day, so that
with every rut and bump and slowly passing kilometer, I was
sealing my own fate and there was no point in arguing about
it anymore, as I would have if I'd been a hostage or even a
mere passenger.

In the next moment I can remember, the undersides of my eyelids felt like they'd rubbed against ground glass. Needles had
punctured the dark cloth of the night sky, letting in the first
stars' thin light. Everything had turned sharp: the coiled spring
underneath my seat; the edge of the doorframe, hard and cold
even through the sleeve of my wrinkled jacket.

Somehow, sleep did come—but only until an unfamiliar
sound woke me. The engine had stopped. I rubbed my eyes
and saw that Cosimo wasn't behind the wheel. I heard again
the dog's low, testing growl. We were at the end of a road,
near the top of a hill, surrounded by farmland, with two small
orange squares of light blazing from a barely silhouetted house

farther up the hill. The Digiloramo family *cascina*, deep in the Piedmont.

From behind the truck, Italian voices drifted—a man and a woman trying to contain their argument in frenzied whispers and the sound of the dog above them, working itself into a lather, whining and growling. Cosimo slapped his leg and shouted, "Tartufa!"—and the dog quieted immediately, following him as he departed. The footsteps faded.

I listened hard, with my hand on the door handle, trying to ascertain whether I was alone. But then I heard the grinding metal of someone trying to raise the truck's back door, pushing hard against a blockage within. The door rattled but wouldn't give. I heard more scraping metal, a high-pitched grunt of effort, a sliding sound, before I realized what was about to happen.

When I leapt out of the truck—shouting, "Don't!"—it was already too late. Hurrying around to the back, I saw her standing with her hands on the door, the dark gap opening. She gasped and pulled one hand away from the door, covering her mouth. I had startled her, compounding the shock of the undignified lump threatening to fall out onto the drive.

I wedged my hip against the unsteady corpse, and in an awkward maneuver wriggled out of my jacket, letting it drop over Enzo's shoulder and battered face, then resumed pushing the body back into the truck, over the lip of the doorframe.

"Rosina—" I hazarded a guess. "Don't be afraid."

"I'm not." But her face gave her away. "Cosimo told me not to . . ."

"So why did you?"

She turned on her heel, profile to me, refusing to meet my glance. "I wanted to see. Go away!"

"I'm sorry." And I was—but I was also flushed with irritation. "You shouldn't have seen him that way. Cosimo should have warned you."

"How do you know me?"

"I saw your photograph. Cosimo had it."

She paused for a moment before completing the turn, her back to me. I tried to tell her she shouldn't misunderstand what she had seen. But she stopped me, answering in German even more fluent than her brother's. "You don't have to explain. Cosimo told me everything."

Truck door secured, I turned to the place where she had last stood and I called her name again, but she had disappeared into the dark night. Walking quickly, I could just make out the faint glow of her white skirt billowing as she turned the corner of a large, white stucco outbuilding, separated from the main house. I caught up with her as she put her hand to the door.

"Where is Cosimo?"

"Restraining Tartufa. The smell of the truck was driving her crazy. Then he is going to tell my mother." She started to tug the door handle, then stopped, turning to face me. "I can't believe it. Just two hours ago, she was serving espresso to the *polizia*. They told her that Cosimo and Enzo had gone missing, and now here, you show up like this." Her voice caught, but she gained control and finished. "You're bleeding."

Dried, rusty streaks stained my wrists and abrasions marked the back of my knuckles, from banging against the inside of the truck and pushing my fingers through the crate's wooden slats.

"No doubt you're thirsty and hungry, too." It sounded like an accusation. "You'd better come inside to clean up."

She stood with her feet set wide apart, each hand clutching the opposite wrist, black hair loose and wild and bushy around her shoulders, looking slightly unhinged.

"I think I'll take a rest here, for a moment," I said. "Or go up to the main house, if that's where Cosimo is."

"Up to the house, is that your bright idea? You're a genius. I can see how you and my brothers got into this mess, all three of you. You're a real good-luck charm! That's what Enzo must have thought . . ."

Her forthrightness disarmed me, as did the power of her words combined with her unruly, unselfconscious appearance. As in her photo, she refused to stand still. I'd been yelled at by my father and upbraided by other men my age in various situations, but yelled at by a woman with large, dark eyes, wild hair, and a semi-transparent skirt? Never.

As soon as she'd finished admonishing me, she turned to go, calling over her shoulder as an afterthought: "If Tartufa gets loose again, be careful. She bites men she doesn't trust."

In the dark, listening to my own breath slowing again, my own confused and irritated sighs, I could make out what appeared to be fields, and farther away, the low, dark silhouettes of olive or citrus trees, and farther yet, darker, wilder woods: oak and willow and hazelnut. In those woods, I presumed, there was flowing water of some kind, a place where I might drink and wash. But I wasn't about to wander around an unknown forest late at night.

Now that we'd finally arrived, I could stop worrying about Cosimo's immediate well-being and begin to worry about both of us: we were fugitives now, like rabbits cowering behind a bush—whether or not Cosimo was willing to face that fact. And I was not only a fugitive waiting to be stalked by Germans, but a prisoner of my Italian hosts, unwanted and untrusted, if Rosina's reaction was any indication. But as long as I was here, I deserved at least a prisoner's rations and perhaps a bath as well.

I followed the sounds of voices into a side door that opened onto a softly lit *terrazza* with an outdoor dining table spread with small coffee cups, a bottle of some kind of liqueur, and a blue plate of white-powdered biscotti. Here was where they must have sat: two or three of the village *polizia*, paying an informal call, social on the surface, business underneath. *We are not meaning to worry you, Signora Digirolamo.*

Had they received a telegram from Rome, or directly from Herr Keller, pretending to be concerned? What version of the truth had reached the local authorities?

The *terrazza* side door led into a large farm kitchen with an immense wooden table at its center, piled with three mounds of pale dough. As soon as they saw me, everything stopped. A matronly, gray-haired woman occupied the spot closest to the doorway, hands on her wide hips. Next to her stood a younger woman, a more fastidious version of Rosina. Beside her was a man—not Cosimo, but close to his age, gaunt and unshaven. And next to him: a doddering grandfather type with silver stubble on his chin, wearing a white undershirt.

The four of them had taken their positions along one long side of the table, like generals planning for a battle. Seeing me, the older woman made a whimpering sound and flung up her hands against her tobacco-colored cheeks. She looked ready to faint, but no one rushed for a chair. The younger woman's lips were parted, mouth open with surprise. The man next to her looked ready to attack me, but he steadied himself against the table, palms flat against the floured surface. The old man remained in place, hands in his pockets, eyes watering profusely.

I had come bearing death. There is no ruder visitor.

"*Buongiorno*," I tried, but no one responded.

On the far side of the kitchen sat a cracked, white, shallow bowl in which stood a large pitcher of water. Condensation freckled its bulging ceramic middle. I hadn't had anything to drink since midday, which explained the pounding headache. I longed for just a sip of water, and to change these clothes, which smelled of smoke and sweat and spoiled milk.

I held my empty hands in front of my chest, speaking in German because it was the best I could manage. "It wasn't my fault. I'm sure Cosimo told you that."

At the sound of Cosimo's name, the younger woman grabbed the sleeve of the man next to her. He risked a quick, irritated glance in her direction before fixing his dark eyes back on me.

"Where is Cosimo, anyway?" *Scheisse*, they didn't understand. "*Dov'è Cosimo?*" Surely I had that right.

I took another step toward the water. To reach it, I would have to squeeze past all four of them. Another step, but this time the matriarch set a hand on the table in front of her, just centimeters from the rolling pin, panting so heavily with her own bottled-up fear that I was afraid she would give herself a heart attack. The old man at the far end was crying silently, the tears dripping unchecked down his cheeks. At least there was no doubt that Cosimo had broken the news.

"I only want a drink of water. That's all for now. Then I'll go."

The younger man, third down the line, lifted his floured hands off the kitchen table and curled them into a boxer's fists, poised for action. A feline yowl exploded from underneath the table, and I glanced down to see a toddler, happily seated beneath the table's stout legs, making shapes from a handful of leftover dough. Her eyes met mine and she dropped the grubby fistful, rolled forward onto knees and hands, and scooted toward her mother's legs.

"*Mi dispiace*," I tried to say, hoping I'd gotten those syllables right. *I'm sorry.*

There had to be some way to explain that I wasn't the enemy. In boot camp, they had taught us many things, but not how to say in Italian, French, English or Russian: *Wait—it's not what you're thinking.* If the war came, as we knew it would, you would need that phrase as you faced a world of enemy strangers. You would advance, village by village and town by town, and see the stunned faces of people who wanted to kill you, who couldn't understand you, whose lives had been going along just fine—the pasta on the table, the laundry on the line—until you and your men came stomping up their garden path. If you were carrying a gun, and of course you'd be carrying a gun, you'd shoot. If they were prepared, they would shoot you first. And not over timeless ideals—the perfection of mankind, art and morals and beauty—but in the short term, over something like this: a stupid drink of water.

Until this point, I'd always thought I feared the trenches, the gas, the bombs. But what I'd feared all along, in fact, was this: meeting other people trapped in a situation very similar to my own, all of us frozen in fear and indecision. Paralyzed. How many of my nightmares, sleeping or waking, contained that feeling; how many of my regrets looked back to moments where I'd done nothing, or done too little, too late?

I advanced another step and then lost heart. It wasn't worth it. But just as I was turning to go, the mother took her own bold step forward, blocking me. The rolling pin was still on the table. Small mercies. But clearly she was comfortable with her small, dark-skinned fists. When she raised them, I pulled my own arms inward and crossed them, elbows over my ribs, like an Egyptian mummy. Let her do it—that was all right. Let her take out her frustrations on me. I wasn't that fragile. And maybe I even deserved it. I squeezed my eyes shut, waiting.

And then those soft, old arms were wrapped around my waist. Baggy flesh enveloped me, and my nose filled with the faint aroma of oregano. Her head was level with my chest, her wide bosom was barely at my navel, and she was pulling me toward her, gripping me, comforting me, dissolving my defenses as she nodded and wept in commiseration: *Va bene. Va bene. Va bene.*

A pummeling would have been easier.

I walked downhill back to the barn where I had last seen Cosimo's sister, checking frequently over my shoulder to make sure that no one had been compelled to follow. I only needed a moment and the cooling evening air on my skin. There was no reason why a grown man should shed tears upon receipt of sympathy when he did not shed tears upon first sight of the thing itself, the real and ugly and inescapable thing. There was no reason a woman should be kind to a stranger and no reason why a stranger should break down within sight of a grieving mother. There was no reason. And so I kept walking until my gasping stopped, until I could breathe normally and put the moment behind me.

At the barn, I turned the corner, saw the open door, and reached for the iron handle, entering the semi-dark space incautiously, only to be stopped short. The center of the room was lit by a kerosene lantern. At the edge of the golden light, Rosina was seated nude on a stool with her legs in a steel tub, pouring water over the curtain of black hair obscuring her face. My lungs got the message quickly: not a sound, not a breath.

She didn't hear me for a moment through the water, but then something alerted her. She tilted her head up. The glossy curtain parted, and now there was a smooth white stomach, and bare breasts heavier and more pendulous than a Greek virgin's, and her eyes, blinking with effort through the soapy, parted hair.

My mind was in several places at once. It was seeing the first original Rembrandt I ever saw, face close to the thickly painted canvas, looking for the source of that Old Master's light. It was with the first woman I knew half-intimately, before Leonie, and before I'd given up on finding a truly compatible girlfriend.

"Cosimo?" Rosina asked, bringing a forearm up to her breasts and twisting away slightly, still blind.

I should have backed away. I should have turned and run. There was still a moment, while the soap was still in her eyes, before she blinked me into clear view. But I was too slow.

She shrieked, held her breath for a moment, then broke into nervous laughter.

Heart racing, I turned away in confusion, quickly averting my gaze. "I didn't know—I expected—I thought this was just a barn."

"You startled me," she said. "It's all right. I have a towel. It was only—your face."

She slipped away on wet, bare feet, leaving dark spots on the outbuilding's rough plank floor, toward a screen-like partition decorated with a still life of pears and peaches and grapes—poorly drawn, I noticed, now that she wasn't occupying my full attention. Then I noticed the large iron bed frame in the corner, the old mirror, the dresser, the glass bottles with flowers on the sill of the building's only four-paned window, the phonograph balanced atop a small fruit crate.

"It *was* a barn," she explained, her voice muffled behind whatever she was pulling over her head.

When she came back out, she was wearing a white blouse,

with her wet black hair draped over each shoulder, making translucent damp spots just below her clavicle.

"*Signorina*," I tried, reaching out a hand.

"I'm a decade older than you."

"*Signora* . . ."

"It's too late for that. 'Rosina,' please." She waited for me to drop my hand. "I offered you a chance to clean up. The water isn't very warm, but it's all right and just a little soapy, if you don't mind using the same tub."

She misread my expression. "Or if that isn't good enough for you, we can dump it. But then you'll have to use cold water."

"No," I said, finding my voice. "Don't go to any trouble. The water is fine."

The warmth of her earlier laugh was cooling fast, retreating behind an armor of grief and understandable caution. I wanted to reach out a hand and catch it before it had disappeared entirely. But at the same time, I was still feeling an acute embarrassment that locked my feet in place. Furtively, I searched her face for any signs of the same unease, but she was moving purposefully, using her wet towel to mop up some extra water splashed from the galvanized tub, hanging the towel on a hook, rummaging on an open shelf. She looked up.

"Forget it."

I nodded unconvincingly.

"You shouldn't be embarrassed," she insisted.

"I was more concerned—about *your* discomfort, I mean."

"Ah, yes—*my* discomfort."

"We haven't gotten started on the right foot."

"You mean, by meeting over my brother's dead body?"

She was right, and there was no pardonable reason for me to be thinking of her hair or her figure, or of the water splashing down into the tub, or of the fact that even now her shirt was open at the throat and slightly wet.

"I'm very sorry."

She swore softly—not at me, as I thought at first, but at herself. "Damn, I can't wear this." She disappeared behind the screen again and came back a minute later changed into a belted black dress, a little too loose in the waist and chest.

"It's all I have in black." She sounded angry and looking for a reason to be angrier yet, if only someone would engage her in argument. She patted the spot at the back of her neck where there was a single small button, just beyond her fingers' reach. "Assist me."

I fumbled until she grew impatient, pulling away, and tried to do it herself, grabbing the button with such force that it popped off and rolled onto the floor and under the bed, sparking a single German curse word that in turn ignited a torrent of Italian blasphemies.

Rosina sat down on the mattress with her face in her hands. The proper thing would have been to step back silently and leave her in peace.

She looked up, finally, scrubbing her nose with the back of her hand. "If you think I'm handling this well—"

"—well enough."

"You would, too, if you had a brother like Enzo. It's just that I'm not surprised. I am, and at the same time, I'm not. I spent too many years worrying."

I nodded, encouraging her.

"Our mother always expected the best from him, but I guess I'm not the charitable, motherly type. I always expected the worst."

When I still didn't move or speak, she began to tell me a story which quickly became a flood of stories—Enzo's gambling problem in Milan; Enzo's bad judgment and a failed business deal involving a cousin in Naples; another time they had to urge Enzo to go abroad, and he did, but he didn't have the sense to stay. But then she heard herself and stopped. "I'm still so furious, but it doesn't matter anymore, does it?"

When I didn't answer, she lifted her chin away from me, eyes wary. "You haven't said very much. All this, and you're still embarrassed about what happened before."

"A little."

"Forget it."

"Yes, of course."

She remembered suddenly. "You met the rest of the family?"

"They barely spoke to me."

"Did you speak to them?"

"I tried."

"They're in shock. It's understandable."

"I wasn't meaning to suggest otherwise. Your mother—" but I couldn't say it without my throat catching. "The old man—"

"My uncle. Zio Adamo."

"He was crying."

"That's probably not about Enzo. It's too soon. Any crisis reminds him of when my father died. How did Gianni handle it?"

"The younger man? He put his fists up and didn't want to let me pass."

She made a noise that was not quite a laugh, but I would take whatever I could get. The awkward silence that followed made the small interior of the low-ceilinged barn seem even smaller yet, the corners lost to the shadows beyond the lamp's reach.

"I'll leave," she said, rising from the bed where she'd been sitting to push a coarse towel into my hands.

Near the door, she slipped her feet into open-backed leather shoes and put her hand on the old handle, black except for the bronzed spot at the top of the latch where a thumb had pressed a thousand times, coming and going.

"Wait. Please. How do you speak German so perfectly? You speak it even better than Cosimo."

"I should. I lived in Munich for four years. They came and visited me. Enzo was suspended from work. Cosimo talked him into going north, and then, of course, Enzo spent every night finding new trouble while Cosimo spent his time studying German and watching me rehearse. It's no wonder Cosimo picked up the language better."

"Rehearse?"

"I sang in the opera there."

"You sang . . . ," I said, searching for the name of the opera, willing her not to push down the door handle, to stay just a moment longer, "you sang *Hänsel und Gretel.*"

"So Cosimo *did* explain."

"No, he said nothing about it. He only whistled."

She looked momentarily confused, then uninterested. "No one likes to mention it. It's the family scandal."

"Scandalous to sing opera?"

"No, scandalous to become . . . *involved* in Munich." She seemed to consider omitting further detail but then shrugged it off. Perhaps it was her natural brazenness; perhaps it was the disarming effect of the day's events. I'd never know how she would have seemed if I'd met her in different circumstances. But then again, in different circumstances, I wouldn't have met her at all.

"I took a lover," she explained. "A local resident, not an Italian. That was the most incomprehensible thing for them. Anyway, it didn't last."

Rushing to fill the awkward silence, I said, "I'm sure your family was glad to have you back. Cosimo emphasized how close you all are."

Her chuckle was hollow. "Close—yes. My family accepted me once I moved back because I married quickly and conveniently."

She saw my eyes widen, looking around the makeshift accommodations for signs of a jealous husband who might lay hands on a snooping visitor.

"No, *he* lives in the main house. The one with the fists up. Gianni. He helped my father and my uncle with the farm. With Papa gone and Zio Adamo getting old and Cosimo and Enzo working in town, we couldn't manage without him."

Her hand was still on the door handle, but she was leaning away from it now, her weight shifted, off balance, one foot pulled out of the shoe, a toe playing with the exposed insole.

"You live apart from your husband?"

"Gianni remarried. He lives in the house with his wife and their daughter because my family needs him here. That is the second scandal."

"And you?"

"I need only to be left alone, if that's what you're asking."

"But they make you live out here?"

"*Make* me? There's something wrong with my little *palazzo*?" At least now she was teasing, though with Rosina, I was quickly becoming aware, a tease could quickly turn sour. "Because if you'd rather wash up at the main house—"

"Is it that easy to end a marriage in this country?"

"When you are physically defective, it is."

Our eyes met, and I was hoping she couldn't read my mind and know that I had seen, and was recalling still, the very absence of her defects.

"You've heard," she added, "of the Battle for Births?"

When I shook my head, she explained, "We are expected to reverse the population decline. A target of five children per family, but ten, thirteen—the more the better. I have not been a loyal soldier."

I must have looked uncertain about that last phrase, because she added in a bitter voice, "I can't make babies. These days in Italy, it is almost a crime."

She opened the door. "There will be a lot to do. I'll find Cosimo and let him know where you are. Anyway, what is your name?"

"Vogler."

"That is your first name? Because I've already given you permission to use mine."

I hesitated. "It is . . . Ernst."

"You say that like you're choking on it."

I could have told her that it was my father's name, which even my mother's gentle voice had never managed to make appealing, or that it always sounded like a brutish grunt to me.

"It sounds . . . very serious," I said.

"And you're not serious?"

"It also means 'to battle to the death.'"

"I take it you have other plans."

"No plans, but no death wish, either."

She paused for a moment, thinking. "Perhaps it only needs an Italian variation, with more vowels. We give them away here, no charge. How about . . ." She pushed her loose foot more securely into the shoe, widened her stance, straightened her spine, inhaled, and announced: "*Er-nes-to.*"

She delivered it with an operatic flourish, bringing each syllable up from a deep place in her body, as if all three of those syllables in that order had long been stored there, fully formed and waiting, and she had only to haul them up, out of the dark and into the light. And isn't that how the important things should feel—beauty and honesty and love—as if they had always been there, only waiting to be expressed?

"The meaning has not changed," she said, stepping through the open doorway, pausing for one last moment on the threshold. "But now it has loosened its belt. Now it breathes."

osina, if only I could stop time there, at that moment where you showed me a different kind of woman's beauty. (Even though I'd slept with several other women, you were the first real woman I'd ever seen entirely undressed, unhidden, unmarmoreal and in the flesh.) If only I could pause there, when you showed me a way of speaking the truth, a way of infusing breath and life into something as unpromising and unrefined as my own name.

I could walk and keep walking through the Piedmont now, through all of Italy perhaps, imagining that you are still waiting, somewhere. It would be easier to find the café closed, to miss you, to take a wrong turn into the wrong town than to find out you have a child, are married, remember nothing of what I am recounting here or remember it all differently, or only in its most dismal form: that a difficult foreigner showed up, inviting chaos, leaving behind devastation.

Walking past vineyards and up into Renaissance towns and down old Roman roads, I could keep reviewing those few moments, putting you on a pedestal, no pun intended.

Should I?

I recall that photo Cosimo used to carry: the look of impatience and irritation. No, you say, of course I shouldn't. Better to choose life and the truth than settle for the false moment, the preserved image. So fine—no dishonesty, then.

You probably don't believe in love at first sight, anyway. But how about love at second or third sight? I would settle for that.

"We need to make a coffin," Cosimo said when he found me a short while later, clean but bone-weary and disoriented, sitting in the dark on the stone stoop outside Rosina's barn. "There is a man down the road, but he needs to go to another town to get milled wood. One, two days at least."

"Days?"

"That's if he doesn't get delayed." Cosimo made a motion with his hand, lifting an imaginary bottle. "I tell him, we have wood. We have nails. We don't need the coffin to be fancy. In fact, it should not be."

A pause. He was trying to put off saying it as long as

possible. "The crate," he finally admitted. "He must take wood from the crate."

"And the statue—?"

"We will wrap it in blankets or mattresses. That is not a problem."

"I'm glad you think it's not a problem. For you, very little is a problem." That's how it had seemed, once we had arrived at the Digiloramo *cascina*. Before, it was Cosimo and I on a mission together; but now that we had arrived, I had become a stranger again, unprotected from angry or confusingly attractive relatives. "Next you will tell me you need the marble for a grave marker—"

His face closed down; his eyes flattened. "You have no idea of the problems I am facing to bury my brother, with no time, little assistance, not even a priest—"

"I thought there were priests in every Italian backwater."

"The problem is that the local priest maintains very regular communications, of course, with Rome. And he is not the only one. You and I, this week, we do not need any outside attention, from Rome or anywhere else." With each syllable he stabbed a finger toward the road, volume rising, until he just as suddenly paused, realizing that he was getting needlessly incensed. He dropped his hands and his chin, directing his report to his feet. "I have discussed this with my family and they agree. For now, it's better that no one know. Gianni will help me carry my brother from the truck into an upstairs bedroom, where the women will help clean him and dress him. Then I will get you something to eat, and you can sleep in a room with my uncle."

"And you?"

"I will start digging the grave, with Gianni, as soon as we've finished eating."

"In the dark?"

"It's better. We have few neighbors as it is, but in the dark, no one will see us."

"I'll help."

"We have only two shovels."

"There's a tool in Rosina's barn, near her dresser." I'd spotted it as I bathed—a long-handled implement ending in a small, sharp-edged blade, halfway between a trowel and a hoe. It wouldn't take much dirt with each scoop, but at least it would be something.

Cosimo puzzled over my statement. "That won't be any good for digging a grave. It's only for pushing around leaves and a little dirt, for digging truffles. Forget that. If you want to help, eat something, then take apart the top of the crate. Stack the wood just outside the truck, and then go to the main house and try to get some sleep."

I had wanted to see it so desperately: in Munich, at mission's end, and before that, in Rome, on that morning that now seemed like years ago, and in the back of the truck, trying to peer through a narrow gap in the slats. But now, facing the crate with a crowbar in my hand, I was no longer sure that I wanted to see the statue. I might notice a chip off a finger, a crack etched by the vibration of rural roads. I might be overcome by the beauty of the statue and feel again the immense failure of not delivering it on time, in a dignified manner, to its proper owner. Or I might feel *nothing*. That was the most terrifying possibility.

The statue had remained essential in the face of tragedy, in the face of death. But here, on this farm, in the light of an accidental encounter and a single conversation and the simple movement of a family tending to essential obligations—in the face of *life*—the statue seemed, or might seem, like something less than it really was. We fall out of love, or we see behind a veil. A myth collapses. Purpose vanishes. That is what I feared most.

But it did not matter what I feared or what I felt. I'd been assigned a chore and now I busied myself with it: prying off one slat of wood at a time, starting at the top and moving around to each side, leaving only the bottom of the crate as a low-walled pallet. I worked hard, prying and sweating and slipping, trying to keep each board whole and undamaged. In the middle of the work, Cosimo brought me a shallow bowl of oily polenta and I shoveled it into my mouth, hardly tasting it, because it was only fuel for this effort of which I did not quite approve. But I would worry about protecting the statue later, when there was hope of being on the road again. I set aside the bowl and the spoon and returned to work. And as I proceeded to loosen more slats—hardly even looking at the object my work was uncovering, so disillusioned and confused were my thoughts at that moment—my memories loosened as well, splintering unpredictably.

Gerhard had been the only one of my colleagues to show up

at my father's funeral in December. He had stood next to me during the perfunctory service and had asked me how I was managing. Later, outside the church, after thanking him for coming, I had let it slip that I'd never understood my father, had never even felt like I'd known him.

"Your father had different experiences," Gerhard had said, expressing gentle understanding toward us both. "The war, a lot of struggle since, just getting by—it's all hard."

"But you've been through all those things?"

He considered carefully: "Yes."

"And none of it made you into a brute."

We were at the top of the steps, and two older men walked past and tipped their hats. They were drinking buddies of my father's, paying their respects. His funeral hadn't been well attended.

"It could have, yes. It might have. But I had joy in my life, too. Things I loved doing and learning. People I loved." This was one of the times—there were more to follow—when he had begun to talk about his memories of Italy. The girl in Perugia, or Pisa. The importance of mere days; the importance of hours. I had countered, argumentative young man that I was, with a point about the importance of the eternal. He had mentioned—before there was even talk of a government trip—that I should make a trip south.

"To see art?"

"Well, yes. But I don't want you to go just to evaluate the art. I want you to go in order that you might *experience* the art. Photographs and sketches can't do the sculptures justice— or the frescoes, or the cathedrals. I want you to stand there, in the light of Tuscany, in the noise and heat of Rome, and see the work of ages."

I started to answer him, but he put one arm around me and lowered his voice to a whisper: "And then, my friend, I want you to forget what you see and know, just for a moment. I want you to experience Italy as the sculptors themselves did. Live as they lived, feel as they felt, on those days when they looked at a block of marble and believed in the humanity that was imprinted even on that cold surface—even inside stone."

I stumbled into the Digirolamo house an hour or so later and found the uncle's room at the top of the staircase where Cosimo said I would find it. There were splinters in my fingertips that I could feel but not see, and though Cosimo had left me a candle affixed with melted wax to an overturned jar lid, I was too tired to light it. I didn't even take off my clothes. Zio Adamo was already asleep on his own twin bed across the room, snuffling quietly.

When the door opened some time later, my eyelids popped open. My heart was beating fast, even before I remembered where I was. Gianni, framed by weak light, stood in the open doorway, legs apart and arms lifted off his side, ready to shoot or duel. He crossed the bedroom and sat down hard at my side, jabbing me in the arm.

"Yes?"

When he pointed to the floor and yanked the top of my sheet, I extracted myself from the warm pocket of bedclothes and stood, confused. He scooted into my place, drawing his long legs up and pushing them under the covers, before turning away from me, face to the wall. His room had been the one converted temporarily into a funeral parlor, so I didn't blame him for leaving it. Ejecting me was understandable, but his dislike for me was so evident that I decided I'd rather be outside on the cold, hard ground than sleeping on the floor at his feet.

I tiptoed down the stairs and downhill to the barn, where the truck was parked, and where at least I wouldn't wake to an inhospitable stranger's face. The next hour crept by as I tried to sleep with my head turned to one side, tightly wedged under the steering wheel, my legs bent, my stocking feet pushed up against the window. Impossible. I was shifting yet again, thinking of trying the back of the truck where there would be less padding but more space, when suddenly there was the sound of frantic clawing coming from the other side of the truck door. Sitting up, I banged my ear against the steering wheel and listened hard, trying to distinguish the scratch of a wild animal from that of a tame one. I tapped back three times.

Tartufa heard me and barked once, then launched into a series of agonizing whines. I rapped at the door, opened it a crack, cursed—all to no avail. She couldn't seem to make up her mind, alternating between a low, wet growl and a needy whimper. Now, the back of the truck wouldn't work at all. With the retractable door open, she'd either jump inside or stand just below the threshold, barking. As for sleeping in there with the door closed, I'd had enough of that.

I was sitting upright, head in my hands against the steering wheel, when a quick rap against the window startled me all over again. Rosina pressed her face against the glass, her hand cupped above her eyes, squinting. "Ernesto," she whispered. "Come."

She clapped her hands once and cursed at the dog, who ran off, allowing me to exit the truck and follow, unmolested. In the barn, Rosina refused to hear my objections and pointed to a pile of blankets in a corner, diagonal from her own sagging bed. She, too, was exhausted and tired of hearing Tartufa whining and growling outside.

"Why isn't Cosimo keeping her locked up?"

"She makes a good watchdog. He's anxious about unwanted visitors coming around the farm tonight."

"I can't intrude upon your privacy like this."

"Stop," she said, turning down the lantern next to her bed. "I'm too tired for all that."

But a moment later, she asked quietly, "Why was Enzo visiting Farfalla?"

"Cosimo didn't tell you?"

"No."

So I explained to her about the failed proposal and about Cosimo's revelation that he and Farfalla had been a couple, before Enzo came along.

"Poor *liebling*," she said. And a little later: "Speak to me. About anything. I like the sound of your voice."

"You like the sound of German?"

"I miss it very much."

"But Italian is more passionate—isn't that what people say?"

"There is romance, and then there is urgency." She paused, and I listened to the whisper of moving sheets and the creak of her bed as she shifted toward me. "The sound of German reminds me of—well, never mind."

"I think . . . I think you are thinking not of me, but of the man from your past."

"What if I am? Given your fascination with classical art, you are living in the past all the time. Who are you to judge?"

The dark made it easier to speak without inhibitions. "It's not very flattering, to have a woman sound interested because you remind her of someone else."

"Isn't arousal usually about memory?"

"I'm sorry?" It wasn't the concept that had stopped me in my tracks; it was the provocative word, *arousal*—a bit more explicit, I was guessing, than she intended, but that is what happens when you are speaking in a second language. It is hard to soften the edges of things, and that is why, perhaps, things can sometimes progress more quickly than they otherwise might. To talk flirtatiously with a foreigner can be like riding in a truck with no brakes.

Then again, perhaps she was not the kind to use brakes, wherever—or whatever—she was riding.

"Come on now," she said, thinking I needed to be convinced. "You see something that excites you, and maybe it's because it reminds you of when you were a boy and looking in a woman's window, or some photograph you saw, or another lover, or all of it together. So what is wrong with that?"

"It leaves one feeling . . . rather left out."

"But maybe later, *you* will be the memory."

"When the woman is with someone else, you mean."

"With someone else, or alone. Who knows?"

"You are an outspoken woman, Rosina."

"And this bothers you?"

"Not at all. You are remarkable."

"Don't say that." Her voice had turned cold. I was reminded of the woman in Cosimo's picture, the woman who did not want to be photographed, who did not seem to desire adoration, who perhaps did not feel that she deserved it.

"I can't say that you are exceptional?"

"No, you cannot. *Gutenacht*."

At breakfast, though I followed her into the house and sat next to her through a tense family breakfast—only Cosimo was missing, off helping the coffin maker—she would not speak to me. I tried a question or two, in German, but she ignored me, and each time I opened my mouth, Gianni stifled me with his dark glare.

"The old jealousy has died hard. He does not like to hear German," Rosina finally said under her breath, standing to remove her plate from the table. "None of them do."

"So you won't speak to me at all?" I followed her toward the counter where the dirty dishes were stacked.

"*Basta*."

Mamma Digirolamo and Rosina were wearing black dresses,

but Marzia, Gianni's wife, seemed to have a special exemption and was wearing a loose, yellow, flower-spotted dress. All three were puffy-eyed, as if they'd been up for hours, tending to all the normal chores in addition to the new ones imposed by this day's necessary rituals.

When Gianni left the room, Marzia carried the dishes just outside where there was an outdoor kitchen established around the paved *terrazza* with a water spigot and a washtub. The uncle sat quietly at the table, plaiting strands of straw into what would become, in the next hour, a woven cross. Mamma Digirolamo and Rosina began filling pots with water, rolling out dough, cutting up pieces of a long, bright-red sausage.

"Can I help with anything?"

Rosina broke her silence. "You'd better."

"But what can I do?"

Gianni scowled.

"You can help with the coffin, I suppose," Rosina said.

"I know nothing about carpentry."

"And you know more about cooking?"

"Not really."

"Then we'll keep things simple. Go find us eggs. At least six, in the henhouse."

After pantomiming with Marzia outside, I found my way around the *cascina*'s various outbuildings: a pigsty; a storage shed full of barrels and jars; the half-finished foundation of a small house—one Gianni was originally building for Marzia and himself before he lost steam and decided the main house would be more comfortable. Finally, I stumbled into the henhouse and fulfilled my mission, returning with a dirty armload of eggs, one of them cracked and dribbling. Back in the kitchen, I helped pound dough; I cut thin strips of dried tomatoes; I crossed the room to fetch plates or reach hanging pots whenever Rosina pointed wordlessly to them. I watched as a lump of risen dough became an elaborate picnic bread, with latticework pieces woven over hard-boiled eggs, still in their shells, and bits of sausage. This last small, sculptural masterpiece, baked in the outdoor oven, would be the afternoon meal eaten at the family cemetery—a shame that so few would get to see it.

Over the next two hours, I yearned to hear Rosina speak. There she was, sitting across the table, and there were so many things I wanted to ask—about her years singing opera, about her perceptions of Munich, about her life here on the farm—but she did not want to hear from me and this seemed the wrong time to make repeated overtures. We were living a relationship in reverse, from the intimacy of nudity to candid conversation, to terse communication, and now to silence. Another hour, and she would look up from the bread she was shaping and fail to recognize me.

At one point, Marzia's eyes happened to meet mine and she offered a tentative smile. Throughout the silent afternoon, I had been struggling to piece together the little Italian I did know, and now I tried a sentence. "This is a big farm."

Mamma Digiloramo looked my way, expression blank.

I tried again, aware that I sounded like a child or an idiot: "I see pigs and chickens. Many."

Marzia giggled into a cupped hand.

"Good buildings," I said. "Hills. Trees. Beautiful." So what if they were single words? They were better than this cursed silence. I had relied on Cosimo and Enzo too much; I hadn't even tried. And I realized now, as all travelers do, that speaking is not just about exchanging information or the essentials of getting by. It makes you feel like a different person.

"*Bello*," I said again, because it was a word I was more confident about, and it felt good to say it. "You have . . . grapes?" There was a phrase I could use again, with infinite modifications. "You have . . . corn?"

Marzia laughed again, without answering.

I was exhausted from the effort, but Rosina smiled. That smile was more important than my dignity.

Just then, Gianni passed through the kitchen and delivered a message that I couldn't understand, except to catch Enzo's name. Mamma Digirolamo exhaled through pursed lips as he talked, head swinging side to side in a pendulum of maternal regret. She turned and put a hand on Gianni's arm. He stood a little taller, ennobled by this bad news he'd brought. Rosina kept her eyes down, cutting a pile of black olives with much more force than the soft little garnishes required.

"Rosina . . ." I tried after Gianni left, when my latest cooking task was complete and there was nothing more for me to do.

She sighed, stood, and left the kitchen, exiting the house without explanation, and I followed, thinking this was a coded way for us to talk privately. My stomach felt queasy with anticipation—an intoxicating thrill I hadn't felt in years. I pictured our moment alone: closing the barn door; or perhaps down in the woods, near some clear-running creek. I

pictured reaching a hand out to her shoulder and running a
finger across her clavicle toward the soft hollow at the base
of her throat. But halfway down the hill, toward the barn, she
turned on me, muttering in German.

"I can't talk with you right now. I need some time, before
the funeral."

"Of course."

But I followed her a few steps more.

"Cosimo says you didn't want to bring Enzo here, for the
funeral."

"I didn't at first. But we're here, aren't we?"

"He says you will leave soon and he'll help get you to the
border."

"This afternoon, as soon as the burial is complete."

"This *afternoon*?"

Cosimo had explained the missed deadline and the importance of delivering the statue. But not wanting to worry her,
he hadn't explained the full extent of Keller's intrigues or the
scale of the consequences facing us, which even in my accep-
tance of recent delays had never been far from my mind.

"You can't be serious," she said now. "These are unusual
circumstances. What does it matter if you take another day or
two? No one could fault you."

"No," I said a little too sharply. "You don't understand.
Things in Germany aren't the same as they are in Italy. People
have expectations."

Her eyebrows lifted. "We don't have expectations?"

"About getting things done. About things going according
to plan." But this was a wrong turn. I hadn't meant to lecture.

"I may visit again, though. I hope to."

"Is that so?"

"I've always wanted to visit Florence."

Her eyes narrowed. "Is that so?"

"It would be"—I could almost hear Enzo's teasing voice—"*very tempting.*"

"Of course—you enjoy art," she said flatly. "What did you see in Rome?"

"There wasn't any time."

"Did you see the Sistine Chapel?"

"No."

"The Pantheon? The Trevi Fountain? Not in your priorities? Not in your plans, even though you are so devoted to history and to art?"

"No."

I was being punished, not for the big choices—refusing to drive Enzo to Farfalla's, to save him from that dangerous and unlit journey—but for the small ones.

"Did you sit, even once, with an espresso perhaps, and look around you?"

"*That*, I did try," I said quickly. "But I could not get a seat."

"All the way from Germany, and you did nothing, you saw nothing. Our country was wasted on you, don't you think?"

"I had a job to do."

"But you haven't done the job." She folded her arms across her chest. "I don't think your art office will send you back. And more than that, I don't think you would want to come. Cosimo has already told me everything about you."

"Cosimo knows little about me."

"What doesn't he know? Convince me." When I didn't respond immediately, she lifted her chin at me with a dismissive flick. "You are all business, he says. You have no interest in being here."

"But I do," I said under my breath. "I am very interested in being here, not in Rome or Florence, but *here* . . ."

"But you will leave today."

"Yes. I must."

"Then stop following me around like a dog."

Gianni came banging out of the main house, hailing Rosina. He strolled up and pushed a wadded shirt into her hand. After he headed back, she inspected the collarless pin-striped shirt, fingering a rip in the sleeve and tallying its missing buttons.

The shirt Enzo had been wearing during the accident was unsalvageable, and this one, provided by Gianni, was only slightly better. All of Enzo's other clothes were in town, in the apartment that he and Cosimo had shared, but Cosimo dared not go now, especially when his own superior thought he was hundreds of miles away, completing an official task for which he had been given time off. Mamma Digirolamo and Marzia were upstairs in the house, taking care of the day's most difficult and tender duty—washing the body, preparing it, brushing out the hair, trimming the fingernails, and shaving the delicate skin. Sewing was nothing compared to all that. And they'd need another hand when it came to dressing him again.

Rosina frowned at the long sleeves with their frayed cuffs.

"It's not a very nice shirt," she conceded. "Gianni would never give away something he actually likes."

The words couldn't tumble out of my mouth quickly enough. "I have a better one in my suitcase. It's much closer to Enzo's size. He once mentioned that he liked it. There's a small stain, but I haven't tried washing it out. It will probably be fine . . ."

"I don't want to go back into the house," she said, touching my arm—a brief, electrical contact. "If I were you, I'd just get in that truck and drive away—alone, back to your home. Anywhere."

"I burned my map." I said it in all seriousness, but when she laughed and brought her arm up to wipe her eyes, I laughed too.

"And now look at the time you are losing here."

I shook my empty wrist. "I can't look at the time. I have no watch. I gave it to a stranger."

Now her smile faded. She moved her face more closely to mine. We were alone but still within sight of the house, near an open window, never far from her family. "Did it ever occur to you that you don't want to return to Germany at all? You burn your map. You give away your watch. Someone might think . . ."

She hesitated when I started shaking my head violently, but then she tried again. "The truth is, you can leave anytime. You can leave now. No one is stopping you."

"Cosimo needs me."

"He has all of us."

The fact of that statement forced me to pause. "Then I need

Cosimo." Truly, I could not picture finding my way to the border without him. But there was that word—*picture*. With or without him, I had no pictures in my mind of the border anymore, or of Munich.

"Was he helping very much, that last day?" she asked. "He told me he slept most of the way. He said he was almost incoherent. He even gave you permission to leave him and Enzo at that farm."

"But he wasn't in his right mind."

"How do you know you are in yours? How do you know that I'm in mine?"

I didn't. And maybe I didn't *want* her to be in her right mind. Maybe I wanted her to be so swayed with emotion that she would need an arm to lean on, something I wouldn't have been asked to provide under normal circumstances.

There is balance, I had once believed, in everything that happens. There is symmetry. The thrower leans forward to balance the weight of the outstretched arm and, behind him, the heavy disc. In my life, again and again, something good had been followed by something bad. Wasn't it time for something bad to be followed by something good?

"Go to your mother," I told her. "I'll bring you the shirt as soon as I have it ready."

An hour later, Cosimo told me they were starting the vigil inside the house. Turning to go, he remembered to ask, "Do you have Enzo's lighter?"

I patted my pocket with the last of the three postcards from Rome, and the lighter, which I surrendered.

Cosimo explained, "We put a few personal items into the coffin with him—whatever he might want, whatever he might need, whatever we can't bear to see again. Do you want to come up?"

"I'll wait outside, if that's all right."

My family was Catholic in heritage only. I hadn't said a Rosary for my own parents. Now, I sat under the shade of a single broad-crowned tree downhill of the main house and drew out the third and final postcard I had purchased for my sister. I'd scratched out the message I'd written on the first one and left it at the bottom of my suitcase. I'd torn up the second and lefts its shreds littering the truck cab. I began again now, thinking of Greta and remembering how kind she had been to me during the difficult end of both our parents' lives, eighteen months apart, and how little I had appreciated her kindness at the time, how I had judged her for creating a dull life for herself and Friedrich, the man she had married. But at least she had created a life. And she had always made it clear that I was welcome to share her refuge: a small island in a sea of uncontrollable events.

Now I wanted desperately to write something heartfelt and true to my sister. The third postcard showed a photo of the Colosseum. I had bought all three directly from the signora at the pensione upon check-in without even consulting their faces—the first had a famous bridge; the second, a crowded scene of some notable piazza. None of the postcards' images had relevance to me or this trip or my Italy. *My* Italy: certain hours, certain changes of light over a landscape that reminded me, more than anything, of certain people, events, and emotions. Nothing that a postcard photograph could depict.

I spent a while under the tree, looking at the kitchen garden near the house, the tidy vineyards further on, and the woods down below, which didn't seem nearly as thick or off-putting as they had seemed last night. I heard, through the open window, the low, repetitive chant of prayer. Rosina came to the half-open window and pushed hard against it until it gave way and she leaned over the sill, looking as if she would have been happy to fall out or fly away. She saw me and stopped for a moment, rosary still hanging from one wrist. She lifted her palm to me slowly, nodded and half smiled, then backed away into the dark, hot room back toward the sound of reverential murmurs.

I watched the empty window for a long while before putting pen to postcard. Then I started writing and kept going until I'd run out of space, so important did it seem to tell at least one person.

CHAPTER 11

t was a funeral party of eight, including Marzia and Gianni's two-year-old daughter. Leaving Mamma Digirolamo to walk holding the toddler's hand, it took six of us to carry the coffin—an oversized, thin-planked rectangle, twice as wide as it should have been, with insecurely hammered corners that squeaked and shifted. Zio Adamo was in the middle right position, hampering more than helping, holding onto the rope handle like it was a hand strap on a trolley car. The two young women, Rosina and Marzia, shouldered the coffin's front corners, proving themselves much more than mere decoration; Marzia's biceps bulged from the loose folds of her flower-patterned dress as we walked.

We made our way from the house, down a path alongside the fields, and up a hill, atop which was some sort of small family burial plot. But just as we were beginning to crest the hill, Cosimo gave the order to set the coffin down. We all stopped and mopped our brows, then hoisted again at his command and found ourselves unexpectedly heading left and downhill, toward the copse of woods. Gianni grunted, reminding us all of the work he was doing. Rosina's ankle turned and she cursed but kept going. The makeshift rope handle cut into my palm.

We crossed into the woods, where the thick green shade provided a sense of momentary relief, but only until the humidity enveloped us, and now we were trudging through green, wet heat. The path was less clear, with fallen branches and rocks underfoot. Near the house, we had been taking measured and dignified steps as best we could, trying to synchronize our gaits. But fatigue had set in. This was no parade, and there was no audience. We may as well have been carrying a big box of coal. Marzia begged for a break. We set the coffin down. Cosimo said something. We lifted it up again and took a hard right turn, and a little while later, another right.

"He isn't lost, is he?" I whispered to Rosina, walking just ahead of me.

"Shhhh."

"Because I think we're going in circles."

The toddler was crying now; Mamma Digirolamo had picked her up, but couldn't carry her for long. Marzia would have to take her. We lost some good muscles on the right.

We trudged out of the woods and up a hill, where we caught

a tantalizing breeze, then down into the green woods again. We set down the coffin, taking a longer break.

I was about to press Rosina for more information when an old man with a flat cap came walking toward us, walking stick over one shoulder, whistling. We gingerly lowered the coffin and stood next to it. He raised a hand in greeting. I was hoping that he was a priest in disguise, that we had been trying to rendezvous with him and that explained the circuitous route. But he approached Cosimo and Zio Adamo and Mamma Digirolamo with too much exuberance and ease for that to be the case. Hugs and kisses were exchanged; Cosimo delivered a rambling address; the neighbor lowered himself onto the coffin lid with a heavy sigh and took out a pipe. Mamma wrapped her heavy forearms around herself, under her wide bosom.

"Are we going soon?" I whispered to Rosina.

"He believes we're having a picnic."

"I thought we *were* having a picnic, after the burial."

"Our neighbor doesn't know about the burial."

"And the coffin?"

"Does it look like a coffin to you? He believed us when we said it was a picnic table."

The neighbor pricked up his ears at the German and said something to Cosimo, who made a show of introducing us. "I told him that you have come," Cosimo translated for me, "to learn more about the truffle-hunting season. You are here three months early, but he is not surprised. Bavarians aren't always the brightest."

"Thank you very much, Cosimo." And to the neighbor: "*Grazie.*"

We gathered around the ersatz picnic table, wiping our foreheads, fanning ourselves with our hands. The neighbor's eye kept flitting from person to person, eyeing Mamma's shoulder bag, round with the bread loaf inside, and the straw-wrapped wine bottle slung over Zio Adamo's shoulder. They hadn't offered anything yet; the neighbor hadn't offered to leave. Sweat glistened on our faces. The hillside promised to be cooler, but we couldn't yet ascend. Finally, Mamma Digirolamo grunted and dropped the bag at her feet—*There, fine, have at it*—and Rosina took out the bread and cut everyone a slice.

We ate in the wood, in the sultry shade, the old neighbor munching happily on his slice of festive bread, peeling his hard-boiled egg, chewing his slice of sausage, eyes squinting with pleasure, while everyone else glanced nervously from one face to the other, nibbling unhappily. Finally, the neighbor stood up and rapped his walking stick hard against the coffin top, making Mamma Digirolamo wince.

As soon as he was out of view, Mamma Digirolamo exploded with a torrent of spitting and cursing, signs of the cross, and gestures up through the heavily leafed trees.

"He's joking with us, she says," Cosimo explained over his shoulder.

"The neighbor?"

"No. Enzo. She says he put the neighbor in our path. She says this is just his kind of humor—to make his own funeral such an inconvenience."

"But Cosimo," I said, ignoring Gianni's scowl, "why are we taking this route? Are we hiding the body in the woods?"

"No, back up to the hill."

"The one we almost climbed, just past the field?"

"Yes."

"But why didn't we go straightaway?"

Mamma Digirolamo unleashed some kind of lament.

"She does not like the talking—from any of us," Cosimo explained, breathing heavily. "To do this right, we must be quiet."

"I know, but really, this is heavy."

Rosina cut in: "We are confusing his spirit. My mother is from the South, and this is her family's tradition. Enzo died a bad death, we haven't done a proper Mass, and he will want to stay on this earth, so we can't make it easy for him to find his way from the grave back to the house. We go in circles—*Sì Mamma, prego!*—until we've walked enough to confuse him. Then maybe he'll stay in the grave long enough to give up and go away to heaven."

She risked upsetting her mother further to add, "You wonder why I moved away to Munich? Because of things like this."

"Maybe we will walk all the way to Munich."

She pushed her face into her sleeve, stifling a small noise. "I'm not laughing."

"Of course you aren't. Who could laugh at a time like this?"

Rosina tucked her chin and cheek down into her shoulder, until she had enough composure to say, "You will stay for dinner, of course."

Mamma Digiloramo shushed us again before I could answer.

I'm not sure what I expected from the burial itself. This being Italy, perhaps I expected opera—or at least oratory. Instead, there was only more work. The walls of the grave sloped and the bottom wasn't wide enough for the poorly made coffin. We all waited as Cosimo stripped off his overshirt and, in white undershirt and dusty trousers, jumped down into the grave to square the corners better. That was the most disturbing moment of the day: seeing him down there, head lower than the level earth above, occupying the space in which his twin brother's body would remain for perpetuity. From above, seeing his tanned shoulders, and staring at the nubby dark-gold hair that had loosened and grown curlier with the day's work and humidity, the resemblance was more clear than ever.

The hole was widened, the box lowered, and Zio Adamo said a slow and halting prayer. Then Cosimo picked up a shovel again and I picked up the other. It took longer than I expected, and it was different than just watching, waiting, or weeping. The physicality of loading each weighted shovelful felt like a very purposeful attempt to put a barrier between all of us and what had happened—but that barrier was not a denial or a distancing. It did not feel peaceful. But it felt necessary. There were worse ways to say good-bye to someone. And there were worse *things*: like not saying good-bye at all.

With the last tamping of metal against earth, Cosimo dropped the shovel and turned to shake my hand, then pulled me into a full embrace. "*Grazie, molto grazie.*"

"I've done nothing, Cosimo. Really—nothing."

But he held me still, so grateful that it only made me feel terrible for what had happened and regretful that I couldn't do more. And still he embraced me, until my own muscles loosened and I stopped resisting, until I returned the full measure of his embrace and the touch itself seemed to change that feeling of frustration into a purer grief, a simpler camaraderie. His strong back weakened; I felt gravity working on him. He was starting to collapse; he was choking up. He had sleepwalked through a long list of tasks, and now that he was nearing the end, there was no relief, only confusion. He stepped back and turned and stalked down the hill, back toward the house, and Mamma Digirolamo hugged me quickly before following him, her worry turned toward the surviving son, who had held up somehow through all this but might not hold up much longer.

The rest of us stayed up on the hill. I wandered away to look at the five other gravestones—an 1896, a 1911, two 1918s, and the newest one, 1935.

"That one is my father's," Rosina said, coming up behind me.

Several paces away, just downhill from the graves, Gianni ate another piece of picnic bread, leaving the eggshells scattered in a half circle around his feet. Then he lay down with a hat over his face. Marzia lay down, too, on her side, her eyes open but glazed. In that position, I could see the draping of her loose yellow dress over her round belly. It had taken me this long to realize she was pregnant—not too pregnant to help carry a coffin, evidently. Regarding her rounded form, and imagining the new baby who would be born just when the olive harvest was coming in, I found myself envying Gianni for all he had here: the family pleasures that would coincide with the changing seasons, and the fact that he and Marzia had an imaginable future together.

Their daughter, Renata, tried crawling over her father's legs. When she was shooed away, she came to sit in front of Rosina, who took the child's chubby hands in her own and played a finger game with her, acting out a story about a rabbit and a wolf. The first time, the little girl liked the attention well enough, but the third and fourth time, she was beside herself with tense glee, understanding now the fate that awaited her, once the wolf came in for the kill, snatching the make-believe rabbit, and all of it ending with a tickle. Every possible emotion flashed across the little girl's face—from worry to joy to surprise to recognition, and just a little horror when the wolf finally pounced. But then it was all fine again, and that was the fun of it, enduring the tension to get the pleasure, understanding one couldn't have the one without the other.

"I'll stay—but just for dinner," I told Rosina.

She smiled. "I thought you would."

■

A feast was laid out, late that afternoon, at a table outside under the trees. Mamma Digirolamo set eight plates for the adults and then caught herself, claiming she was really setting one for Renata, who was old enough to have her own plate now rather than eating off her mother's. There was too much food. It would have been the right amount for a normal funeral, if everyone had been invited: farming neighbors, old schoolmates, cousins from faraway, Farfalla and her family, other hope-filled young women who'd stayed available as long as they could, Enzo's *polizia* colleagues and the eight or ten men in town with whom he had most frequently shared talk of fast automobiles or football. They would have filled the house and covered the *terrazza*. They would have emptied the cellars and the cupboards and scraped clean all the plates.

But instead, this: the only seven adults who knew of Enzo's death, the only seven who would know for a few more days. So, the plates remained full. But there was no sense of waste. It seemed that the Digirolamo family needed the look and the smell of abundant food—the splitting crust of bread, the fruity gold of olive oil pooling at the bottom of a shallow dish of potato gnocchi—to remember that they were not the ones who had stopped living.

Pushing away her plate, Mamma Digiloramo began to tell a story about Enzo, using a deep and castigating voice, but it was clear from the reactions of her listeners that the story was more mocking than serious. Marzia erupted into laughter first, holding her daughter's curly head loosely in her hands, playing with the silky strands as she listened; then Rosina laughed, and even Cosimo managed a crooked smile. No one translated, but there was no need. We were hearing, I could guess, about the time Enzo first got lost in a market; next, about some confusion over a farm animal; later, about an early girlfriend who—this made clear from the way Mamma pushed her own shelf of cleavage up toward her neck—was amply endowed. I didn't struggle to understand the words;

I just sat, glad to be forgotten, and studied the faces and voices of this family, the differences and similarities, the way Rosina's throaty laugh resembled her mother's, the way fatigue and sadness showed on Zio Adamo's face, as they did on Cosimo's, even when he was smiling. When they toasted some anecdote I couldn't understand, I raised my own glass, toasting what perhaps only a stranger could see and what is so hard to appreciate in one's life: the continuity of family; the elastic, accommodating permanence that persists despite the transience of flesh.

When even the light conversation had stopped, even the occasional mumbled request for another slice of bread or another glass of water or wine, Gianni pushed himself back from the table and began to deliver an address that I mistook as a eulogy of some kind until I saw Mamma Digirolamo's hands go to her cheeks. Cosimo leaned forward in his own chair, then stood with a hand up, signaling Gianni to desist.

Cosimo addressed me directly for the first time since dinner had begun. "We should leave as soon as possible, but we still have to wrap the statue again, for safe transport."

"But what did Gianni say?"

"Take your time. Finish your meal. I will go look for some blankets and padding and then meet you by the truck."

I turned to Rosina. "What did Gianni say? What did your mother get upset about?"

"He said that the carpenter who made the coffin heard things in town. The head of the *polizia* is coming here again tomorrow morning, for a friendly visit."

"If they know something, why didn't they come today?"

"Because they had a telegram today. They are waiting for visitors coming to join them from Germany."

One day late, and the gears were efficiently turning. I seemed to be the only one who was not surprised.

"*Buona notte*," Cosimo said to his mother, but Mamma Digirolamo objected, fingers grasping at his forearm.

Marzia, with sleeping Renata clinging to her hip, began to pick up the plates, but then Gianni said something to her and she set the plates down and entered the house behind Zio Adamo. Gianni delivered terse instructions to Rosina and followed his wife, leaving only Mamma Digirolamo arguing with Cosimo, Rosina, and me.

Cosimo twisted his arm away, extracting himself from his mother's grip, and with a regretful, tired look, turned his back. She stood, whipping the napkin out of her lap. She approached me and I stood as well, lowering my head slightly, ready to accept another of her wide-bosomed, maternal embraces.

With my eyes down and my arms slightly out, I could smell the warm blend of yeast and oregano on her approaching breath. I was starting to say "*Buona notte*" when she slapped me with astonishing force.

"Mamma!" Rosina shouted with horror.

Mamma Digirolamo pursed her lips and walked into the house.

Rosina ran around to my side, holding a wet napkin, which I took and touched absentmindedly to my face.

"She caught me by surprise," I managed to say, working my jaw, still registering the heat of that small handprint on my cheek.

"She's mad at you for taking Cosimo away so soon."

"But he has to go. Gianni said it. The *polizia* are coming. We have to get the statue out of here."

"Believe me, she wants you and the statue to go. But she doesn't want Cosimo out of her sight. He's in no condition to travel."

"He isn't, but I need him." I touched my face again. "I thought your mother liked me."

"She did. But now you're going to betray her. She doesn't forget."

Rosina turned away and lost herself in contemplation of the table loaded with leftover food, glasses, and dirty plates. The other women had left. The men, except for Cosimo, who was occupied, couldn't be bothered with domestic details. From the droop of her shoulders, I gathered that this was nothing new. She stood and stacked several of the dishes, moving around the table haphazardly, carrying them to a tub on an outside counter.

"Do you want me to bring the other plates?"

When she didn't answer, I began to carry them one at a time, stacking them next to her and standing for just a moment to catch the scent of her skin before returning to the table. Another plate, stacked on top of the last; another intake of breath. It was possible that she was waiting for me to go away, that she was annoyed by my presence. But then again, her head was tilted just to one side, as if she were trying to catch something too—a sound, a smell, a memory. I lingered next to her after I'd stacked the last one.

"We shouldn't wash them," she said without turning, holding a plate caked with sauce. "We should break them."

"Break the plates?"

"It's a tradition." She sounded distracted. "Like taking a long route to the grave. Like the picnic bread and putting mementos in the coffin."

"Really?"

Instead of answering, she turned and flung the plate into the air, over the table, and into the stone oven at the far end of the *terrazza*, where it smashed into a dozen pieces. The noise woke her from her half trance. She pressed her hands to her face, horrified and gleeful.

"You're certain this is a tradition?"

"Hand me another."

The first had been a lucky hit. The second missed the mark and went flying to one side, landing in the soft grass unbroken.

"I'm sure you could do it better," she said, breathing more heavily now, cheeks flushed. "Show me the correct way. Don't you spin around, before you let go? Show me how to hit the oven again. I want the biggest possible explosion."

I hadn't thrown a discus in years, and these plates were too big and greasy besides. She was more likely to fling a plate into the house.

"Come on, Ernesto. Show me."

"Your mother will be upset, seeing all this mess."

"*Let* her be!" Rosina's voice had jumped, like a violin string cranked taut, to a higher pitch. "She's been upset with me for years. She's never stopped being upset! And your time is up as well, don't forget. She slapped you. Don't you feel angry about that?"

"Just surprised . . ."

"Then throw one for Enzo. Throw one because he got you into this mess."

But I'd long since stopped blaming Enzo.

My silence and inaction only enraged her more. "You should be furious!"

"I am furious," I said, but my voice was only weary.

"You're not!" She grabbed another plate, used the back of one hand to scrape away the messy sauce, rearranged her grip and prepared to let it fly. "I'd love to *see* you furious!"

"No, you wouldn't." Her increasing volume made me feel only more subdued. "I have to help Cosimo with the statue. I have to go."

She returned the plate to the counter, looking disappointed. Bringing a dirty finger up to a wayward strand of her hair, she dragged more sauce across her face, which she tried to wipe away discreetly with the back of her wrist. "I saw your statue. I went and took a good look today in the back of the truck after the burial."

"And?"

"It wasn't worth all this."

When I said nothing, she continued, emboldened. "That is the problem with a *thing*—a thing that one person owns and sells to someone else, and that everyone wants."

"That is the world of art."

"Not music, fortunately." She tried to sound flippant. "You can't own a song. It can't be taken away from you."

"And do you still sing your opera songs—the ones you performed in Munich?"

Her forced smile faded. "No."

"So you lost them somehow. Or someone took them away. You *let* someone take them away."

Her fiery anger, the anger I had missed the opportunity to share, had burned down to a private smolder.

"Anyway," I continued, "The *Discus Thrower* is a marvelous work of art. You can't possibly disagree with that?"

She looked down at her stained dress, as if noticing for the first time what a mess she had made, with broken crockery scattered over the *terrazza*, out into the yard. "I don't know anything about art."

"You have an opinion. Tell me."

She reached for a cloth behind her, wiping each finger slowly. "You want an opinion? All right. The body is perfect—young, muscular, athletic, and realistic, of course. I understand all that. But the face is empty."

"You're not understanding. It's an issue of development over periods. This isn't a Renaissance—"

"See? I knew you would say that."

"I'm sorry. Go on. Please."

She took a breath before starting again. "The eyes are empty. The face has no personality . . ." The cloth was now balled in her hand. "There is no emotion, no intellect or individuality. For the sculptor, everything above the neck was an afterthought."

"That's a matter of style."

"No, it isn't, Ernesto. It's a statement about ideals."

"Well, it was ideal in its time, a very long time ago."

"No. It is an ideal in our time—among *some* people, the people who were willing to pay millions of *lire* for it. I'm sure you have a great respect for the past, for history and art, but this isn't about that. It's about using an icon from the past to justify the future, don't you think? Why else would they go to so much trouble to purchase it?"

"Are you blaming me for working for such people?"

"No."

"Do you think those are my ideals—to be thoughtless and without emotion, to be without individuality?"

"I don't."

"So?"

"So I just want you to be more, for one night."

"Be more than what?"

"I want you to be more than the reason you came here. That's all."

Cosimo had appeared at the edge of the *terrazza*. His eyes widened, taking in the yard's broken dishes and the spatters on Rosina's forearms.

"I'm sorry," she continued, ignoring her brother's silent arrival. "I've hurt your feelings. I've insulted your favorite sculpture."

"Who said it was my favorite?"

"I've insulted your work."

"Of course I'm not insulted. It's all very interesting." But as soon as I said it, I heard myself sounding again like the person she didn't want me to be: detached, pedantic, single-minded, able to lecture at length without divulging anything that really mattered. But how could I, when even I hadn't decided which parts of the past could be safely remembered, and which should only be forgotten? "Let me tell you—I'll show you a book, my di Luca guide. A colleague—a very good friend—gave it to me. It has excellent pictures. You will see the progression, from Greco-Roman to Renaissance, including some of the same developments you've noted. It's very interesting, all the same."

Cosimo said nothing as we walked to the truck together, climbed into the back, and surveyed the statue and the remaining crate bottom. We took everything he had hauled outside—an old stained and ripped mattress, several blankets and lengths of rope—and formed a cocoon around the statue, lashing the padding down to the pallet-like bottom and stuffing extra padding between the crate and the inside walls of the truck. If anything, it was better protected now than it had been before.

"I'm glad to see you've washed up," I told him. He had refused to shave until after the burial and had begun to look like a walking corpse himself. Now, there was some improvement. But still, he looked on the verge of collapse. "You didn't sleep last night, I imagine."

"Not really."

"How long would you last tonight?"

Cosimo looked up at the sky, a washed-out blue. "We have maybe two good hours, then some difficulty driving in the dark, but we can go a little ways. At least we can start heading for Milan, and after Milan, tomorrow, the roads will be much better."

"You'd have every right to stay here, to make me go alone."

"But how would you find your way? Mechanical problems, language problems—and you're still not such a good driver, even with practice. And then, someone has to return the truck."

"You're not thinking about the truck."

"No." Cosimo attempted a smile. "But you got my brother here. So I will get you to the border. It's only fair."

"Thank you, Cosimo."

"For what?"

"For everything."

He put a hand on my shoulder. "We are not leaving tonight?"

"We're innocent, Cosimo. That should stand for something."

His empty look told me that he stopped seeing the world in those terms long ago. Perhaps it was the policeman in him, or perhaps the Catholic, or perhaps simply the grief-stricken man who feels we're all being punished for something.

"*Domani*," I said firmly. "*Meglio*. Better, early *domani*."

Cosimo lifted his eyebrows—whether at my slowly improving vocabulary or at my questionable decision, I'd never know.

CHAPTER 12

An hour had passed when I pushed open the barn door. Rosina looked up from her bed, startled and guilty, closing the di Luca guide with one finger still holding her place.

"You said it had excellent pictures. It was just sitting on top of your suitcase. I thought—"

But I could see it in her face. I remembered, now, sitting under the tree and then sliding it into the book, for safekeeping.

"You found the postcard."

"Were you really going to send this to your sister?"

"I don't know."

"Why did you write it?"

"I needed to tell someone."

"But you weren't going to send it."

"I hadn't worked that out. This entire trip has shaken my faith in the idea of planning ahead."

I walked over to the stool next to the washtub, carried the stool across the room, placed it next to her bed, and sat down opposite her. She was sitting with one leg folded under the other, wearing a silky gray-and-blue robe patterned with gingko leaves—out of place here, but not out of place in the world she'd once inhabited. I could imagine her in an opera-house dressing room, with her hair piled on top of her head, in front of a brightly lit mirror.

She noticed me staring at the robe and pulled her legs up to her chest, arms wrapped around her shins. "Pretty wrapping for a plain box, I'm afraid."

"You're forgetting. I've already seen the box."

"I'm not forgetting anything."

There was an awkward moment as she scooted to a more upright position, back against the headboard. She patted the side of the bed, and I left the stool to sit closer to her, still not touching.

"Do you want to talk more, about art?"

"Not at all."

"*Va bene.*" She smiled, self-consciously. "Perhaps you should tell me more about yourself. I've told you a lot about me."

"Not so much."

"I've told you I was married. I've told you I'm defective. That should frighten you away, unless you think it is a convenient defect."

"You're not defective, Rosina. Anyway, how long were you married?"

"Two years."

"That's all?"

"It was two years too long. And trust me, a man like Gianni can't wait to see his face reflected in new faces all around him." Now she laughed. "You have no idea. You're so young! At least ten years younger than I am. No, don't tell me."

"You *are* trying to frighten me off, aren't you?"

"Look at you—not a wrinkle, not a blemish." Her fingers touched the front of my shirt. "And you probably have no idea that you are good-looking or athletic because no one your age can appreciate—"

"Now you're being condescending. You're trying to make me feel young and foolish, so I'll leave you alone." I unbuttoned my shirt, methodically, and left it hanging open. She watched, a serious look in her eyes.

"I will tell you something," I said.

"What, you can't get pregnant either?"

I didn't laugh, didn't smile. Then I started to tell her, slowly at first. It wasn't easy to talk about. I'd never told a soul, not the librarian who had befriended me and first showed me the great books of classical art; not the antiques dealer who had given me my first job; not any of the coaches who'd been annoyed by my tendency to dress and bathe away from the other boys; not Gerhard or any other work colleague or friend. Only Doctor Schroeder had known, and my mother and I had left his office before I was subjected to his questions or procedures.

I told her about how I hadn't noticed at first, as a boy; about how my mother had helped me cover it up; about how it had embarrassed and later enraged my father. I explained about the summer campouts and group hikes I had missed, as well as the youth organizations I had failed to join, and the impact that had made on my life in a day when military preparedness and group affiliation and the appearance of cooperation were everything. Even now that the problem was no longer visible or tangible, it had left a stain on my life.

Maybe it was my fault for building it up, for leaning closer and closer, for lowering my voice at the awkward moments. Our foreheads were nearly touching. "I don't have it anymore. But I did, as small a thing as it was, and that's the story."

Her brow furrowed as she listened, trying to understand.

"But what is it—what *was* it—exactly?"

"A mark."

"But what kind of mark?"

I opened my shirt and let her see the long, puckered scar across my ribs.

"But is that it? Or was it there before?" She ran a delicate finger along the jagged, salmon-colored line.

"The scar came after. It was much smaller."

"But what was it?"

When I told her, she pulled away. She threw her hands to her face. She buried her eyes. It was a reaction that made my heart race because I had visualized it so often before—the revulsion and judgment of a stranger. She couldn't help it; she was trying to hide it and squelch it. It took me a moment to realize she was convulsing, not with disgust, but with laughter.

"That's all?" she said, just beginning to catch her breath. "It probably looked like a mole. That's really all?"

My face blazed.

"I'm so sorry." She reached for my shirt, my chest—and missed, because I had scooted back and was leaning as far away from her as I could lean without falling off the bed. "No, I shouldn't have laughed. But don't you realize how common that is?"

When I didn't answer, she reached for me again, hand on my knee. "My goodness—hundreds of people have an extra nipple, I'm guessing. Thousands of people. I knew a girl with the same oddity. I knew a boy with six toes. I had a *cat* with six toes. I'm sure extra nipples are just as common. *Liebling*, I'm sorry. I'm not trying to embarrass you. Wait—don't go."

But I was only going as far as the stool. I didn't want to be touched, or laughed at, or condescended to, or sympathized with; I didn't even want to hear the word she had said twice already, the name for the extra thing I once had. I had in fact already learned, in just the last few years, that my own birth defect—the visible part, anyway, because there always would be the question about what lurked inside, what other cellular strangeness or hereditary weakness existed—was minor and common.

"As common," I said, continuing my thought in midstream, "as being an imbecile. Or an incestuary. Or a gypsy. Or a Jew. Or infertile." I was clutching the bottom of the stool just to keep my hands occupied. I was afraid of my own hands. "Yes, I am well aware that it is common."

"I'm sorry."

"It was a mistake to tell you."

"I'm very sorry. But Ernesto—"

"Ernst. I'm not Italian. Call me Ernst."

"But what happened after? Why is there a scar?"

"Another time."

"Never mind," she said, swinging her legs over so that she was sitting on the edge of the bed. She touched her lips to mine, waiting for me to respond, which I couldn't help doing—which I did and kept doing, until she needed a breath. She let her robe fall open and she whispered into my neck: "Never mind."

We were experts at starting again, newly coined experts at seizing the moment, but perhaps that was the natural outcome of burying someone. There should be something good that comes from it.

My hands were inside her robe, on either side of her waist at first, holding fast to this first rung on a ladder that stretched farther than my mind dared picture all at once. I moved my hand, and she pressed closer. I followed her curves, surveying everything quickly, anticipating many subsequent explorations, adoring and memorizing her.

When my poorly shaved cheek rubbed against her skin, just above the line of her camisole, she murmured, "You missed a rough spot there," and when I pulled away, she pulled me back. "I didn't ask you to stop."

A moment later, she broke away to whisper, "Tell me what you wrote on the postcard."

"*Ich bin verliebt.*"

"So soon?"

"*Ich liebe dich.*"

"Again."

"*Ti amo.*"

"You've been consulting your dictionary."

"That one was easy."

"But I don't believe it," she said. It was a game, but one she didn't mind playing. It was a game she had played with someone else who sounded like me, maybe even looked like me. What was the harm in that? At least that was her view.

I rolled onto my back, taking her with me, and then changed my mind. Now I was on top, she underneath, and perhaps I was pressing too fiercely. She flinched, and I thought I'd reached a limit, done something wrong or moved too fast. But it was only the sound she had heard. She froze, listening—there it was, the soft, swift scratching. She cursed under her breath, pulling away from me.

Tugging her robe closed, she hurried to the door and slipped through it, hand low to the floor, pushing away the would-be intruder, Tartufa. In a minute she was back.

"Couldn't we have ignored her?"

"She would have kept it up all night. It's because I let her sleep in here sometimes. She would have started barking, until Cosimo came and found her, and found us."

"You scared her off?"

"I put her in the back of the truck and pulled down the door." Rosina laughed at this, at the desperation of it.

"Won't she still bark?"

We listened together, and there was the sound—a single muffled bark, a long pause, then another testing bark. But it was very faint.

"That's all right," she said, pulling me closer, resuming what we'd started, but more gently now. She reached to unfasten my belt. "Let me help you."

"I'll get to that."

More gently, more slowly, nothing wasted or forgotten. But it was like a phonograph slowing down—not just slower, but changing pitch. The new sound was one of uncertainty, with—here, the truly unfortunate thing—canine accompaniment.

There was nothing fluid in this. Nothing elegant or well practiced. I tried harder, but harder was not better. Like a man drowning, I was only making things worse with my struggles, losing track of the woman beneath my weight—not just a woman, but *Rosina*—losing track of what had excited me, of all that she possessed when I had first seen her, not only physical beauty, but lack of shame. And all the while, I was still thinking of that dog, pushing its paws up against the door, scrabbling to get in.

"I heard something."

"She's fine."

"Maybe someone . . . maybe Cosimo . . ."

"We're alone." Then, joking: "There are no ghosts."

When I stiffened, she apologized. "I shouldn't have said that. Kiss me." *Küss mich.*

But if I was afraid of any ghost, it wasn't Enzo's.

Something was off. The interruption, the distant barking, the time pressure, my own recall of her love for someone else, the question of what would come next, the argument we'd been having before which had returned to prick me, a thorn ignored but not forgotten. Something had hollowed out the moment. My hand paused too long, and she noticed, too. She pulled away slightly, though without closing her robe, so that she was sitting on the bed, half reclining, her body in full view.

Her beauty was undeniable. I was not any less drawn to her.

"I'm worried about the dog," I said, because that was the easiest part to explain.

"Still?"

When I didn't answer, she began to pull her robe closed again.

"Please don't. I want to look at you."

And though she complied, my own body betrayed me. My own vitality had ebbed, my own self-consciousness had returned, and yet the adrenaline was still there, poisonously unspent. Of course she wouldn't love me. Of course she wouldn't have desired me if we had moved more slowly, if she had looked carefully and examined me more deeply and considered what she was doing.

And the act itself—it might have been disappointing. While this—looking at Rosina, seeing and memorizing her every contour—was a pleasure that would sustain me for months and years to come. Just as Rosina herself had predicted: a memory for later, but a memory of *before*.

The moment before had always been the best moment. The moment at the starting line, just before the struggle and before the striving, before the questionable euphoria. None of it used up. None of it tainted, in the way that everything is ultimately tainted—everything and everyone. The moment just before the discus flies, when nothing has happened, when no one has succeeded or failed, won or lost. When everything remains possible.

That's how it had been, once.

That's how it should have been, still.

Looking at Rosina was a pleasure, even with the poison in my veins, and the anger. But with whom was I angry? Not her. Not Enzo. Not even Keller.

"I'm just going to close my eyes," she said, releasing my hand before she rolled away. Could she really fall that quickly from frantic passion into unguarded sleep? But perhaps more time had passed than I realized. Yet more time passed as I listened to the soft, uncertain sounds outside and stared at the bunched sheets, the sensual slope of her robe-draped hip. My shirt and belt were flung across the stool, but I was still wearing my unbuttoned trousers.

"Stupid dog," I whispered, though the bark was so irregular, so faint, it was bothering no one.

"Will you turn down the lantern?"

"Must I?"

"You can stay," she said sleepily. "But don't forget the light."

"Rosina—" I began. But what more could I tell her? What more could I ask? And anyway, she was already nodding off. "I'll move to the floor later. Cosimo will be looking for me just before dawn."

She didn't care what Cosimo thought, so why did I say that? Perhaps to cloak my own lack of performance in chivalry. I had spared her and her reputation. She had not asked to be spared. And still, she gave off warmth, and forgiving softness, which I found in the dark and curled up next to, wishing that sleep itself were unnecessary.

It's hard to remember how deeply a child sleeps, how deeply and without care, but that's how I had slept once. Deep enough not to hear arguments, or the radio, or a barking dog, or neighbors coming and going, slamming the doors, even on a hot summer night with the windows open. I used to fall asleep with the smell of dinner cabbage in my nose and not wake again until there were different smells—a combination of bleach and potatoes that meant my mother had been scrubbing floors and making breakfast well before the rest of us awoke. In between were hours of safety and ignorance, which I had nearly always slept through, without complaint.

So my father's hand was already on my shoulder when I awoke in the near dark. He was pushing hard, pinning me to the bed. I thought at first he was falling onto me, that he had consumed a few too many beers and had been ejected from my mother's bed and had come to share mine—because that had happened two or three times, when I was even younger and his own belly wasn't quite so stout, when it was possible, just barely, to share a narrow mattress.

But this time I was sixteen years old, and though beer was on his breath, he wasn't anywhere near losing consciousness. In fact, he was strong. He pushed so hard on my shoulder that I thought it might dislocate. I tried to squirm away and felt the pop of my pajama button flying off—a comical sound, a comical feeling, except for the ache at my collarbone and the knowledge that more was coming.

A moment of suspense and paralysis, next, as my mind located itself, clearing away the cobwebs of sleep: here was the room where I'd never feel comfortable again, the room I had to myself, slightly bigger than Greta's, though she was older; a room I would have shared with my brothers if my mother and father had ever had any more sons—but they didn't. I was his only hope, and his greatest disappointment. Across the room was the wallpaper patterned with pale blue and silver leaves that glinted in even the faintest light, leaves that turned into slim fishes, swimming under the surface of night; fish that would break the surface for many nights to come because I would never sleep as soundly again.

I felt the fabric of my opened nightshirt bunching oddly beneath my armpit, followed by the strange, hard, flat pinch of something cold pressing against my bare rib cage. The pinch became a burn, and when I recoiled and cried out, he sat down on my right leg, pinning me even harder to the mattress. When I twisted my head to look, I saw the knife in my father's hand, and the shaky, inexact surgery he was attempting to do.

It hurts and it doesn't hurt, when it's your own flesh and you're seeing the damage done, at close range. The hurt comes later. The nausea and lightheadedness come first.

I always told myself later that it was because he was my father, *mein Vater*, someone I must obey. But maybe I would have been paralyzed by anyone cutting into me unexpectedly like that, as something wet spread across one side of my rib cage, the warmth turning immediately cold, as if I'd had a nighttime accident.

Over the years, I tried imagining a different response: reaching up with a hand to dislodge the knife. Reaching up with two hands to push him off. Turning hard on one side, bumping my hip to his, rolling out from underneath him, using my greater youth and clearer mind to escape. Obviously, I was at the peak of my own strength and health. Obviously, it should not have been hard to get the better of him. If I had only reacted quickly enough, before my body and my brain shut down. If I had worked it out ahead of time, somehow. I imagined these scenarios so many times I must have burned them into my consciousness. I know I became a less sound sleeper, tossing and turning, practicing the escapes all too late.

But what was done was done. He wanted it gone, and it was gone—the flesh on my side, the singular anomaly and patches of previously unblemished skin above and below, cut to ribbons. The blade had stayed mostly flat to my rib cage. It hadn't pierced between the bones into any organs. As it happened, I simply lost a lot of blood. Later, I would acquire an infection from the dirty knife and the infection would do more damage than the quick surgery itself, and the memory would do more damage than the infection.

My mother came rushing into my room as soon as she heard my confused whimpers. He fled to the living room where he collapsed into a chair, the knife still in his hands and the rambling excuses ready on his lips, justifying himself with every trembling syllable: "Now, he can join any team, any squad, any platoon. No more hiding or covering up. It was for him I did it. For him!" Greta dressed and ran to a neighbor's home to use a phone, to call and wake a doctor, who came and found me wide-eyed in my bed, clammy and confused, every bit of color run out of my face and into the sheets and onto the floor.

"Will you come to the funeral?" I asked Gerhard seven years later.

"Of course."

"You understand, I don't love him."

"Shhh, *mein Junge*, you don't need to say—"

"I'm not sorry he's gone."

"That's all right. But he isn't gone. You'll see. Fathers never are."

CHAPTER 13

'd been caught off guard once, but never again. This time, I was ready. So when something bumped the foot of the bed, when the electric torch clicked on and swept across the bedclothes and into my eyes, I reacted quickly. My hand thrust sideways to the nightstand, where at home for months after the incident I had kept a heavy volume of Aesop's *Fables*—innocent-looking enough, but a weapon of last resort. Discovering no book, not even the electric lamp with a railcar-shaped base that I'd had since my tenth birthday, I kicked out with one leg and heard an answering expulsion of breath that confirmed contact with a doughy stomach.

But that didn't send him away. It only made him angrier, and I felt his hands wrap around my leg, just above my knee, pulling me off the bed and onto the floor. I felt his hands around my waist, pulling me sideways, tackling me to the ground. The torch had gone flying, its illuminating arc catching a flash of silver before falling to the ground. I fell back, rolled, and got to my knees—reaching, reaching, in this room that was bigger than it should have been, bigger and unfamiliar, until the fragments of reality slid into place: a rough wood floor, not the polished planks of my childhood bedroom; the iron-looped handles of a clothes dresser, not my own; a smell that was not cabbage or bleach or beer, the pedestrian smells of my childhood home, but an aggressive and somehow familiar cologne. I evaded the grasping arms and crawled forward, one hand patting everything I could reach, finding the side of the dresser, the right angle with the wall of the barn.

Rosina, meanwhile, was shouting in the dark and scuffling around on the other side of the bed—trying to get under it, I thought at first, until I saw the light come swinging again, the found torch held in her shaking hands. "There's a knife! Ernesto, I saw a knife!"

Another desperate reach and I had something long and thin in my hands: a stick, no, the trowel-like, steel-ended truffler's *vanghetto*. When the hands grabbed my bare calf, nails pressing into the flesh behind my knee, pulling me back with surprising force, I turned toward the groping. There was no question. There was no confusion. I knew what I needed and wanted to do, and when I felt the hands on my waist again, I twisted and leaned back, raised the tool, then pushed it in a downward motion with every bit of energy inside me. The steel made contact, cut, and separated from the shaft, but I lifted and thrust again.

The splintered end of the *vanghetto* sank into the man's chest, hit an obstruction, and sank a little further before I leaned too hard and broke the shaft in two. But it had done its work. The torchlight swept and stopped. Blood bubbled out of his parted lips, darkening the tips of his shaggy mustache.

"I know him," I managed to say.

This only confused Rosina more. She was whispering to herself frantically, crouching down on the other side of the bed, searching for the missing knife and a dress to pull over her shivering body.

"Opportunist," was all I could say, indicting us both.

He wore pin-striped trousers, a white shirt and tie, and polished shoes that glinted in the sweep of the torchlight. Between the folds of his fleshy neck, his Adam's apple kept working, up and down. His left leg kicked out weakly, the motion pushing up his pant leg, revealing the knife holster wrapped around his upper calf, the knife gone missing—somewhere on the floor around us, having just missed its mark. The leg finally stopped, but the Adam's apple wouldn't, even after his shirtfront was stained black.

"He's still alive," Rosina said from beyond the far side of the bed, head and shoulders peeking just above.

"It takes a long time."

Eight years, in fact. Eight years of poor sleep, until I finally woke in time to fend off the ambush that had waited for me, interrupting my sleep all that time.

His eyes remained open, unblinking.

And suddenly, he was only Keller. Which was bad enough, but still, only Keller. What had I done? I put my head in my hands and got sick on the floor just next to him.

This was the end of one thing, finally; the beginning of another, but not the beginning of anything I would have desired most. The day of individual happiness had passed. There was no such thing as a small, quaint, rustic farm where a couple might hide away for years, sketching still lifes and playing old phonograph records of nineteenth-century operas. There was no such thing as a city life of books and statues and index cards—not really. Not anymore.

Keller had not moved for several minutes when we crept outside, scanning the darkness for any sign that he was traveling with a companion, but there was no sign, only the oblivious insect noises of deepest night.

"I'll run up to the house," Rosina said, one hand nervously raking her bare neck.

"Yes—wait. But how did he come? If there is a car . . . perhaps he walked in . . . if there is someone else out there, waiting . . ."

"It can't be far."

"It can't be far," I repeated, unable to locate my own thoughts. "He wasn't much of a walker."

We proceeded together, silently, staying to the side of the road, ducking under branches overhanging the natural berm that flanked one side. Just around the first curve, not even a quarter of a kilometer away, there was the little red Zagato Spider in which Keller had arrived, keys still in the ignition, and a valise and crumpled map on the passenger seat. During the last stretch, at least, he had traveled alone.

I started and restarted the engine a few times before I managed to shift into the proper gear and drove slowly up and around the back of the barn, then a little farther, up and over the grass toward the pigsty, leaving a light track of flattened grass and tire-printed dirt. All the while, I kept the headlamps off, as if Rosina and I were still sneaking around, trying not to let Keller hear.

Even without lights, the sound of the car had alerted Cosimo. He came out of the main house in pajama pants and no shirt just as we were approaching. Rosina fell into his arms, trying to explain. Gianni appeared, fingering his tousled hair. After a moment, he disappeared around the side of the house and returned with a shovel in his hands, blade up and poised to strike.

"I'm sorry," I said, interrupting Rosina. "I did it."

"Yes, we know," Cosimo said, trying to move past me on the path, to see the scene for himself, with Gianni just behind him. "You've said that several times already."

"Have I?"

Cosimo asked his sister, "Only one man? One car? You're sure?"

"I don't know." I reached for Cosimo's arm.

"It was self-defense," he announced. "And we must keep defending ourselves in any way we can."

I hadn't been preparing to offer an excuse. I had been preparing only to thank him, to apologize, and to surrender myself if it would make his life any easier. He could drive me into the village right now, into the village where the local *polizia* were perhaps beginning to roll in their beds, to groan and stretch, irritated by the ridiculous hour the visiting German Gestapo agents had asked to meet for this emerging investigation. I felt sure they were unaware that one man had gone ahead without them: the eccentric German liaison from Rome, eager to sniff things out for himself on the pretext of looking for any sign of local corruption, ahead of the local *polizia* whom no foreigner should trust, when perhaps he saw this as his last chance to make a deal and cover his tracks, simultaneously.

"You wait here," Cosimo said, stopping Rosina at the doorway to the barn. When I tried to follow, he stopped me, too.

"It's my doing. I want to help."

Gianni handed me the shovel, blade up, but I fumbled, my hands shaking so badly that I dropped the thing onto my foot.

"Sit down," Cosimo ordered, pointing to the stone stoop. "Put your head between your legs. Was he still moving?"

I assured them he was not. But Cosimo muttered something to Gianni, who picked up the shovel and gripped it close to the blade, ready.

The sound of dull blows came from inside the barn, continuing even as Gianni came out, pacing several times before going back in. Perhaps it wasn't so easy to kill a man, through and through. I had forced Cosimo to finish what I could not, to finish what he had threatened the morning we'd found Enzo, though I had never believed him.

They came out several minutes later with the inert body slung between them, grasped at armpits and knees—a drunken reveler hoisted by two friends out of a tavern, one would have liked to pretend. Rosina turned away.

Cosimo, struggling against the large German's weight, jacked up his end with a shrugging motion. "We'll need someone to burn his clothes. Ernst—"

Rosina objected. "Don't leave me here alone. Someone else might be coming. And what about the car?"

Cosimo reconsidered. "Stay together, then. Cover the car with anything—a blanket, branches. Scuff up the tire tracks. Check for personal belongings and hide them, but quickly. Then return to the barn, push everything back into place, clean up and wait.

"There's no hiding what I've done," I said to Cosimo's departing back.

Forty minutes later, Rosina and I were sitting on the tidied bed together, hands washed but still shaking, catching a pungent smell of smoke, not a smell bad enough to explain how they are disposing of the body itself. I left it to Cosimo, who, in his line of work, probably knew ways I couldn't imagine. The surrounding landscape, in my horrified mind, became a map of morbid options: an algae-covered pond here, a collapsed cellar, a sty full of hungry pigs. That last image was the hardest to shake, even as I felt Rosina's hand on my back, tracing light circles with her fingertips.

"*Bitte*," she said, and I realized it wasn't the first time she had said it. I'd been hearing it faintly without apprehending.

Ja.

Bitte.

Ja.

Then silence as we traveled down a path we had begun to travel before, but this time without banter, no attempt to study or adore, to hurry or delay; no references to past or future, or to any people other than ourselves. The consequences of what I'd done were rushing toward us, but strangely, I felt a sense of release. The worst had already happened.

I closed my eyes without any thought of vigilance or scrutiny. I shed each layer without any thought of self-consciousness. We stopped kissing long enough to turn the covers down, but carefully, as if we were only preparing the bed for someone else. Of course, this is what we should be doing now. Of course, this is what we must do.

And how beautiful her body was, how soft and how singular. We took our time, and there were no interruptions or regrets and no awkwardness or shame, as if we'd made love a dozen times before, as if we'd always been lovers. How fortunate I felt, and how ready, once we were finished and I had dressed again and rolled up each sleeve with meditative care, to accept whatever would come next.

Sitting on the bedside later, fully clothed, I laced my fingers with Rosina's one last time as we watched the sky outside the barn's one small window turn from black to gray to lavender, dark hills cleanly divided from lightening sky. "Now we wait for Lady Fortune. That's what Enzo would say."

Rosina looked skeptical. "He never understood that she is bad fortune as well as good. Fickle and unlasting—the symbol of the turning wheel. Attracted to displays of youthful violence, some say."

A moment later, I asked, "Maybe you could sing something for me?"

"Who would think of singing at a time like this?"

"Later, then. Do you promise?"

She turned away, but I'd already seen the thickening lens of tears darkening her eyes. "*Prometto.*"

Then I heard the sounds of tires on gravel, the assertive application of brakes, the sharp metallic scrape of four car doors opening. "They're here. I'll go to meet them."

"Wait for Cosimo." Her fingernails dug into my forearm.

But we heard him calling out to the visitors from the hill beyond the barn, sounding falsely hale and hearty, as if he'd just been feeding chickens and shoveling manure. "*Buongiorno!*"

When I stepped out of the barn, buttoning the top button of my shirt, I came up against two Germans in suits, one with a small, slim-barreled pistol in his hand, pointing. Closest to the car was a man in police uniform, an Italian supervising officer of some kind, chatting amiably with his hand on Cosimo's sleeve. His face met mine, saw the gun pointing at me. He looked even more shocked than I was.

"*Essere attento,*" the Italian said, searching his brain for foreign words. "*Achtung.* Easy, easy."

Another Italian policeman stepped out of the car, yawning, and stopped mid-stretch, alarmed by the scene unfolding. The two Germans wanted to search me, search the barn, find the truck. The two Italians wanted to go up to the main house, maybe wake up with some espresso if Cosimo or his mother would be so kind, take out their notepads and ask us some questions.

"*Va bene, va bene,*" Cosimo soothed, striking a compromise. He shouted out to his mother in the house to prepare for guests. To the men gathered, he suggested, in both carefully enunciated Italian and then German, that we go directly to the truck, where the statue of the *Discus Thrower* awaited us. That was why they were here, was it not? It was fine, well cared for, and ready for the final leg of its transport. We would go to inspect it, without delay. When Rosina slipped out of the barn, Cosimo directed her up to the house, out of our way: *Help Mamma.*

As we walked to the truck, the second German, who introduced himself simply and without rank as Herr Fassbinder, began to question me. But it was the unnamed one with the polished chestnut-colored holster riding high against his hip—Herr Luger, I'd tagged him in my mind—who held my attention.

"Why are you here?" Fassbinder asked gently.

"There was . . . an incident. A series of incidents."

"We have a report that someone was trying to steal the statue you were transporting."

I lowered my voice. "Someone *was* trying to steal it. Not these Italians. I think they're ignorant of the entire matter." The presence of a sympathetic listener encouraged me further. "At first, I suspected some Roman policemen, but now I think it was a private ploy, an attempt to take the statue, not to return it to the government, but to sell it on the black market." Should I implicate Keller, or would that only prompt them to ask me if I'd seen him? Should I tell everything I knew, as fast as I could, and rely on the truth to save me?

"Very helpful, very interesting," the German said, returning my whisper. "We are also missing someone—a man who came out this way earlier this morning. It would be our luck if he got lost here, motoring between farms, surveying the country-side for pretty girls, no doubt." He glanced over his shoulder at the yawning Italian walking behind us. He started to catch the yawn himself and shook it off. I couldn't tell if this casual manner was authentic or just a tactic to earn my trust. Either way, I preferred it to the point of a gun. "They haven't given us much help, I have to say. I was in Genoa, on vacation, when they called me. The other man—he's on duty, sent by The Col-lector himself, who is waiting to hear."

I repeated the dreaded words back to him: "*Der Kunstsammler.*"

"Yes, there is unhappiness at the highest levels."

Cosimo, the Italian police captain, and the German with the reholstered Luger were ahead, talking just as animatedly. Up at the house, the side door opened, and I saw Mamma Digi-rolamo waving, with a tray in her other hand. The espresso wasn't ready yet, but it soon would be. All this would be set-tled. For a moment, this felt like a cheerful reunion, and I could imagine all of us making a best effort to sort through the confusion, in two languages, with all due respect. If only Keller *had* gotten lost. I could almost believe it myself. I could see him accepting breakfast in a farmhouse, dancing a waltz on a *terrazza*, falling in love.

But that would have been a different Keller, not the one who had fallen in love with profit and fineries, whose distinc-tive cologne even now was so strong in my nostrils I was sure others could smell it, too. I brought my arm to my face as if I were just rubbing my nose, and there was the source of it, on the underside of my forearms, where I must have pressed hard against his chest as the *vanghetto* sank into his lungs. I unrolled my sleeves, buttoning them, but still, the sickly sweet perfume lingered.

Up ahead, Cosimo threw open the back of the truck and was startled when Tartufa came leaping out, escaping her all-night confinement. She landed on all fours, sized up our assembly, darted forward a meter or so, and then turned to bare her small white teeth. For a moment, she seemed to be snarling at me—at the smell on my arms, at the clear look and aroma of my guilt—but then I saw her take a threatening step toward the other strangers. She picked out the Germans, perhaps because they were closest, their erect posture mimicking her own nervousness. She quieted for a moment, a gurgling sound dying in her throat, then pulled back her lips again.

And fell, tumbling to her side. There was a yelp and a gunshot—or most likely, the reverse. Of course. The gunshot followed by the yelp, followed by the fall. My mind was still struggling to see it unfold, to understand why she had gone limp.

Cosimo knelt down, cradling the dog's head, while the rest of us turned toward the sound of the shot. The sleepy Italian policeman was no longer sleepy. The Italian captain, Cosimo's supervisor, was outraged. Even Herr Fassbinder, hands anchored in the front pockets of his trench coat, looked surprised. I heard a house door slam and the sounds of women's voices, plus a man's—Gianni's—ordering them back inside.

"Remove the animal, please," the German with the Luger ordered, and my former ally, the off-duty vacationer in Genoa, shrugged off his last vestige of casual impartiality and got down to business. He carried the dog to the side of the truck, just out of view.

"Now, let's get to work," the first German ordered. "How much does this statue weigh?"

When I told him, he laughed. "Good God. What a nuisance. I suppose we paid by the kilo?"

No one responded to his joke.

"All right. Five of us then." He pointed to me, Fassbinder, the Italian captain, and the secondary officer. Cosimo was left to stand, staring down at his stained hands. "And if anyone sneezes, or drops this *verdammte* thing on my foot, I still have ammunition left."

Even Fassbinder failed to smile.

We were told to remove the statue from the truck for inspection, to unwrap its makeshift wrappings and stand it up in the yard. It was harder to do now that the crate had been mostly disassembled; it would take some time and some rope and a good deal of sweaty cooperation, handling those hundreds of kilograms of marble. It wasn't a good idea to do haphazardly, I wanted to say. But since when had any of this been a good idea?

I was too nervous to look closely until it was fully upright, until it was done. Then I took off the last blanket and put a hand to the *Discus Thrower*'s side, on his exposed right ribs, holding him upright until we knew the round base was secure on the pebbly ground, and then I paused for a breath to look. Once I looked, I was unable to stop looking. This is what I had wanted to do all along—not only to look at it up close, but to touch it, unhurriedly, as I would never again be able to do, once the statue was in powerful hands, on private or public display.

There was the taut pectoral muscle, and beneath it, the smooth and shadowy indent just below the first rib, the second, the third, the fourth and the fifth, all the way down to the muscular iliac crest. Where my hand rested, along the middle of the rib cage, was the place where I had been strong once, where I had been ashamed, where I had been attacked, where I was now healed. I ran my hand over the marble, feeling all that this statue was, and all that it was not—nearly unfathomable artistry, but not everything. Both more than and less than life. The fact that it would outlast us all was, at this moment, both an injustice and a relief.

There was a dark line near the *Discus Thrower*'s hip, but when I reached down and touched it, the darkness wiped off easily. It was only soot from the truck fire, not a crack. There were no lines or new signs of breakage anywhere along the statue, from toe to fingertip, from back to front, other than the cracks that had been apparent before—on the discus itself, just below the right shoulder, a few other places, all well documented.

The gathered men were all looking at me. They would have to believe what I had to say, or better yet, I could show them the di Luca guide. The two nubs at the top, like the faint traces of two little devil horns—of which Herr Luger asked, "Did something happen there?"—were part of the authentic Roman statue, artifacts of the molding process. I could explain everything in fine detail about what didn't matter, and almost nothing about what did: *Was it worth all of this, including what would come next?*

"There it is, safe and sound," I said as we all looked on with some awe. At the very least, we had not damaged a masterpiece.

Maybe that thought made me believe we were past the worst of it, or maybe I was not optimistic at all but only reckless, intoxicated by the presumption of imminent liberty, ready to accept the lash rather than cower from it.

"There is money," I stammered. "Money from the people who were trying to steal the statue, who paid Cosimo's brother, Enzo . . ."

Fassbinder translated this into Italian. Now I had everyone's attention.

"Enzo?" the Italian police captain asked, looking worried. But not nearly as worried as Cosimo, whose eyes grew wide.

He stared at me, entreating. But he couldn't worry about Enzo's reputation now. It was too late for that. We had to save ourselves.

Fassbinder squinted into the pale yellow dawn breaking over the farm, still wanting to be back in bed. "This implicates you, I'm afraid."

"How could it? If I were going to be paid for stealing the statue, I would not have received the money yet—not from people who didn't know or trust me. No, this money went to a local man, a member of the *polizia municipale*, who was trying to misdirect us."

The Italian police captain didn't like this. Now it was more than just Enzo's reputation at stake; it was all of his police force. But then again, who were these German investigators to meddle in a local affair? Was this a police matter now or a diplomatic one? Shouldn't there be higher-ranked officials involved?

The German, ignoring all questions of rank and policy, continued pressing me. "And how did you get it from him?"

"He died in a road accident. We found it in his pocket. It's a large quantity, in *lire* and *Reichsmarks*. There is a German you should suspect, that's true, but it isn't me."

Cosimo was still staring, shaking his head slowly. I felt for him. He had suffered the worst of this, he had helped me at every turn, but his judgment was not sound.

"Cosimo. You must give them the money."

"I don't have it," he said, nearly choking on the words.

"You must. There is nowhere else it could be but here."

"No one wanted it."

"No one wanted it? It was a small fortune."

"It was *sfortuna*." *Bad* fortune.

The police captain said something to Cosimo, who translated: "Perhaps you men should go for a drive, looking for your colleague. The captain says he will interview us and get to the truth." But neither German showed any interest in that, not with the scent so near and the whiff of money added to the intrigue. There was some disagreement in two languages, a patronizing tone that did not please the Italian police captain. I missed most of it, thinking of the unwanted money, of who would have wanted it most, who would have needed it, where it might have been put and never seen again.

"Follow me," I said. I turned away from the statue. "I know where it is."

The trigger-happy German raised his Luger again and ordered me to stop.

"If you shoot me, then you'll have to do the work yourself. This is going to be a hard enough job without you waving that thing. Cosimo, where is the shovel?"

I hadn't seen him look this unwell since the moment he had found his brother alongside the road. If anything, he had looked more tranquil then, as if that moment had been a confirmation of a long-lived fear, whereas this moment was a complete, terrible, and unnecessary surprise.

"Up on the hill," Cosimo whispered.

"That's where I'm going, then." And I turned and strode without hesitation, followed by the sound of several pairs of heavy footsteps hurrying to catch up with me.

CHAPTER 14

The mound was still fresh when we got there, less competently tamped down than I remembered it. I began to dig, watched by the two Germans, two Italians, and Cosimo. No one offered to assist. The rising sun burned away a scattered bank of clouds. A few bumblebees danced over the bright green grass, and we continued to hear them even when we couldn't see them, the buzz of floral exuberance. After a few dozen shovelfuls, I stopped to roll up my sleeves, then changed my mind and unbuttoned my shirt, tossing it aside, unfolded.

In the Labor Service, we were never allowed to take off our uniforms, even on the hottest, longest days, and that had always been fine with me. But now, I didn't care about propriety; I hadn't a self-conscious bone in my body; I didn't care that this was one of the worst days of my life because the work wasn't so bad really, and the sun on my shoulders felt good for now, and now was all that mattered anyway. I didn't have to think, only dig.

I didn't have to think, that is, until sometime later, when my shovel hit something soft. I poked around. I dug more carefully and felt around with the blade, aware only now that what I had thought was the insistent buzzing of an insect had become, in the last few minutes, the sound of Cosimo praying under his breath in rapid Italian. He was praying for the Lord's mercy, for forgiveness. He was praying for the Germans' patience. He was praying for our lives.

Let me stop and go back here, to this moment I have failed to remember properly, a stuck frame in my mental camera. Let me see Cosimo, who is not only praying frantically, but holding something. The Germans have moved Tartufa out of view, but just before following me up the hill, Cosimo picked her up again, cradling her like a baby in his arms—all damp, dark, speckled fur and black paws, the tail peeking out from underneath his left arm. He is a policeman who has investigated murders and transported the body of his twin brother. He has helped to hide a corpse. But there is one thing he does not understand: why a stranger had to shoot his dog, without even a warning.

So when the German with the Luger begins to hold it up again in response to the appearance of something strange coming to the surface—the back of a head, a few wisps of hair like the sweeping end of a broom mysteriously buried in the dirt—Cosimo stops praying. He tucks the limp dog more firmly under his arm, between hip and armpit, and with his free hand forms a fist.

The German takes a step closer to me, closer to the grave, fascinated and repelled. He lifts the gun higher, even as his gaze drops.

"Put that away!" Cosimo shouts, voice trembling. "You have no right!"

Rosina has left the house, in defiance of Gianni. She has climbed the hill. She is watching, too, from just behind the two visiting Italians and the other German. She is pressing her knuckles against her lips, trying to hold back any ill-advised sounds.

I have stopped digging. I have realized my strategic error. I, too, am trembling.

The German can't believe what he is seeing. "Is that . . . ?"

Cosimo makes his demand more clear: "Put it away!"

Rosina calls out to her brother—too late.

Cosimo's fist comes up, catching the unsuspecting German on his left jaw. My shovel drops, the pistol with its deceptively narrow barrel swings—and then the popping sound that changes everything.

I stumble forward, hands sliding on the edge of the grave, trying to pull myself out. But Rosina gets to him first. Cosimo has dropped to his knees, he is falling, his head is in her lap, he is trying to speak. The German is still holding his weapon as he pushes toward the grave, down on his knees at the edge, his legs level with my face, trying to see for himself.

"You did this?" he demands, and I am sure he is talking to me, but then I look, and he is facing Cosimo.

Cosimo says something none of us catch. The lips move, words the Germans don't understand—"*Mio fratello.*"

"That's right," the German says. "Now you've got something to say about it."

They think he is confessing, but he is doing nothing of the kind. He is only calling out, as one would hail a friend on the street. He isn't implicating me, he isn't sacrificing himself for anyone, he is simply trying to be heard before the figure turns the corner and is lost. "*Mio fratello.*" My brother.

I howl, "You've got the wrong man!"—but at that moment, there is a rush of sounds—a second carefully aimed shot and Rosina's shriek, followed by a commotion as she attempts to interpose before there are two men shot instead of one: "I saw it all happen!"

"And you?"

They are asking me now. I am staring at Cosimo's closed eyes and softened jaw and parted lips, still moving slightly, still filtering air, but only barely.

Rosina shouts, "It was self-defense! Can't you just leave? We hate you!"

The Italian police captain closes in on the German with the gun. He steps between the German and Rosina, a brave man for doing it, a brave man waving his arms and using every gesture and facial expression God gave him to try to calm everyone down. In anger, I make a grab for the German's ankle and, in return, hear another *pop*. I feel a hot spike of pain run through my hand, and hear yet another *pop* that makes my shoulder throb. If any coherent thought runs through my brain at all, it is only: *this is how things end*. But it will bring balance. It will be a punishing symmetry, to meet my end after the end I have inflicted upon these others: Enzo, Cosimo, and even Keller, regardless of his faults. And more than that: a punishing symmetry considering how I came here, and what I refused to acknowledge.

"Gerhard," I whisper, only to myself, yielding to the shock as the left side of my body begins to go numb.

A flurry of questions over my head: "Who is this Gerhard? Another thief? Is he here on the farm?"

No, he is—was—in a place called Dachau. When he entered, he was an old man—the opposite of a survivor, unwilling to censor his own thoughts, unwilling to please his superiors in the way that might have saved him, and physically unwell besides. They'd let him take nothing with him, his servant girl had said: not clothing, not his medicine. Almost certainly, at that moment, he was already gone, no more alive than Enzo, his spirit even more lost than Enzo's because he had never been mourned.

And still, these ten years later, I am forcing myself to replay the scene I've never allowed myself to envision in full since the day it occurred, while stopping short at full disclosure. But why stop short? Why not just say it? Why not admit that at the moment I was sobbing for Gerhard, I believed that his survival had been unlikely. But not impossible. A small distinction, but the only things that matter are small: the differences between a man and his brother, the distinction between a mere copy and a masterpiece.

I know more about the shame of Dachau now—a place that was bad enough from its founding, in 1933; a place which would become horrific on an entirely different scale with the start of war. But I also knew, even in 1938, that there had been a brief window of time—maybe only days, maybe only hours, those hours in a life that end up mattering most—when I and Mueller and my coworkers at *Sonderprojekt* could have done something. That *I* could have done something much more than stand once outside Gerhard's door, accepting the gift of the di Luca guide, accepting the gift of an Italian detour, signing the pact of silent paralysis that is to blame for everything, not just in Germany, but everywhere—the darkest moments of the last two thousand years.

I had betrayed my mentor in one way: by making no protest at his disappearance, by voicing not a single question out loud among the many of us who had worked alongside him. I had obeyed him in another: by taking the trip he believed would change me.

"Gerhard," I continued to whisper on that final morning, waiting for the last shot that did not come, mute to the questions being shouted all around me in the chaos of that graveside moment, and hearing the echo of Rosina's desperate shout, "Can't you just leave? We hate you—all of you!"

CHAPTER 15

They carried me out to a waiting car, still conscious but only half alert. They did not let me communicate with anyone in the Digirolamo family. Herr Keller was brought out of the twice-used grave and loaded into the truck with the dirt still clinging to the folds in his neck and the waves in his hair. Also loaded into the truck was the *Discus Thrower* and all the treasures found within Enzo's coffin—the money, and even the lighter, which I saw the Luger-toting German using later at the consulate where I was questioned, flicking the thing open and shut.

In Turin, I was given medical attention and phone calls were made, and I was brought into the consulate there, where the questioning began and then was halted, to be continued on our own soil. Two more vehicles joined our caravan, and by Milan, we were back on faster roads, up through northern Italy and to the border.

In Munich, following my recovery, I was roundly abused for defaming Herr Keller, though my claims and Cosimo's apparent confession cast enough confusion over everything to make any simple conclusion or dissemination of justice impossible. I was stripped of my position and told I wasn't good enough for regular prison, wasn't good enough for a simple execution, but they'd find a hard, miserable job for me somewhere—which they did, in Neuengamme, a new camp in Hamburg, on the grounds of a defunct brickworks.

There we built the facilities that would hold hundreds of prisoners, and later thousands. Day after day, I dug through heavy, peaty soil. I excavated foundation pits where barracks would soon stand. Alongside many others, I dug a canal that would be used to transport the bricks made by camp inmates. I dug and dug—and every bit of soil I moved was creating one thing only: the next grave. The next million graves, ordered by Hitler.

Even at *Sonderprojekt*, I had rarely voiced *Der Kunstsammler*'s actual name; even now, I try not to say it. But I will say it once, and remember one last time how Gerhard referred to him: not as the failed artist, but as the failed father figure. He had said, when I told him once about the animosity I felt toward my own *Vater*, to be wary of replacements. "It is in wanting to replace, to reach out for false hope or false comfort, that our nation has stumbled so dangerously. Sometimes, we must simply accept an absence in our lives."

But of course, it isn't easy. If I hadn't been so eager to replace the father figure in my own life, I would not have been drawn to the men who all resembled my father in some way—including Gerhard himself.

Furthermore, if I had not been a replacement for some German lover that reminded her of happier days, I find it hard to imagine Rosina would have allowed me into her heart and her bed. In the end, this was the unhappy uncertainty that followed me for years, not knowing whether Rosina had enjoyed me only as a pale echo of someone else. If so, it would have been a fitting punishment for the man who had failed to save her brothers. It would have been a fitting punishment, too, for a man who had been obsessed with a lifeless marble icon—to be remembered as merely a stand-in for someone or something else, rather than loved as something real, inconvenient, flawed.

I might have kept making bricks for many more years if it hadn't been for the war, which started in earnest with the invasion of Poland, in September 1939. In Warsaw, later, they took down an enormous bronze statue of Frédéric Chopin and melted it. Had I ever really believed the Nazis wanted to preserve artwork? Had I ever really believed they wanted to preserve anything?

Following the first rounds of casualties that drained away the best of German's youth, the Wehrmacht Heer decided it needed me back, and I went, my sins forgiven as long as I was able to tie my boots and carry a rifle. The other soldiers thought we were underfed in the army, and we were—but not in comparison to where I'd spent more than a year. In my first two months, I managed to gain back ten kilos.

I didn't expect to survive. Why should I, when so many others had not? Even my sister Greta and her husband failed to make it through. They perished in 1944, their home leveled in an RAF bombing run. Sometimes, it seemed like everyone had been wiped out by the war—everyone and everything.

As it turns out, even some fragile things did manage to survive. Later, I would discover that Italians had done a remarkable thing to preserve their statues, ancient columns, and historic monuments that could not be moved to safety, out of bomb's reach. With the help of wood and sand and mounds of brick, entire massive works of art—including Michelangelo's *David*—were entombed. What a strange thing it would have been to visit the Accademia in Florence and to have seen those domed and beehive-shaped mounds, like the ziggurats or pyramids of a new and tragic age.

I did the same thing with my feelings for Rosina and my question of whether I would ever see her again, or even know if she had survived the war. I entombed that subject, not heartlessly, but lovingly, knowing that in dangerous times, the walls must be built to withstand great damage. And because the walls were indeed built strong and tight, it would take a while to dismantle them.

◼

Three years passed between the end of the war and my life's return to relative normalcy. I got a job with an international commission, cooperating with the U.S. Army and the governments of several other nations, to sort through and repatriate hundreds of thousands of great artworks through several collecting points and back to the dozens of countries from which they had been bought, or more frequently, stolen.

In 1948, I was still only thirty-four years old, though I felt much older, with ruined feet, an arthritic left hand, deafness in one ear, and chronic back pain (my own passport of disability, with stamps from Neuengamme and the Eastern Front). I was only a lowly assistant in an incomprehensibly vast effort, the most important job of my life, far more important than the job I'd been given in 1938. It was a chance for me to redeem myself, the first time I even dared to think about what life could become again.

Railcar after railcar traveled across Europe, returning one item after another: the *Bruges Madonna* back to Belgium, da Vinci's *Lady with an Ermine* back to Kraków, Holy Roman regalia back to Vienna. Each returned object helped me feel as if I had gotten a piece of myself back, as well—the part of me that had always loved art, not only because of my own search for greater perfection, wholeness, worthiness; but also, simply, because each work was its own story, its own world. These artworks placed no limits on humanity. These artworks only enlarged it.

The *Discus Thrower* was one of the last pieces to be returned—to Rome, ten years after it had been removed—and is, of course, the reason that I am in Italy now. It is fitting, in a way, that it took so long. One of the first and most ancient masterpieces acquired, one of the last to be returned. Tapped gently back into place like a puzzle piece. Other gaps remain, to be sure, and some masterpieces—and many more people—are lost forever, never to be seen again. But the *Discus Thrower* was one of the earliest of The Collector's coveted items. One of the earliest symbols of our questionable intentions.

There is nothing worth recounting about the first part of that trip from Munich to Rome—a few delays, perhaps, and one ancient Perugian woman in the seat opposite me, muttering that at least the trains had run on time before the war. But I knew it wasn't true. The trains had never run on time, and why should they? Is there something so terrible about the occasional unexpected delay?

I traveled with the repatriated statue, saw it unpacked and documented—all very quietly, and all without incident. *Ohne Zwischenfall.*

When all was done, the relief was far greater than I had anticipated. The bricks that I had expected to dismantle slowly, one a time—someday, perhaps when I was a wizened old man—came tumbling down, and the sand spilled out. And there were the feelings, and the question. There was the thing inside that I had to do, that I wanted to do.

Clearly, my subconscious had seen this moment coming, as the contents of my suitcase proved. I had packed a little more heavily than I had on this same trip, a decade earlier. Three shirts, instead of two. Better shoes, so that I might blend in with the Italian crowds. A nicer jacket, dark blue instead of brown, suitable for a dinner or a drink with a friend, should the opportunity arise.

CHAPTER 16

1948

Which brings me to this road: long, but perhaps not long enough—could I turn back still? And to this town, just waking from a late-afternoon lull, the autumn sun soft between the trees, soon to drop behind the close-packed stone buildings that wind along the narrow streets.

There are only two cafés, I've been told. I wander into the first, dark and sour smelling and unpleasant—the wrong place, I'm immediately certain—and continue down the street, to its more successful competitor, where there is not only the smell of good coffee and warm bread, but the sounds of life.

The cigarette smoke, the tap of glasses on the bar, the sounds of women laughing in a corner and three young boys clamoring for gelato—all of it makes me feel old and foreign and out of place. I tried memorizing something clever to say, but when Rosina comes to take my order, wiping her hands on her apron without looking up, all I can utter is *"Fragola"*—the word on a label attached to the bin behind the glass. I don't know if it is strawberry or some other red fruit, and I don't care.

The three syllables are enough. She catches the accent, stops wiping her hands, and looks up.

"Gelato?"

"Sì. Io voglio . . . Vorrei . . ."

"Fragola?"

"Sì, fragola."

I sound more infantile than the dirty-kneed boys milling around me. She takes her time with the scoop, pushing it into the soft ice cream. I watch her face, trying to distinguish between anger, fear, or repulsion.

When she comes back, she has relocated her German vocabulary, rusty from a decade of disuse, and delivered brusquely. "Wait for me outside. Five minutes."

"I'm sorry to bother—"

"Just wait. I have to take care of the other customers and talk to the owner. Go."

When I try to pay, she waves her hands in frustration.

Outside, I can't eat the gelato. My stomach is turning.

Five minutes pass as I wait for Rosina outside, then ten, then fifteen.

Perhaps I am remembering things inaccurately, after all. We slept together, certainly, but so what? I can't quite recall her last private words to me; I remember a promise about something, about singing, I think, but perhaps not. Possibly I have left things out, or added things, or simply made too much of a few days in Italy long, long ago.

I am wondering if I should leave, if I should have never come, when she exits the café, pulling the kerchief off her hair as she walks, shaking out the dark waves.

"First," she says, standing in front of me without so much as a hello. "Take a look. Tell me what you see."

"I was only hoping—"

"No, tell me. Inside the café, it was smoky and dark. Here we are in the sun. Tell me a single lie and I won't talk to you again. Tell me what you see."

I take a step back and look her over, top to bottom.

"Your hair is turning gray. And I'd say, maybe five more kilos, on the arms and across the middle. But maybe that isn't from ten years passing. Maybe that's just from working too close to the gelato."

She crosses her arms, deciding.

"But you are still beautiful, Rosina. You are still an exceptional woman."

"I am forty-four years old, you bastard—" and she attacks my chest with both fists, pummeling without vigor. "Why did you have to take so long?"

I hesitate. "Your last words, if I'm not mistaken: 'Can't you just leave?' And: 'We hate you all.'"

"Hate who?"

"Germans. The Gestapo who came." It's difficult to say. "And me. Perhaps not that other Munich lover you had all those years ago, or maybe him, too. I could never be sure. It would be understandable—"

"Oh, *liebling*. You're wrong about so many things."

"Am I?"

"That lover who meant nothing. I mentioned him only because I was flirting and wanted to sound more confident than I felt, so you wouldn't take advantage. And then I had to flirt even more, so that you *would* take advantage." Hands on her hips, shoulders back, she's on the verge of smiling. But then the light in her eyes dims. "And those last minutes at the graveyard. You're all wrong."

"I'm sorry," I say, trying to reach for her, though she resists at first. "I'm so very sorry."

She lets me hold her, there on the street, on the pavement, with the dropped gelato in a bright red starburst at our feet. It is the most wonderful thing to feel her crying, her chest heaving and her arms softer than they were ten years ago—not quite her mother, but getting there, and making the most of it, hugging me and hitting me at the same time.

"And what are you doing, coming for gelato? Buy me a drink, *figlio di puttana*."

"Must you keep swearing?"

"I get to swear for a day at least. A night and a day, Ernesto," and she begins to cry again, pushing her balled-up kerchief into her eyes. "Couldn't you have written to me, at least?"

When I don't answer, she confesses, "I didn't remember your last name. I only thought to ask it when my son was seven or eight and started to ask questions—about his uncles, about the farm and the old days—and then it was too late. There was no one to ask."

"It's Vogler, by the way."

"Volger."

"Almost." I say it again.

"Did you tell me that, when we first met? I should have remembered. Why couldn't I remember?"

And I share her worry, that we both had it all wrong, that things didn't happen quite as we remembered, that we are gambling too much on past events and interpretations.

"Ernesto Vogler," she repeats, and it thrills me just to hear it transformed by her voice, her lips. "Ernst Vogler."

"Either way. Whatever you prefer."

She's gotten control of herself now, eyes dry. "My uncle must have been shocked to see you."

"He was. He said I'd changed."

We've been holding each other's hands, there on the street. She takes a step back, studying me as I studied her, without comment, refusing additional assurances.

We cross the street to go to a restaurant she knows, but on the way, we walk past a window and see white tablecloths, and on the wall, a print by Van Gogh—that peculiar man, painter of green skies and blue fields—of sunflowers.

"There," I say. "This one."

"You're sure?"

"I'm sure."

We enter the restaurant, order wine and dinner, espresso when it seems that we are wrapping it up, and more wine again when we decide to hell with it, there's no reason a good dinner can't last three hours or four. I can't stop staring, except for those brief moments I look down at the tablecloth in order to focus on the sound of her voice, the lilting accent that I could remember even after other details had faded. At the end of the evening, she touches the back of my hand and says, "I should be getting back. He is with a neighbor, she's very kind, but she'll be worrying by now. And he'll be worrying. He's like that, very protective."

"I understand."

"Will you be here tomorrow morning?"

"As long as you'd like me to be here."

"You'll find a hotel?"

"Why not?"

"That's good. It gives me time to think, time to explain." She pulls a lipstick out of her purse and applies it at the table, trying to remake her face, though by now it is a lost cause—splotchy and puffy—and I don't mind at all, not how she looks, nor that she has dropped my aching hand. She has been squeezing my knuckles for the last hour, as if she expects me to vanish as soon as she turns her back.

"I named him Enzo," she says. "I know that is unusual, but I wanted to remember him. I wanted to remember everything. I hope you think it's all right."

"But why not 'Cosimo?'"

"I was saving that for the second boy—which only shows how foolishly optimistic I was."

"So—things didn't turn out."

"What things?"

"With your son's father, I only meant."

She stops, and closes the compact. "*Ernesto.*"

"Yes?"

"Are you paying attention?"

"Completely."

"You didn't have an idea, as soon as you talked to Zio Adamo?"

"Idea . . . ?"

She states the facts again, directly, and I am left speechless, as speechless as when I first saw her, bathing nude in the tub, awestruck.

"He is completely normal. Ten fingers, ten toes, nothing extra and nothing forgotten."

I probably look queasy, but so does she, reacting to my own surprised expression. "Is it all right?"

"It's better than all right."

"Are you sure?"

"*Certo*. It is beautiful and unexpected news, Rosina. It is a gift I don't deserve."

"None of us deserve anything," she says, reaching up to wipe my cheek.

This is what I always expected her to say—that in the light of what happened to Cosimo, and to so many others, too, we do not deserve happiness, perhaps no one does.

"But," she continues, "we can always hope for more than we deserve."

I am still absorbing everything she has said when she asks, "Where would we live?"

I hadn't expected that question, hadn't expected to come to Italy again and have my life change so suddenly. But that's the way it happened before; that's the way it can happen now. Isn't that why I had come?

"There is Munich, or Florence, if you prefer. Or maybe

somewhere far from all of this," I say. "I don't know. We can discuss it."

"I'm not saying it will work. I'm not saying I'll stay if it doesn't work, Ernesto."

"Of course."

Something new comes into her face. It relaxes slightly, filling with the light of a new confidence. "But it could work, couldn't it?"

"Yes." And I have never felt so certain in my life of anything: "*Certo. Ja.*"

She rests her chin in her palm. "I might want to go somewhere new . . ."

We consider the possibilities that are close at hand, then allow our imaginations to take flight, to new continents where neither of us ever expected to travel, much less settle. Australia. The Americas. She seems open to anything, and that openness confirms what I remember and promises new discoveries to come. I want this conversation never to be finished—not because I dread that shift from perfect stasis to uncertain forward motion, as I once did, but because the conversation alone makes the world seem a better and more promising place than I have let myself believe for so many years.

We have drained our glasses, but continue to grasp the stems as if they are not empty. We are the last people in the restaurant. They have swept it out and stacked the outdoor chairs and removed all the white tablecloths except ours, and the owner is standing in the open doorway, smoking a cigarette, ready to be home himself but willing to give us this final unhurried moment, as if civilization depends on it.

AUTHOR'S NOTE

This novel is populated by fictional characters whose lives are shaped by a factual event: the purchase of the ancient *Discus Thrower* statue by Adolf Hitler in 1938, against the objection of many Italians—a first step in what would become a seven-year looting campaign of Europe's greatest artistic treasures. I have used some historical details from that ultimately-thwarted Nazi cultural project, while inventing others (including some minor variations in chronology) to suit this novel's needs. Hitler's most ambitious plans to collect art for a new museum in Linz, Austria, started taking their clearest shape about one year following the fictionalized storyline in this book. The *Discus Thrower* was repatriated from Germany to Italy in 1948, ten years after its original purchase;

it can now be seen in the National Museum of Rome. For a broader historical context, including the work of America's "Monuments Men," who helped track down and protect stolen art during and following World War II, I recommend *Rescuing Da Vinci* by Robert M. Edsel. Another entertaining book that inspired my (and Ernst Vogler's) ideas about classical art and body image was *Love, Sex and Tragedy: How the Ancient World Shapes Our Lives*, by Simon Goldhill. Much of my information about sculpture and historical context comes from trips to Munich and Rome, including visits to the National Museum of Rome and to Munich's Glyptothek, where the *Discus Thrower* was on display for one year. (A brief history can be found in an excellent museum guide, *Glyptothek, Munich: Masterpieces of Greek and Roman Sculpture*, by Raimund Wünsche, translated from the German by Rodney Batstone.) Aside from research, inspiration for this story may have originated with my own hybrid identity: My first name is Greek, my heritage is Italian and German, and I married into a Jewish family. All of those threads shape my interest in 1938 Europe and the strange confluence at that time of influential and sometimes dangerous ideas about classical art, genetics, and politics.

My most sincere gratitude goes to Juliet Grames, my Soho Press editor and a person who won my respect even before this book brought us into closer contact, and thanks to my agent, Gail Hochman, who championed this project and made helpful editorial suggestions, as well as to the many people at Soho Press who shared their time and their talents: Bronwen Hruska, Ailen Lujo, Scott Cain, Anna Bliss, and Michelle Rafferty. The

Rasmuson Foundation supported this project with a fellowship, without which I would not have been able to travel to Europe in 2009.

Thanks are due my sisters Honorée and Eliza, practitioners of art and lovers of travel, with whom I should have visited Cold War-era Berlin more than twenty-five years ago, when I had the chance, rather than heading my own way to Barcelona. For being a general source of family support extended across many miles, thanks to Nikki and Leona; my mother, Catherine; my mother-in-law, Evelyn; and to all of the extended Lax clan, for ongoing support, as well as to my most trusted first reader, Brian, and my children, Aryeh and Tziporah. I am indebted to Alaska writers Bill Sherwonit, Lee Goodman, Kathleen Tarr, Doug O'Harra, Amanda Coyne, Eowyn Ivey, and the 49 Writers community of writers and readers, for literary advice and camaraderie. Thanks to Amy Bower, my childhood friend and fellow believer in detours and other life adventures; and to Stewart and Karen Ferguson, who have been helpful readers, listeners, and running partners, willing to share ideas and rants while pounding away stress. For assistance with language questions (any remaining errors are mine alone), I thank Charles Beattie, Keith Jensen, Nausicaa Pouscoulous, Filippo Furri, and Henriette Zeidler.